"I'm Detective Lieutenant Jake Delancy," he said. *"I've been assigned to protect you."*

Rebecca studied him.

His assessing gaze made the young widow and single mom self-conscious about her appearance. And it made her way too aware of this cop as an attractive male.

She noticed his firm chin and sexy mouth, his full, sensual underlip, the slight crook in his nose. His thick lashes brought the term *bedroom eyes* to mind—except for the coldness in them that reminded Rebecca of his deadly purpose.

Delancy had a tough, no-nonsense air about him that should have been reassuring. Yet Rebecca suddenly dreaded bringing him into her cozy little home.

His blatant study of her made her feel like a woman again.

He made her feel as if a brand-new danger was walking right through her door....

Dear Reader,

Merry Christmas! I hope you'll like Intimate Moments' gift to you: six wonderful books, perfect for reading by the lights of the Christmas tree. First up is our Heartbreakers title. Welcome veteran romance writer Sara Orwig to the line with *Hide in Plain Sight*. Hero Jake Delancy is tough—but the power of single mom Rebecca Bolen's love is even stronger!

Terese Ramin is back with *Five Kids, One Christmas*, a book that will put you right in the holiday mood. Then try Suzanne Brockmann's *A Man To Die For*, a suspenseful reply to the question "What would you do for love?" Next up is *Together Again*, the latest in Laura Parker's Rogues' Gallery miniseries. *The Mom Who Came To Stay* brings Nancy Morse back to the line after a too-long absence. This book's title says it all. Finally, welcome Becky Barker to the line as she tells the story of *The Last Real Cowboy*.

Six books, six tales of love to make your holidays bright. Enjoy!

Leslie Wainger
Senior Editor and Editorial Coordinator

Please address questions and book requests to:
Silhouette Reader Service
U.S.: 3010 Walden Ave., P.O. Box 1325, Buffalo, NY 14269
Canadian: P.O. Box 609, Fort Erie, Ont. L2A 5X3

HIDE IN PLAIN SIGHT

SARA ORWIG

Published by Silhouette Books

America's Publisher of Contemporary Romance

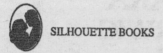

SILHOUETTE BOOKS

ISBN 0-373-07679-7

HIDE IN PLAIN SIGHT

Books by Sara Orwig

Silhouette Intimate Moments
Hide in Plain Sight #679

Silhouette Desire
Falcon's Lair #938

SARA ORWIG

lives with her husband and children in Oklahoma. She has a patient husband who will take her on research trips anywhere from big cities to old forts. She is an avid collector of Western history books. With a master's degree in English, Sara writes historical romance, mainstream fiction and contemporary romance. Books are beloved treasures that take Sara to magical worlds, and she loves both reading and writing them.

With thanks to Lucia Macro and Angela Catalano.
Thanks to Jeri Cook, Lynn Holmes and the
Austin Police Department, for answering questions.

Prologue

"**W**ill the foreman please read the verdict of the jury?" the judge instructed.

Feeling certain she and the other jurors had done the right thing, Rebecca Bolen rose to her feet, standing in the front row of the jury box. Thunder rattled the long, narrow windows of the Texas courthouse and sheets of rain beat against it. The air inside was stifling—as if a storm were brewing within the room. Her gaze ran across the courtroom, encompassing spectators, the detectives who had testified, the prosecution. Then she looked at the defendant, Lenny Meskell.

Thick-shouldered, sandy-haired, dressed in a tan suit and a dark brown tie, Meskell looked more like a successful businessman than her idea of a hardened killer. Yet the evidence was damning: A camera had recorded Meskell holding a gun on the convenience-store clerk and then shooting him.

A witness had picked Lenny Meskell out in a lineup. Another witness had turned in the license number of the car he had used. Police witnesses had testified about the high-speed chase he led them on. Then detectives had testified about the shoot-out in which Meskell gunned down a policeman. It hadn't taken the jury an hour to reach a verdict.

Lightning flashed and another clap of thunder reverberated in the room. The courtroom walls were cracked and a faint smell of mildew was in the air. Throughout the trial, the hall had been filled with deputies with metal detectors. The press had wanted interviews constantly, although the jurors had been cautioned by the judge not to talk to anyone. She was anxious to get home and away from the tensions of the trial.

Rebecca straightened the jacket of her beige linen suit. As she lifted her head, she felt compelled to glance across the courtroom. The defendant's icy gaze was fixed on her. She felt a slight chill, because she knew he had killed more than once, knew he had threatened to escape during the trial.

Trying to ignore his unwavering glare, she glanced at the slip of paper in her hand. "We, the jury," she read in a steady voice, "find the defendant guilty of murder."

"No!" Meskell yelled, bursting from his chair.

Pandemonium broke loose. Lenny Meskell's chair crashed behind him. He sprang over the table and ran toward her.

Rebecca looked into cold blue eyes and raised her hands, fists doubled, to defend herself as he lunged toward her.

In a flash, one of the detectives jumped over the railing. He caught Meskell's shoulder and spun him around. The detective pivoted so that all his weight was behind the blow as he slammed his fist into Meskell, connecting with his jaw. The crack of bone on bone was loud, and Meskell staggered.

"You!" Meskell snapped. "You damn bastard!" he screamed at the detective, lunging for him.

Instantly, court deputies grabbed Meskell's arms and tugged at him as he fought them and yanked one arm free, pointing at Rebecca.

"I'll kill you for this!" he shouted. "You're dead!" His blue eyes met Rebecca's, and she looked directly at him, feeling the lash of his rage. "I swear I'll get you!" He shoved a deputy, yanking his gun from its holster.

The detective kicked Meskell's hand, and the pistol went flying while another deputy grabbed Meskell's arms and pinned them behind him.

"I'll get you, too, cop!" Meskell yelled, struggling with the deputies as they shoved him to the floor to cuff him.

Rebecca shivered, the hairs on the nape of her neck standing. The judge banged his gavel for order as reporters buzzed. While noise hummed around her, she stood in stunned surprise at Lenny Meskell's outburst.

Thinking about her children, Rebecca felt icy. To do her civic duty and serve on this jury, she had rearranged her schedules, missed work, lost sleep. She'd had no choice about serving, and she'd felt she was doing what she should. Now she wished she had never been called for jury duty.

The detective turned to look at her, his hazel eyes meeting hers, as a deputy stepped over to her.

"All you all right?" the deputy asked.

"I'm fine," she answered perfunctorily, caught in the detective's steady gaze. She was aware of his height, hazel eyes, firm jaw and thick brown hair. In the melee, locks of his hair had tumbled across his forehead, and he raked his fingers through them now, combing them back. What was his name again? she thought dazedly. Delancy, yes. Jake Delancy. He nodded at her and then turned away, straightening his coat and tie.

Suddenly she realized that the other jurors had scrambled to the far end of the jury box and she stood alone. Now they slowly began to move back to their seats.

The deputies shoved Lenny Meskell down onto a chair. Quiet was restored. Judge Driskell ordered Lenny to reappear for sentencing, set the date, and finally turned to thank the jury.

As if the outburst had never occurred, Judge Driskell told the jury what good citizens they had been. He told them how patriotic they had been by doing their duty. Still stunned by the outburst, Rebecca barely heard him. Her gaze moved across the courtroom, trying to avoid Lenny Meskell, meeting the hazel-eyed stare of Detective Delancy.

She looked away, focusing on the judge. Finally they were dismissed, and a deputy guided them out a back door to avoid reporters. A few jurors went down the hall to the elevators. When she looked over her shoulder, she saw them standing in clusters of reporters, who snapped pictures. She noticed Detective Delancy crossing the hall in long strides and disappearing into an office.

"This way, folks," the deputy said, closing the door to the hall behind them. He pointed toward the stairs. "If you don't want to be interviewed, you can get out the back without anyone asking questions."

Outside, when she ran through the rain to the parking garage, she inhaled deeply of the spring air. The trial was over, Lenny Meskell would be locked away, and more than likely given a death sentence. She would never cross paths with him again. She hurried along a glistening sidewalk, avoiding silvery puddles of rain. Had Lenny Meskell been terribly shocked by the verdict? The jurors had found him guilty swiftly and unanimously.

You're dead! I swear I'll get you! The words echoed in her mind, and she saw again his cold, blue eyes staring at her with hatred. Rebecca shivered and hurried a little faster, her heels clicking against the wet pavement. She crossed the street and rushed along another block, pausing at the corner, finally feeling the tension leave her shoulders as she became more aware of her surroundings.

Waiting for the light to change, she looked at the tall buildings of downtown Austin. High above the buildings, a rainbow arched across the sky. The rain had diminished to a fine mist, and the air smelled sweet and carried the freshness of early spring.

Now the outburst in the courtroom seemed less frightening, a momentary explosion that had been brought under control. Lenny Meskell was locked away and soon would be headed for the penitentiary. He would never have a chance to carry out his threat against her.

It was early April, and within the hour she would be home safe with her girls and the incident would be forgotten.

Chapter 1

Two Months Later

"Lenny Meskell is armed, dangerous, and in this vicinity," Detective Captain Richard Vance said, looking at the men of the robbery-homicide unit of the Austin Police Department. Six men were seated around a table. Fluorescent lights were bright overhead; the only sound was the rustle of papers as Vance flipped through a file on Meskell. The special meeting had been called early this morning, and Detective Lieutenant Jake Delancy knew his quiet weekend was gone.

"We don't know if he's still around here. If I had been given the death penalty, I'd be in Mexico by now," Detective Sergeant Will Gowdy said.

"He's threatened every juror that served at his trial and sworn to get them. It's just his style. He's a sociopathic killer—two killings that we know about. Look at his record of prior arrests and the time he's served," Vance said, thumping the file, and then continued.

"The D.A. is having fits. If Meskell gets even one juror, the killing would wreak havoc on our jury system. We have to operate on the assumption Lenny is here and he will carry out his threat." Vance spoke impatiently, running his hand over the top of his head, his frustration clear in the tone of his voice.

Jake Delancy shifted, sharing Vance's frustration, wanting to get his hands on Lenny personally. He had been the detective in charge of the case against Lenny, the one who brought him in after the convenience-store killing. He had been there the night Lenny Meskell gunned down Dusty Smith, a fellow officer, and memories of that night still brought a stab of pain. It was particularly frustrating to know that after more than a year's work, work that had resulted in a solid conviction, Lenny had escaped.

"This is top priority," Vance continued, his brown eyes looking at each man. "Now, here are the jurors," Vance said, passing out eight-by-ten glossies. As soon as the pictures had been distributed, he cleared his throat.

"You have on the table in front of you information about each one of these people."

Jake studied the faces in the pictures, the light reflecting off the glossy finishes. His attention returned to one face in particular. Rebecca Bolen. He remembered her name and the moment when Meskell had gone for her in the courtroom. Her hair was pulled back behind her head in the picture the way she had worn it at the trial. As he fingered the photograph, he could see why she had received so much media attention. She was a looker.

"The women will be the most vulnerable, and there were seven of them on this jury. Who will be the biggest risk?"

"He said he would get the woman who was foreman," Jake Delancy said. "And if Lenny gets her, it'll generate publicity beyond his wildest hopes."

"I agree, and so does the D.A.," Richard Vance said. "We can assign uniformed men to all these women except Rebecca Bolen," Richard announced solemnly. "The D.A. wants her protected at all costs. We'll place one of our own men with Rebecca Bolen."

Jake looked across the table at Ray Holder, who rolled his eyes. Several of the detectives exchanged glances, and Jake knew none of them wanted the task of baby-sitting a juror when Lenny was on the loose.

"I'll volunteer for the blonde if she's single," Jay Werner quipped, and several men chuckled.

"Plenty of men would volunteer to be her bodyguard," Jake remarked dryly, studying her picture. He leaned back in the chair and pushed open his coat, stretching out his long legs. He was barely aware of the weight of the pistol in his shoulder holster.

"Here's our plan," Vance continued. "Rebecca Bolen will be a decoy—within limits. We'll place one of our men with her, keep a cop outside in the area and wait for Meskell to come after her."

"With constant protection for the juror, what makes you think Meskell will attempt anything?" Jay Werner asked.

"He'll go after her," Jake said dryly, remembering the thick file he had built on Lenny Meskell. "He'll try to carry out his threat."

"Jake's right," Vance said. "Meskell isn't the kind to wait. He wants instant gratification. And we'll be waiting for him."

"You're making her a decoy instead of placing her in a safe house," Jake said.

"She's aware of the risks. I've talked with her at length about this. And I've told her we'll give her all the protection she needs." He looked directly at Jake, and then his gaze went around the table, taking in each detective. "I want her to get through this unharmed. I think we can protect her or I'd never agree to this. Meskell's going to make a move.

We might as well set things up so we know where he'll make the move, who it'll be against, and hopefully, when and how he'll attempt his revenge."

Vance unfolded a chart and spread it before them. "Here's her house," he said, pointing to a small black square. "She lives on an acreage on the edge of the city, in our jurisdiction. Here's the highway past the place, and her drive. There are woods near the house. We're going to keep a man on the place around the clock."

"Just one man?" Werner asked.

"With a man inside, as well, we think that's all we'll need. We'll have surveillance points set up on a back road where we can watch anyone approaching the place. There's no other way to get to her house except hiking cross-country. Jake, you know Meskell—how likely is he to do that?"

"Not likely. He's no country boy. He's pure city."

"That's right. And this is hilly terrain. If he does go cross-country and we miss him, we'll still have a man inside the house with the family. We should be able to close in on him before he can do anything."

"If the surveillance guys see him drive past on any of the access roads," Jay Werner said thoughtfully, "we close in and surround him. He may make a desperate run for the house."

"The minute he's spotted, the SWAT team will be sent to the house. We'll cover the grounds and get the chopper out. The man inside will be notified immediately."

"Who gets that great job?" Werner asked.

"This is top-priority," Vance said solemnly, "and we're giving it all the manpower we can. Kurt, you'll head up the search for Lenny. Jay, you'll be in charge of surveillance."

Jake's first reaction was disappointment. But his surprise at not being chosen to head the surveillance team turned to wariness as Richard Vance's gaze swung around to rest on him. Vance gave him one of his scowling "We all must sacrifice" looks, and Jake got a sinking feeling.

"Jake, we've got to protect these jurors. Everyone's on my back about that. I'm putting you with—"

"No!" Jake blurted out, knowing what Vance was going to say. "Let me go after Lenny," he said tightly. "I watched the bastard gun down Dusty. I want to get him!"

"You're to stay with Mrs. Bolen," Vance announced firmly, and Jake knew what that implacable tone meant. It was useless to protest further.

For the remainder of the meeting, Jake listened to Vance, making notes, offering his opinion. Then when the meeting broke up, Vance asked him to wait.

As soon as the two men were alone, Vance faced him squarely. "You understand why we need you with the widow."

"Dammit," Jake exclaimed, leaning forward, feeling his muscles tense. "I don't want to baby-sit some blonde while everyone is out after Lenny!"

"Sorry. She's the one he'll go for. You said it yourself. She's high-profile—the foreman. We've got to protect her, and you're the man."

"C'mon, Richard. For Lord's sake, don't put me on that assignment. I'll go nuts out there!"

"Jake—"

"Let the woman hire a bodyguard," Jake persisted.

"Even if she'd do it, I'd still send you, because I need a man with brains, not just muscle. You're to watch her. Come hell or high water, see to it that Lenny doesn't get to her. Remember, he has a rape charge way back in his record. He got off light because he was a juvenile."

Vance looked beyond Jake and took a deep breath, his forehead knotting in a scowl. "She has an etched-glass business, and she did the windows in the governor's house before he was elected. He's putting pressure on us to protect her, too. We can't send a uniformed cop—we've got to have a detective. The woman is beautiful and the media loved her during Meskell's trial. They will crucify us if

Meskell guns her down. Get out there as soon as you can. I told her you would be there today.''

"Oh, dammit!'' Jake said, looking down at the dossier in front of him. Widowed, two children—Tara, seven years old, and Celia, five years old. Lives on an acreage on edge of Austin city limits. No men in her life.

"She's on an acreage, for Lord's sake. Put her in a safe house and let me hunt down Meskell.''

"We thought about it, but we need her to seem vulnerable if Meskell is to make a move. When he does, we'll be there to protect her and stop him.''

"Dammit, Richard, this is a woman with two little kids. I'll go nuts.''

For the first time since the meeting started, a hint of a smile flitted over Richard Vance's face. "It'll do a confirmed old bachelor like you good.''

"The hell you say.''

"For as long as I can spare the manpower, I'll put a man on the grounds, as well as you with her. As soon as I get someone, I'll let you know and tell them to check in with you. We'll have the surveillance set up by two o'clock today.''

Richard Vance gathered up his things and dropped a scrap of paper in front of Jake. "Here's her phone number. I'm counting on you, Jake. And don't forget, Lenny threatened you, too.''

"And I hope he comes after me,'' Jake said grimly.

"Frankly, we expect him to. That's all the more reason we'll be ready and waiting.'' At the door, Vance paused. "How many weeks would you give him to make his move?''

Jake thought about Meskell, about all the times he had tangled with him in the past. "Knowing Lenny, I'd say we have anywhere from two to four weeks.''

"That was my estimate, too,'' Vance replied with satisfaction. "You be careful.''

As he left, Jake picked up the scrap of paper. He crumpled it in his fist and stood so swiftly his chair toppled over with a crash. He wanted to put his fist through the table to vent his anger. Instead, he gathered up his papers and headed for his desk, leaving the chair where it had fallen behind him.

When he thought of Meskell, he always remembered Dusty. He had watched Meskell lean out of his car and shoot Dusty and then speed away. He'd been unable to do anything about it. Jake swore under his breath, clenching his fists. He hated Meskell and he knew it was mutual. When they caught Lenny, Jake had been the one to cuff him.

Jake drove to his tenth-floor condo, which was west of downtown. Two hours later, after throwing what he needed into a small case and packing his shoulder holster, he changed into jeans and a navy T-shirt. Jake tucked the weapon he preferred, a 9 mm semiautomatic, into the waistband of his jeans at the small of his back. After locking up his condo, he turned onto San Antonio Street and headed north to take the freeway through Austin, turning onto the road leading to her house.

The road slashed through rolling hills dotted with feathery mesquite, bright yellow black-eyed Susans, wild pink and yellow lantana and tall green grass that bent in the June breeze.

In minutes the tenseness left Jake's shoulders. As he glanced at a herd of white-faced Herefords grazing nearby, he relaxed, thinking about the land he had purchased. After retirement he would settle in the country, where it would be quiet and peaceful. But his thoughts strayed back to the task at hand.

A widow who was an artist. Probably about as tough as spring tulips. Well, maybe a little tougher than that. He remembered her quick reaction at the trial in April when Meskell had lunged at her. She had doubled up her fists and had thrown her hands up to defend herself. She had been ready to fight. Jake smiled at the memory.

"Damn," he said softly. If he had two kids and his life had been threatened, he wouldn't continue to live isolated on the city's edge. He prayed the house was set back miles from the highway, near neighbors, and behind a high fence, with a vicious guard dog.

Weekend traffic was heavy and he pressed the brake as he came up behind a bright lime-colored Volkswagen. In minutes he was swearing impatiently under his breath because there was no chance to pass on the two-lane stretch of road and oncoming traffic was steady. The usual wide shoulders the state provided were missing along this stretch of pavement, and on every rise the glow-in-the-dark wreck in front of him slowed to thirty-five miles an hour. Downhill, the car picked up speed, getting to forty.

In minutes a glance in the rearview mirror showed a string of cars behind him. Finally, at the top of a hill, he had a chance to pass and stepped on the accelerator, barreling around the creeping car and settling back in the seat with a shake of his head.

Twenty minutes later, long before he reached it, Jake saw the Bolen place. The small one-story frame house was set back from the road about a quarter of a mile on a slight hill and was clearly visible from the highway, as well as from the stand of oaks across the road, and from any number of places in any direction around it.

A dilapidated one-car garage with a tar-paper roof and a weathered barn stood yards away from the house to the west. Three wooden steps ran up to the front porch, where a porch swing hung from the ceiling. Along the drive in front of the house was a battered metal mailbox on a post.

Winding along the hilly drive, Jake slowed and parked in front of the house and stepped out, feeling a surge of anger as he looked at a stand of pines behind the place. "Dammit," he muttered. Anyone could hide with a high-powered

rifle and pick Rebecca Bolen off, and no one would see who
had done it. Meskell couldn't have asked for a better ar-
rangement.

A plume of dust rose in the air near the highway, and Jake
studied the road he had just traveled. In seconds the green
Volkswagen topped a hill and then went down out of sight,
dust following in its wake. Jake's eyes narrowed and he
prayed it was someone coming to visit. As he watched the
approach of the car that backfired loudly, he could see three
heads through the windows.

"Oh, for God's sake," he grumbled again. She lived in
plain view, drove a car that couldn't outrace a kid on a bi-
cycle and wouldn't be more noticeable if it had her name in
red flashing neon across the top.

The car slowed and stopped and two little girls climbed
out, wearing matching pink shorts and white T-shirts. The
taller child had a long brown pigtail.

She was the one who noticed him first, speaking to the
other little girl, who turned to look at him. He recognized
them from their pictures: Tara and Celia. The tallest turned
to pick up a sack of groceries and hand it to the smaller
child.

His annoyance shot up another notch. The mother should
have kept them in the car until she knew who was waiting.
They could all see him, and yet there was no hesitation in the
children about getting out of the car. As he started toward
them, Rebecca Bolen emerged and came around the car, and
for an instant Jake forgot where he was or why he was there.

Golden hair fell below her shoulders in a slight curl. Wide
blue eyes gazed at him with arched brows raised in question
and full red lips made him think about kisses. She had
flawless creamy skin and pink cheeks. The pictures hadn't
done her justice, and she had looked different in the courtroom.

There was a lively sparkle in her eyes that made him forget what he had been about to say. His gaze lowered to her

slender throat, the green knit shirt that fit and clung to lush curves and a tiny waist. Pale jeans hugged her hips. He pulled his gaze up again in time to see her eyes narrow.

"Take the groceries inside," she said, giving the taller child a key and waiting, staring at Jake. As the girls went to a side door, he moved toward Mrs. Bolen, stopping only yards away, momentarily forgetting his purpose and thinking she had the bluest eyes he had ever seen.

Rebecca watched Detective Delancy stride purposefully toward her, and suddenly her heart began drumming. She remembered the moments in the courtroom, remembered Detective Delancy slugging Lenny Meskell and stopping him in his tracks. And she remembered Captain Vance talking to her on the phone, assuring her that Delancy "is as dependable as sunshine. He's damn good at his job."

Looking at the tall man striding toward her, she could imagine that he was very good at his job. He looked decisive, confident and fit. She should have felt relief, but the closer he drew, the less relieved she felt, because he had an aura about him that made her too aware of him as a man. And made her conscious of herself as a woman.

It was a unique, troublesome feeling that she hadn't experienced since her husband's death, and she didn't want to experience it now, not with the man who was going to be their bodyguard. Thank heavens he would be outside in his patrol car!

"I'm Detective Lieutenant Jake Delancy," he said finally, "and I've been assigned to protect you."

Rebecca nodded, studying him. His assessing glance made her conscious of her appearance and too conscious of him as an attractive male.

She remembered Detective Delancy from the trial, remembered his tousled, thick brown hair. Now she noticed his firm chin and his sexy mouth, with its full, sensual underlip. There was a slight crook in his nose, and his features combined into a rugged handsomeness. His thickly lashed

hazel eyes would have brought the term *bedroom eyes* to
mind, except that there was a coldness in them that was a
reminder of his purpose.

She dreaded the disorder he was going to bring into their
lives, yet she remembered Meskell lunging across the courtroom, his blue eyes fixed on her, and she knew this was
necessary. Delancy had a tough, no-nonsense air about him
that should have been reassuring under the circumstances,
yet his blatant study of her made her feel as if a new danger
had just entered her life. He made her feel like a woman
again.

"Captain Vance told me you were coming. I'm Rebecca
Bolen."

When Jake offered his hand, she extended hers. Her hand
was soft and warm as he gave a brief shake. "I'll get the
groceries," Jake said, glancing up the road again. "You go
inside."

As if she hadn't heard him, she turned to get sacks out of
the car, and he reached out, touching her arm. She swung
around, her eyes narrowing, and he wanted to groan. She
was a single mother who owned her own business—probably as independent as an alley cat. She was going to have to
learn to take some orders during the next few days, whether
she liked it or not.

"Get inside, Mrs. Bolen. You're in danger. I'll bring the
groceries."

Looking startled, she glanced past him at the road and
then turned to hurry inside. He watched her walk away,
watched the seductive sway of her hips, her trim bottom and
long legs encased snugly in jeans. Turning to pick up sacks
of groceries, he mentally swore at Richard Vance once more.
This assignment would be a lot easier if Rebecca Bolen
weren't so damned pretty.

Jake strode toward the small house, gravel crunching beneath his feet as he walked along the drive. A narrow grav-
eled walk led to the door, and beds of pink and purple

periwinkle grew beside the house. As he went up the back steps, an eerie prickling crossed his nape.

Jake glanced over his shoulder at the shadowed woods. He felt vulnerable, standing in plain view of the trees with his arms filled with groceries. He yanked open the door, entering and letting the screen slap shut behind him.

"Pow!" came the soft word, the sound not carrying. The hairs in the rifle sight made a dark cross against Jake Delancy's head as he stood on the step to Rebecca Bolen's back door.

The barrel of the rifle lowered. Lenny Meskell grinned as he watched Delancy disappear into the house. They'd sent Delancy to protect the bitch. Meskell chuckled. Now he'd get them both.

He could have gotten them only minutes ago. He'd had them both in his rifle sight, yet he wanted Rebecca Bolen alive for a while. He wanted her to worry first. Then he would take her with him, head down to Mexico. She would regret the day she'd stood up and declared him guilty.

He would kill Delancy, then take her and kill her later. And she would go with him willingly, to protect her children. He knew women like Mrs. Bolen. Uptight, self-righteous, worried about their kids.

The cops thought Delancy could keep her safe. Meskell took a drag on his cigarette and tossed down the butt, studying the house. He could get into the house any night. Once he got in her bedroom he knew Delancy couldn't make a move, because Mrs. Bitch would then be a hostage.

But they'd sent Delancy out—what if there were others? he thought suddenly. His grin fading, Lenny looked around, hating the eerie silence of the woods, his eyes peering through the shadows. Was Delancy alone?

Lenny inhaled and stepped back from the edge of the woods, moving cautiously, placing the rifle sling over his shoulder and drawing his pistol.

He studied the trees, watching for movement. Damn, he hated the outdoors. Worse than a cell. Damn worse than a cell. Better not see a snake. He hated snakes. He moved through the trees. He'd come back tonight. No hurry. He'd come back and check to see if the police were going to stand guard outside or if the detective was considered sufficient.

Lenny fingered the grip of his pistol as he moved through the woods. Give them another day. This was Saturday. By tomorrow night, or in the early hours of Monday morning, while it was still dark. Let them wait and wonder when he'd make his move.

Payback was coming. The cop and the bitch. He'd get them both, and they'd regret ever crossing paths with Lenny Meskell. Lenny glanced over his shoulder. Through the trees, he could still see the white square of the house. He'd be back soon enough.

A sudden thought occurred to him, and he grinned again, looking over his shoulder. "I'll give you something to think about, Delancy," he muttered, moving faster through the woods, away from the house.

Jake kicked the door closed with his foot and set the sacks of groceries on the wooden table. The compact kitchen was filled with oak cabinets, pots of green plants, pictures held by magnets to the refrigerator, and an antique round oak table.

As the little girls stared at him, he smiled at them.

"Girls, this is Mr. Delancy. Mr. Delancy, this is Tara and Celia, but we call her Sissy."

"Hello, Tara," he said. He nodded at Sissy, who was studying him intently, her tiny mouth pursed as she stared. She was blond like her mother, with the same blue eyes. He wiped his forehead, thinking it felt like a hundred and ten degrees in the kitchen.

"I'll turn on the air-conditioning, and you can have a seat in the living room while I put away the groceries," Rebecca said, switching on a window unit.

"I'll help with the groceries," he said, joining the girls, who were already putting things away.

Shrugging, Rebecca took a head of lettuce from a sack. He noticed tiny cuts and scratches covering her slender hands, and he leaned forward, pointing at the back of one finger. "A cat?"

She shook her head. "My job. I work with glass."

Nodding, Jake picked up frozen cans of orange juice. The girls were staring at him, and he wondered if they had any idea who he was or why he was there.

"We're finished," Tara said. "We'll be in the backyard, Mom."

He watched them go, knowing he was going to change this family's lifestyle and wondering how big a task it would be.

"Would you like a glass of tea, Mr. Delancy?"

"It's Jake. No need to be formal. We're going to see a lot of each other in the next few days. And yes, tea sounds good," he replied, wondering if the window unit was the only one they had. He watched her move around the kitchen, and in minutes she held out a glass of iced tea to him. Short tendrils of blond hair clung damply to her temples, and she pushed them away, shaking her head and causing her fall of hair to swirl across her shoulders. His fingers brushed hers as he accepted the cool drink. He looked down at her, knowing he needed to keep his mind on business.

"You seem annoyed," she remarked.

He gazed beyond her at the back door window.

"This house wasn't built for security," he answered, checking the simple lock, making up an excuse. The truth was that he was annoyed because he found himself attracted to her. "If she wanted to, your daughter could break in here in less than three minutes."

"We've never had to worry about that before."

"You don't own a dog, you live in isolation, and you're on a major highway in full view of the road. You need more security all the time, not just now."

"Thank you, Detective," she replied frostily. "We can go to the living room," she said without moving, and then he realized she was waiting for him to get out of the way. He stepped aside, and as she brushed past him, he caught a faint enticing scent, like summer flowers.

While he followed her down a narrow hallway, his gaze drifted down to the sexy sway of her bottom. Had he been so wound up at Meskell's trial that he hadn't noticed Rebecca Bolen? Or had it been her conservative hairdo and clothing? He had been in court only to testify and to hear the verdict so he had paid little attention to the jurors. And he'd been more interested in Meskell than the jury. Now he wondered how he could have not noticed Rebecca Bolen.

Pausing, she pointed to an open doorway. "That's the girls' bedroom, and mine is across the hall." She slanted him a look over her shoulder. "Does someone else come this evening for a night watch?"

Taking a long drink of the iced tea, Jake shook his head. "No, I'm here full-time," he said, glancing at a room with twin beds, pink bedspreads, a rocking chair, dolls, shelves lined with toys and books. A small fan stood on the floor.

"You're the only one?"

He turned back to find her staring at him with a frown. "Yep, I'm it—around the clock."

Rebecca stared at him in consternation. Jake Delancy would be living with them in this tiny house. The idea plagued her—she wasn't accustomed to having a man in the house anymore. She thought about Dan and felt a pang of longing and need. She couldn't help thinking that if Dan were here, none of this would be happening. If only— She closed her eyes, remembering her husband, knowing he would have taken charge in a situation like this. She felt the old pain resurfacing and was surprised that it still could take her breath away and make her ache. In twenty years, would it still hurt as badly? she wondered.

"Are you all right?" Detective Delancy asked, and she inhaled deeply, fighting to get her thoughts on the present and her emotions under control.

He studied her, his probing gaze boring into her, jangling her nerves.

"At Meskell's trial you were ready to fight him when he lunged for you," Jake said quietly. "Have you taken a course in self-defense?"

"No," she answered. "And I definitely wasn't ready to fight him."

"You had your fists doubled."

"I didn't know it at the time. I owe you a thank-you for stepping in."

"It was a pleasure," he said, his voice becoming cold again, and she realized he felt strongly about Lenny Meskell.

Jake entered the girls' room and tried a window, which slid open easily and silently. He closed it and turned the lock, then locked the window next to it. The screens had holes someone in times past had cut, and he sighed.

"We sleep with the attic fan on and the windows open at night," Rebecca said from the doorway. She was leaning with one hip against the door, and he saw disapproval in her eyes.

"You'll have to start sleeping with the windows closed. These windows need to be locked, and I'll get better locks."

"Look," she said, straightening up, her eyes becoming frosty, "I'm afraid of Meskell." She folded her arms in front of her. "But we have to live our lives and keep some kind of normalcy. As much as possible, I don't want to terrify the girls. And last winter I opened my own business, so I'm on a tight budget. I can't afford to run the air-conditioning around the clock."

"Do you want me to show you how easily I can step through one of these windows when it's open?"

Her lips tightened as she shook her head. "How much danger are we in?"

He gave her a level look. "I watched him gun down my co-worker."

She closed her eyes momentarily. "What about my girls? I don't have relatives I can send them to stay with."

"What about a friend?"

She shook her head. "My friends either have too many kids to take on two more, or they don't have any and wouldn't know how to cope. There just isn't anywhere else for the girls to go," she replied, her voice filled with worry.

"Okay, but if you ever think of someone, let me know. Until Meskell is caught, your girls should stay in the house."

"I'll get them to play in the kitchen now." She left and called the girls. He knew he had frightened her, but she needed to realize fully what danger they were in.

While he waited, he crossed the hall and looked at a room with an old-fashioned brass bed, a pale blue spread, another rocker, more bookshelves, and hanging plants. A braided rug covered the plank floor.

The house was modest, simply furnished, but everything was neat and tidy, with a homey charm. He glanced at the brass bed and an image of Rebecca Bolen sprawled on it, her golden hair spread over the pillow behind her head, flashed in his mind. The fantasy sent his temperature soaring, and he ran his hand across his temple.

He paused beside the bed to pick up a picture. In it, Rebecca Bolen was smiling, wearing a white wedding dress. A brown-haired, blue-eyed man stood with his arm around her as he smiled at the camera. Jake could see a resemblance between the oldest child and her father in their oval faces, brown hair and straight noses. He set the picture back down on the bedside table and went to the windows to lock them.

"The girls will paint in the kitchen and there's a small television on the counter they can watch," Rebecca said from the doorway. She studied him, thinking he dominated the small room. "I thought they'd send someone in uniform."

"The governor and the D.A. are worried about you. You did some glasswork once for the governor, so he requested that a detective be assigned to you."

When they moved down the hall, she was aware of him beside her. She pointed to another open door. "Here's the only bathroom." She turned again to face him. "If you're here around the clock…" She frowned and hesitated. "I just thought we'd have guys in police cars taking turns outside, watching the place."

If she wasn't frightened by Meskell's threat, he suspected, she would want him around about as much as he wanted to be there.

"I'm going to be your shadow. And there will be a uniformed man outside, at least for a while, and he'll stay here in the house when we're away from it."

The frosty look came into her eyes again, but she kept quiet and turned to walk toward the room at the end of the hall. He glanced at the bathroom as he passed it. It was tiny, but clean and neat, like the bedrooms and kitchen.

"This is the living room, and you've seen the whole—"

Jake heard her sharp intake of breath and saw her stiffen. Instinct told him something was frightening the hell out of her. Setting down the glass of tea, he brushed past her and stopped.

Chapter 2

Rebecca stared at the object on the floor in the center of the room. A dead blackbird with a switchblade knife through it was in the center of the room, in the middle of the braided rug. A folded piece of paper lay beside it. Feeling as if she had suddenly been drenched in ice water, she stared at it as Jake Delancy passed her. "I'll be right back," he said, going to his car and returning with a kit in his hand.

Realizing she was staring, she shifted her attention to the windows. "The window's open," she said. "He came in through the window." She shivered, her fear mushrooming. "The girls could have come in here and found that."

Taking a picture of the bird and knife, Jake opened the note, holding it with his handkerchief to avoid leaving prints. She stepped close to look at the note. Large printed letters gave a message:

You will be next.

"He just wants to scare you," Jake said flatly. She stood beside him, looking at the tan, blunt fingers holding the paper. His calm voice was reassuring.

"It's difficult to ignore the fact that he's been in our house."

"He won't be back."

She experienced a flicker of surprise at the tone of certainty in his voice. "You don't know that."

"You have protection now," he said, looking down at her. She met Jake Delancy's hazel gaze and realized he would relish Lenny Meskell attempting to get into the house again.

From a kit, Jake removed transparent plastic covers and placed the note between them. He picked up his cellular phone and punched a single key to dial a preprogrammed number.

When he turned his back to her, Rebecca's gaze ran across his broad shoulders, and she felt better because he looked strong and tough and competent.

"Yeah," he said, while he carefully picked up the bird with his handkerchief and placed it along with the note into the kit he had brought from the car. "Yeah. Okay." He punched a button to end the connection, and then he glanced around. "Where can I put this until someone comes to pick it up?"

"He's been in our house," she repeated, still in shock.

"Meskell wanted to frighten you, but he's tipped his hand now because we know he's close. We've staked out the roads around here. He broke in before we had the surveillance teams in place or I would have heard from them. Either that or he's still out there in the woods."

"Great heavens!"

"The police are on their way, and the surveillance team is in place. We'll check out the area when the others get here."

She ran her hand across her head. "You can put the box on top of the bookshelf. The girls won't bother it or ask about it. I'd rather they didn't see it. It would only upset them."

"Sure," he said, stretching his long arm to slip the box up high. The navy shirtsleeves stretched over his bulging biceps. She studied him again, feeling reassured by his presence. She hated the thought of Meskell being in the house; she felt invaded and uneasy.

"Everything else seems untouched," she stated.

Jake looked around a living area that held flower-patterned chintz-covered chairs, an oval braided rug, toys, lamps that looked like ten-year-old garage-sale bargains, brass candlesticks and a brass clock that rested on a mantel, bookshelves holding worn books. He hunkered down to look out the open window. The screen had been tossed on the ground. His gaze drifted to Rebecca's car, almost out of sight at the side of the house.

"Why do you drive that Volkswagen? It would draw attention in a midnight fog."

"When we had it painted a few years ago, I let the girls help me pick out the color. I didn't think I'd ever have to hide from someone."

She met his gaze squarely and he realized she was frightened. "Remember, I'm here to protect you."

"It's the girls I'm worried about. And I guess it scares me that I'm in jeopardy, because they need me."

"He'll be caught soon."

Jake closed the window while she moved to the adjoining window to turn on the air-conditioning. It started with a *whumpf* and puffed noisily, and he knew it would muffle sounds, adding another security hazard. She stood only a few feet away, and Jake thought again that she was a breathtakingly beautiful woman. He remembered that the dossier had said there were no men in her life. Why not? She was a knockout.

"Are you dating anyone I should know about?"

Her blue eyes were wide and clear. "No. I'm busy with my shop and the girls, and I don't meet many single men. I really haven't wanted to date, anyway," she added quietly, and he realized she hadn't recovered fully from the loss of her husband. Had she moved to the acreage to isolate herself until the pain subsided?

"Do you have an attic?"

She gave him a startled look. "You think he might still be in the house?"

"No, I don't, but we've been all over the house except a basement or attic. The closets in the bedrooms were open, and no one was in them."

"There's an attic, but the attic's not floored and there aren't any stairs to it, just an opening in my closet. You can get a kitchen chair and shove my clothes aside if you want to look. That's what the electrician had to do when he was up there to see about the attic fan. We never go up there."

"I'll check," Jake said, disappearing into the hall. She waited, feeling edgy and vulnerable, hating the thought of Meskell in their house and wondering if he had prowled around.

Jake stood in the bedroom, looking at the small square opening with a piece of wood over it. Below it were her clothes, and he noticed a filmy red nightgown and for an instant imagined her in it.

Trying to get his mind back on his work, he pushed the clothes aside, stood on his toes and slid the board away from the opening. He jumped up, hooked his hands in the opening and hoisted himself up, feeling as if he were climbing into a furnace.

The space was empty, dust-filled, with a thin layer of insulation. He saw the large attic fan, the wire mesh over the opening above the front porch.

He dropped back down, standing on his toes to ease the board into place. As he returned to the front room, he brushed insulation and dust off his jeans. "Everything is fine." He retrieved his glass of tea.

"Won't you sit down?" Rebecca waved her hand and perched on the sofa as Jake sank into an overstuffed chair.

Rebecca was staring at the box. "I never thought he'd really carry out his threat."

"He hasn't carried it out. Now I'm here, and we'll have a man outside soon in addition to the men staked out watching the roads. We'll get Meskell," Jake said solemnly.

"I hope so!" she exclaimed, catching her lower lip with her teeth. Looking at her rosy mouth, Jake forgot business momentarily. He propped one foot on a knee, pulling at a string from the frayed knee of his jeans.

"If you have men watching all the roads and a man circling around in the woods—why are you needed in here?"

"Murphy's law," he answered dryly. "Things can go wrong in a flash. We hope he'll never reach your house, but if he does, I'll be ready." She seemed lost in thought over his answer, and he changed the topic.

"Do you have any relatives outside of Texas?" Jake asked. "Somewhere you could take your family and stay until this blows over?" This was not in the plan he had discussed with Vance, but it would get her out of his hair and would get him back into the action again.

"No. We don't have other relatives and I'm not that close with my deceased husband's family."

He'd struck out on that one. He surveyed the room, his mind working on a plan for them to achieve maximum safety. "All right, we have to make your house secure."

A scrap of paper lay on the coffee table, and he leaned forward to read it, wondering if it was something else left behind by Meskell. Jake read:

Saturday—seven o'clock, breakfast, seven forty-five to ten o'clock, chores, ten until eleven, grocery and shopping. Twelve, lunch. One, nap time for Sissy and music practice for Tara. Two, read to girls.

He stopped reading and looked at Rebecca, realizing this was a very orderly woman who was going to have her life turned upside down.

"Here's your list for Saturday." He stood and held out the paper.

"I try to keep organized," she answered, crossing the room to take the note from him. His fingers brushed hers as he gave her the list.

"You're cold. Everything is all right now."

"I know," Rebecca answered, aware of the slight contact and the warmth of his hand. "When I heard about Meskell's escape, I felt certain he would want to get as far away as possible."

"Not until he accomplishes what he threatened. He doesn't have anything to lose now," Jake answered, his voice becoming deeper. She stood only inches away and he was becoming increasingly aware of her. "I'll secure the house as much as possible."

"A burglar alarm seemed unnecessary and frivolous. I tend toward the practical side," she said.

"Not too practical, or you wouldn't have set aside a special time for reading in your scheduled day."

Rebecca was aware they were standing too close—his hazel eyes were devastating. She should step away, yet she stood rooted to the spot. This disturbing, appealing male was going to be staying with them. The idea made her fluttery.

"You would be safer if you'd curtail your activities," Jake said.

"Are you married?" The moment the words were out of her mouth, she wished she could take them back. "I shouldn't ask, but I suspect you know a great deal about me, and we don't know anything about you."

"I'm definitely not married," he replied curtly. "Relax. We'll know each other pretty well before long."

She was held by his unwavering gaze, aware that silence was stretching between them, and it took an effort to turn away.

Jake watched her stuff the note into her hip pocket before she returned to her seat. Her jeans fit snugly, and she sat down gracefully, folding her legs beneath her.

"This house is a good target. There are too many trees. Someone can hide and watch the house without being seen."

"I wanted the girls in the country. I thought we could manage better and it would be good for them and cheaper for us. I didn't know this would happen." She looked around. "Look how small this place is. Where will we put you?"

"I can sleep on a chair right here."

"No, you can't. The girls share a room, and I have a room. I suppose we can sleep together."

He looked startled, and she realized what she had said. "I meant the girls and me!"

As she felt her cheeks flush, she noticed a flash of amusement in his eyes. "I'm accustomed to this, and I'll stay awake during the night to check on things."

"This," Rebecca said, waving her hand, "all of this seems so complicated. How long were you after Meskell before you caught him?"

"It took a year to bring him in."

"A year! You were the one who did that?"

"Not alone. There were a lot of us who worked on catching him." He paused, thinking about her small daughters. "You'll have to keep a closer watch on the kids. Until he's caught, keep them inside with us."

"They'll do what they're told. These are really small quarters. If you're not accustomed to having children underfoot, I'm not sure you're going to like it."

He gave her a look, and she realized that he disliked being there at all. "Why are you here if you don't want to be?" she asked in dismay.

"It's my job," he answered gruffly. "If you see anything suspicious, let me know at once. Emphasize that with the kids. If you get any strange phone calls, let me know and keep them on the line as long as possible so we can try a trace."

"Are you afraid?"

"No. You can't imagine how much I'd like to get my hands on him," Jake replied with an obvious note of determination in his voice.

"That must be why you're a cop," she said, letting hurt surface momentarily, and his brow arched.

"You don't like cops?"

She tried to control the hot surge of anger. "You should know, Detective Delancy. You should have all the facts about me, what I do, what I like, who I see, the man I was married to, how he died—"

"He was with the Austin Fire Department and died fighting a building blaze."

"That's right," she said, feeling the hurt return. Having a strong man in the house made her think more often about Dan. "I appreciate the work of men like my husband and men like you, but I hate it and never want to be involved in it again." Realizing he was studying her, she closed her mouth.

"A lot of cops' wives feel that way, too," Jake stated in a cynical voice.

She considered him a moment, and then her practical side took over. "I'll have to go to the grocery again and stock up. I didn't know you'd be here full-time."

"Make a grocery list and I'll see that we get everything."

She inhaled as if she were going to argue, but she clamped her lips closed and remained silent. But the sparks in her eyes gave away her feelings, and he wondered how long it would be before they had a full-fledged clash.

"As soon as we talk to the girls, I want to check out the area. I'm going to put simple locks on the windows. I'll get bigger locks as soon as possible."

"What about my business?"

"You'll have to close your shop for the time being."

"Lord, my business is just getting started, and I have five orders right now. I can't close the shop!"

He ran his fingers through his hair, and for a moment she was distracted as she watched his brown locks spring back in waves. His hair was thick, slightly unruly, giving him a tousled appearance that softened his rugged looks and added to his appeal. Was it her jangled nerves that made her more aware of him? One glance from him, and she knew that was not the reason. There was a sexy charisma about Detective Delancy that had nothing to do with the circumstances.

"Can you work at home?" he asked, breaking into her thoughts.

"Here?" she asked, looking at the tiny living room. "I do etched and stained-glass windows. I need space."

"What do the girls do while you work?"

"Right now they have dance lessons and swim lessons in town at the YWCA on Mondays, Wednesdays, and Fridays. The Y has a summer program—the girls eat lunch there and have craft activities in the afternoon after the swimming and dance lessons. I've been taking them to town, and then, when I pick them up, they come back to the shop with me."

"You need to move your work home and cancel their activities temporarily." Jake was sitting back on the chair, looking relaxed, his ankle crossed on his knee, yet his demeanor still held an unmistakable air of authority.

"I can't do that!" she exclaimed, aghast at the changes he wanted to make. "My customers couldn't find me out here! That would ruin my business. It would be like putting a flower shop out here in the barn."

"What I'm suggesting is necessary," he added. Even though he spoke without raising his voice, she detected an inflexible tone that annoyed her.

"My *business* is necessary," she argued, suspecting she was not getting anywhere with her reasoning.

"Your life is in danger, and driving into town every day will make you a sitting duck. We can eliminate the extra risks by your working here temporarily."

"All right. We'll do everything your way," she snapped, knowing she had lost this argument.

"For the time being, and then I'll be out of your life."

She studied him, remembering Dan and feeling another pang of loss. "You're all alike," she said, knowing that he could hear the bitterness in her voice. "You like the adrenaline rush. You love your work."

"If I didn't, how long do you think I could stand to do this?"

The tension rose between them. Their sparring had an edge to it that disturbed Jake because he found her so appealing. "I'll get your work things moved here."

Rebecca wanted to refuse, yet she had to think of the girls' safety. "I suppose I could work in the barn. It's empty because we don't have a horse. The girls would like one, but I just can't afford to keep a horse."

He glanced out the window at the barn, and she took the opportunity to study him. He was the first man she had been acutely aware of since she'd been widowed. He was single, but even if he was interested in her, she wouldn't want to date him. She thought about Dan's violent death and how it still hurt. Jake Delancy was another man who courted danger. She never wanted to risk falling in love with a man who lived that kind of life again. Even though he had been a fire fighter, Dan Bolen had been gentle, kind, full of fun. Jake Delancy looked dangerous, determined and strong-willed. Not the man for her, no matter how physically attractive she found him.

"I don't like the idea of you going back and forth to the barn."

"Detective Delancy—"

"Jake," he reminded her gently with a smile, and she caught her breath. The man had a charming side that would win over a zombie. His smile brought creases to either side of his mouth, an appealing crinkle to the corners of his eyes, and a mellowing of the harshness of his rugged features. His voice was warm and coaxing, quite different from his gruff, take-charge manner.

"Jake," she repeated, thinking it sounded more personal than it should. "I have to get these jobs done on time or give them up to someone else. Surely I can get from here to the barn. I need this business to survive."

"Not if your life depends on it," he answered flatly, all the charm gone from his tone, swept away by an arctic chill.

"The barn is only yards away. I have to get out of the house occasionally—groceries, gas."

He fell silent again, as if lost in thought, and then looked at her. "The barn it is, but I go with you." He wasn't going to yield, his tone was implacable, yet he hadn't raised his voice in the slightest.

"Do you do this often?"

"No. The last person I had to protect was a politician who had been threatened by organized crime. And that incident occurred over eight years ago."

"Don't the women in your life worry terribly about you?" Again the question was out before she could think about it. It was too personal. If she kept everything businesslike between them, it would be easier to deal with him.

"If they worry too much, they break off seeing me," he said, his voice becoming lighter. "Believe it or not, I do have a date every once in a while."

She knew he was teasing her, yet beneath his amusement, there was a hint of anger. She couldn't resist giving him a smile.

Jake's pulse jumped as he saw the flash of her white teeth and a dimple appeared in her left cheek. Her smile was irresistible, and he wanted to coax her into smiling again.

"Jake, Lenny Meskell is a threat, but I'm not going to let that man ruin my life or ruin my girls' summer."

"I think he'll make his move soon. Once he does, this will be over and your life will return to normal. Until then, you can't take unnecessary risks and neither can they."

Anger surged in Rebecca, anger at Lenny Meskell. She knew Jake was right, so she nodded. "You'll have to move a table out here."

"Fine. I'll have the arrangements made."

She opened her purse and withdrew a small datebook, flipping it open. She glanced up at him. "There's another problem."

Jake braced for the worst. So far, Rebecca Delancy was a disaster waiting to happen, with her unlocked windows, her noisy air conditioner, and her house in the middle of nowhere. What other disasters awaited them?

Chapter 3

"What problem?"

Rebecca braced for his objections, raising her chin and looking him in the eye. "I'm supposed to be the dinner speaker at the Austin Businesswomen's Annual Banquet tonight. I'm the main speaker, and it's entirely too late to cancel something important like that."

Jake wondered if Richard Vance had known about the banquet; he suspected Vance had decided to let him learn about it on his own. "Call and tell them you need a substitute."

She shook her head. "They asked me to be the speaker a year ago. I can't call hours before the banquet and cancel. This is the only thing I have to do! Surely you can protect me for a few hours in town. I have to do this."

"It's totally against good judgment."

"I can't cancel on a big organization like that. Do you want me to show you the article in today's paper about the banquet tonight?"

"It's in the paper?"

"I'm not mentioned. It's just a listing about the banquet. I feel I have to do this. I won't cancel this late in the day."

He mentally ran over what he could do to beef up security at the banquet. "How do I have to dress?"

"It's a banquet. A suit will do."

"Then we have to go to my condo on the way. What had you planned to do about the girls?"

"I have a friend in town who's keeping them with her six girls."

Jake thought a moment. "You might put your friend at risk. I can call my brother and his wife. They live in Round Rock, so that's far enough away that your girls should be safe."

"That will just put your brother and his wife at risk!"

"No. Meskell won't know anything about them, so the girls should be out of harm's way. My brother is with the FBI. He's armed, trained, and the girls should be safe. My brother and his wife don't have any children, but Sally is good with kids. She's a kindergarten teacher at Lowell, in Austin. Would you trust them with your girls?"

Rebecca stared at him, thinking that she suddenly had to trust a lot of strangers. She thought about Leah and her children and knew she didn't want to put them in danger. She had a friend whose children went to Lowell. She would call Angie this afternoon and ask if she knew Jake's sister-in-law.

Rebecca nodded, praying she was making the right decision. She thought about the girls. "Shall I bring the girls back in here to talk to them now? Is there anything else to discuss before they join us?"

"Nothing they can't be privy to."

Rebecca left the room, relieved to get away from his direct gaze for a few minutes. The girls were eating apple slices.

"Mr. Delancy wants to talk to all of us. Let's go back to the living room."

When they entered the living room, Sissy crossed the room to Jake and leaned against his leg, holding up the bowl of apple slices.

"Would you like some apple?"

"No, thank you," he answered politely.

She munched a slice and continued to lean against him and study him. "Do you shoot people?"

"I carry a gun to protect people, not to shoot them."

"Sissy, come sit down here," Rebecca said, and Sissy crossed the room to perch on the sofa beside her.

"We need to take some precautions. Your mother can tell you," he said to the girls.

Rebecca went through everything and received a groan from the girls when she said they had to stay inside. "You're to stay inside unless you specifically ask and receive permission to play outside."

"Lenny Meskell's a wanted man, and everyone is on the lookout for him," Jake said carefully. "His picture has been in the paper and is posted all over the country. The Texas Rangers are involved, as well as the Austin police and the FBI." Jake leaned forward to reach into a hip pocket and withdrew a picture. "This is the man. I want you to look at his picture so you'll know him if you see him. If you see a stranger around the house, come tell me at once, okay?"

"Yes, sir," Tara said, and Sissy nodded, as they walked up close to look at the picture. Rebecca stared at it from across the room, remembering too clearly Lenny Meskell's blue eyes and long face, his blond hair and muscled arms.

"He doesn't look bad," Tara said.

"No, he doesn't, but he is," Jake answered matter-of-factly.

"Is this man going to hurt us?" Sissy asked with wide eyes.

"I'm here to see that he doesn't," Detective Delancy answered with quiet assurance. "But I'd like you to be careful, so you stay where I can see you."

Sissy nodded as if satisfied, and Rebecca was grateful for his calm manner, because the girls didn't seem unduly alarmed. Was Jake Delancy accustomed to children? He was relaxed and at ease with them, and the girls seemed drawn to him.

She heard a car motor and watched through the window as two police cars stopped in front. Men spilled out of the cars. With a lithe unfolding, Jake Delancy stood and crossed the room. As he left to meet the men, he took the kit off the shelf and carried it out. Rebecca saw Tara watching him.

"What was in the box?" she asked Rebecca.

Rebecca didn't know whether to tell them or not. She saw Tara waiting while Sissy switched on a cartoon and flopped down on the floor in front of the television.

Rebecca motioned for Tara to come closer. "That man was here and left a warning note for me. Detective Delancy is taking it to some policemen who want to look at it for fingerprints."

"The man was in our house? Here?"

"Yes, he was. He came in through the front window. Mr. Delancy is going to put locks on all our windows. Tara, I want you to keep Sissy with you all the time when you're outside."

"Yes, ma'am. Is Mr. Delancy going to stay with us now?"

"Yes, he is, and another policeman will be outside. They're here to protect us."

"Good. I'm glad Mr. Delancy's here." Tara went to the window to watch the policemen, and soon two men entered and crossed to the window to study where Meskell had entered.

Rebecca carried the empty glasses to the kitchen. Through a front window she could see Jake standing with his hands splayed on his hips while he talked to one of the men. She phoned her friend Angie and in minutes replaced the receiver, reassured about Jake Delancy's sister-in-law.

Watching the men through the window, she saw Jake striding toward the woods behind the house, a pistol in his hand. The wind caught locks of his brown hair and blew them away from his face. His gait was confident, as if he were looking forward to meeting Meskell. Her skin prickled as she looked at the shadows cast by the trees. Jake was walking toward them without hesitation. What would it take to make him afraid? He seemed to have nerves of steel.

Outside, Jake stalked across the ground, his gaze running over the pines and the dark, shaded area beneath them. Drawing his pistol, he lengthened his stride.

He stepped into the cool shade of the trees, standing still and looking around. Birds sang, a slight breeze blew. He glanced down at the pine-needle-strewn ground, knowing it would be difficult to spot tracks. He moved through the trees, trying to decide exactly where he would stand if he wanted to watch the house, thinking he would want the back door in full view, because that would offer the best shot.

An object caught Jake's eye, and he knelt. Pulling out a glove and a plastic bag, he picked up a cigarette stub. A few feet away he found a scrap from a package of gum. A few more feet and he found another cigarette butt. There were more cigarette butts on the ground a few yards away. Jake burned with anger at the thought of Meskell standing out in the shadows waiting to take a shot at Rebecca.

Hatred for the murderer boiled up in him. He easily remembered Meskell leaning out of the car and firing at Dusty, watching Dusty fall. Jake recalled the moment when he had arrested Meskell, the surge of satisfaction he'd experienced, especially after he had punched him out. He'd love an opportunity to do it again.

He pulled out his radio and spoke softly to one of the other men in the area, giving them what he had found. Jake surveyed his surroundings again while listening to the response, looking up in the branches overhead, his attention shifting to the house.

Inside, Rebecca moved from the kitchen windows to the living room, looking for the men. They were nowhere in sight, and she guessed they were searching through the woods and around the house. She turned away to get some household chores done, trying to forget the threat hanging over them.

It was over an hour later before the lawmen piled into their cars and left, and as they drove away, Jake returned to the living room. He crossed the room with deliberation, his hazel eyes studying her, and her pulse started drumming. He reached out to take her arm, and the moment he touched her, she tingled with awareness.

"Stay back from the windows, Rebecca."

Her name, said in his bass voice, affected her deeply. On one level, she was acutely aware of him. On another, she was annoyed by his autocratic ways.

With a frown, she stepped back, conscious that he had dropped his hand to his hip. "It's going to take me a while to get accustomed to this."

"Not used to taking orders?" he asked quietly, his hazel eyes holding her gaze.

"No, I'm not, and I don't like becoming a prisoner in my own house."

"Get over it," Jake said forcefully, knowing that for her own safety she had to cooperate with him. "Someday I'll be gone, Lenny will be in prison, and you'll be your own boss again." Jake flashed her a smile. Something flickered in the depths of her eyes. She had to be aware of the currents tugging and flowing between them, Jake thought. She gave off sparks like metal in a microwave.

He felt an urgent need to put distance between them. If he didn't, he'd reach for her. He mentally swore, because he did not want to be drawn to someone he was assigned to protect. Rebecca Bolen was business. And he didn't want to be attracted to the kind of woman she was. He was not into lasting relationships, and she had an air of permanence that hovered over her like a guardian angel. He turned away to gaze out the windows, trying to shift his thoughts to Meskell.

Rebecca's pulse raced as Jake moved away. The quick smile he had given her was devastating. As tough and assertive as he was, his smile could still disarm, melt and captivate a woman. His teeth were even and white, a contrast to his tanned skin. There were moments when he seemed likeable and nice, moments when she felt far more secure because he was there.

As swiftly as those thoughts came, caution followed. She did not want to be attracted to a cop. Not in the next ten lifetimes. She never wanted her life bound to a man who courted danger again. She looked at him standing in front of the window from which he had warned her to stay away. He flirted with peril, she reminded herself as her gaze ran across his broad shoulders and down over slim hips and long legs.

"Was there any sign of Lenny Meskell outside?" she asked.

Hazel eyes met her squarely. "He's been in the woods behind the house. He must have left the area before we staked it out. He's gone now."

"How can you be sure?"

"We've been over the area thoroughly, and another team of men are still out there and beyond the woods. They'll make certain before they stop the search."

Jake studied the windows. "If you don't mind having a small hole drilled in your window frames, I can get these windows secured easily."

"No, I don't mind. The house isn't a candidate for an elegant-homes magazine."

"I'll get my tools," he said, and left to go to his car. He returned in minutes with an electric drill, and a small box. The moment he switched on the drill both girls came to watch. In seconds he had bored tiny holes in the frames of each window.

"Whatcha doing?" Sissy asked.

"I'll show you," he said, unplugging the drill and placing it carefully on the floor. He opened a box and removed a tenpenny nail. "See, we'll slide the nail into the hole I just drilled, and no one can raise the window, but if anyone inside the house needs to get out," he said carefully to the girls, "just pull the nail out and raise the window. I'll put these around the house and over the air conditioners so no one can slide the window units out of the windows easily."

Knowing her routine had already been destroyed, Rebecca tore up her schedule for Saturday and tossed the pieces in a wastebasket. As Jake Delancy worked, the girls trailing after him, she went to the kitchen to get dinner for the girls.

Twenty minutes later, while she checked a pan of steaming carrots, Jake drilled holes in the kitchen windows. She turned from the stove at the same time he turned, and she bumped him.

He steadied her, his hands going to her waist. She had been conscious of him before, but now the tension was electrifying. His hands held her lightly, yet she felt the imprint of his fingers and palms on her hips. She gazed up into the hazel eyes that met hers. His expression seemed to hold mild curiosity, and his gaze lowered to her lips. She felt trapped by a force that took her breath. Her lips tingled, and she experienced an intense physical response to his merely looking at her. And what frightened her most of all was that she wanted to lean closer to him.

"Sorry. I didn't realize you were close behind me," she said, moving away from him. She was talking too fast, unnerved by her reaction to him. Had he felt something, too? And had he been as startled by it as she had been?

Probably not. The man surely dated regularly and responded to many women. She hadn't dated in a long time, and maybe that was the problem. Yet she knew that wasn't the answer because she knew men through her work and through organizations and church, men who had been friendly, but to whom she'd had no such fiery response.

She prayed they caught Meskell soon.

Jake stood staring at her, his gaze going to her hips, drifting over her legs. The past few minutes had shaken him. He'd never had difficulty keeping business separate from pleasure. He was here to protect her and her family. He didn't even want to be here, he'd rather be out looking for Meskell. He didn't want to be attracted to the beautiful Mrs. Bolen. She wasn't even his type. Any woman who hadn't dated for years would definitely be in earnest when she started. He picked up his tools and left the room.

He walked outside into the sunshine, his thoughts still on her and the startling reaction he'd had to her. And he suspected she was equally surprised. What was it about her that made him so intensely aware of her? It couldn't be sympathy for her. She was too snappy to inspire sympathy. She wasn't deliberately flirting with him—far from it. She looked as if the whole matter were chilling including his staying with them. Yet there had been sparks between them; his erratic pulse testified to that. That and his wayward thoughts. He had to fight the images of her in his arms, in his bed, that kept flashing through his mind. And the curiosity that made him wonder what it would be like to kiss her.

He groaned, striding to his car to retrieve his briefcase, hurrying back to the house. "Forget her, Delancy. She's business. Anything beyond business would be pure trouble."

Inside, Rebecca checked on the golden chicken breasts baking in the oven. She called the girls, and explained what the plans were for the evening. While they ate, she went to dress and shower. She had long ago decided on her green linen dress for the banquet.

She gathered lacy underclothes to take to the bathroom. Remembering Jake, she hunted in vain for a robe, finally finding one of Dan's old blue chambray shirts. It would have to do for a robe. When she stepped across the narrow hallway into the bath, she heard the detective talking to the girls in the kitchen. He was good with kids; too bad he couldn't stay with them for the evening and make himself useful.

As soon as she finished showering, she wrapped her hair in a towel and put on her underclothes and the faded chambray shirt. She opened the door and collided with Detective Delancy.

He caught her, his hands going to her waist again, sending another electrifying jolt through her. She responded to him like a sun-drenched plant in a spring rain.

"Sorry! We seem to have a knack for collision," he drawled, and she felt her cheeks burn, wondering if he thought she was deliberately running into him.

She was aware of his hands on her, of his nearness, of her skimpy clothing. "I thought you were in the kitchen. I heard you talking to the girls."

"I was, but they've finished eating now," he said. His hands stayed on her waist, and he stood only inches from her. Her toes touched his shoe and she slid her foot away.

"I told you it would be crowded," she said, pulling the collar of the shirt closed. His gaze dropped down to the collar, and then lower, and she responded, her nipples becoming taut, a tingling racing through her. The shirt was old, not transparent, but soft, clingy, and too revealing, and she was certain he could see her body's response to his gaze. "You can have the bathroom now."

"I don't want it, thanks," he said in a deep voice, his hazel eyes raising to look at her, and as silence stretched between them, she felt her heart thud.

"I should dress," she finally managed to say, and hurried past him, feeling as if she had just brushed too close to a raging fire. She closed the door to the bedroom and stared across the room at her reflection in a mirror, but she was seeing Jake, his hazel eyes probing her as if he were peering through a microscope. She didn't want to respond to him, not in a sexual way—not in any way!

She thought of Dan then, unexpectedly. She moved across the room to pick up their wedding picture. "Dan," she whispered, missing him, feeling such an enormous void within her. They had been a close-knit, happy family. He had been wonderful with the girls, so full of life and zest and cheer.

"I miss you," she whispered, setting the picture back in place and wiping away the tears that had sprung to her eyes. It still hurt so badly, and now Jake was a constant reminder of what it had been like to have a strong man in their lives.

She took a deep breath, still feeling the imprint of Jake's hands on her waist. Why did he get her so rattled? If she re-acted this strongly to him after only a few hours, what would it be like when he had been there for days?

She dressed, her thoughts swirling. When she was ready, she took a deep breath, opened the bedroom door and headed toward the living room.

Chapter 4

Jake sat reading the paper while the girls played with cards on the floor.

"Is everyone ready?" Rebecca asked from the hallway. He glanced up as she entered the room and for a moment he felt as if all the breath had been punched from his body. Looking as if it were streaked with sunlight, her hair was a cascade of gold framing her face, falling softly over her shoulders. Her luminous blue eyes were highlighted by a faint touch of shadow that made them seem a deeper blue. The short green dress clung to her figure, and he realized his imagination had never come close to doing justice to the pair of legs beneath the jeans. Long, shapely legs, high-heeled green pumps.

His gaze slowly returned to her face and he stood, his pulse thudding. The woman was drop-dead gorgeous. He knew he was staring, and he couldn't stop. You're here to protect her, not date her, his conscience shouted.

"Are you ready?" she asked the girls, and they scrambled up, Tara gathering the cards.

"I won, Mr. Delancy," she said happily to him.

"You sure did," he answered without taking his attention from her. She didn't even seem aware that he was staring. If there were no men in her life, it had to be her choice.

The girls ran from the room. "We'll get our things," Tara called as Rebecca opened her purse and withdrew her small notebook to flip it open. While he still stared, she made notes with a tiny silver pen. The dress had a square neckline that was low enough to stir his imagination, but too high to reveal anything except her collarbones. I'm losing it, he thought to himself. I'm fantasizing about the woman's collarbones!

"You look gorgeous," he said in a husky voice.

"Thank you," she answered briskly, but for one brief moment, she flashed her big blue eyes at him and she looked startled and pleased before she went back to scribbling in her notebook. And he noticed a faint flush in her cheeks that hadn't been there before his remark. The dress had a tiny row of pearl buttons down the front, and he wondered how long it would take to get them unfastened. As she moved closer to him, he caught a scent of lilacs.

"Here," she said, handing him the slip of paper. "This is tomorrow's schedule."

He was not interested in her schedule. Her skin was smooth and flawless; her full lips were enticing.

"You can have the bathroom first before seven," she was saying. "I don't think it will be possible for you to sleep later than that, anyway. Then I'll get in the bathroom so I can start breakfast. We'll breakfast from seven to eight. The girls will be up and need to bathe for church."

As she continued down the list, he realized what she was saying. "No."

When she looked at him, he shook his head. "Sorry, but church is out. Too dangerous. I agreed to the banquet—that's a one-time special deal for you. Sundays you'll stay home until Meskell is caught."

She opened her mouth as if to protest, and then she crossed out church. "At nine, I'll go to Austin to my shop."

"This would delight Meskell," Jake said dryly.

"Excuse me?"

"A schedule. Do you follow a routine every day?"

"Yes. Sunday is the different day, because of church. Weekdays, I go to work at eight."

"If you have a regular routine, do you know how easy it is for him to decide when and where he'll try to get you?"

Realizing he had a point, Rebecca stared at the paper. "This place is so small. If we don't schedule everything we do, we'll have chaos."

Warm fingers took the paper she was scribbling on from her and crumpled it, along with the schedule she had handed him. "Live on the wild side tomorrow," Jake stated quietly. "Let the day unfold. You'll see. We'll all get to use the bathroom and we'll all get dressed and Meskell won't know what to expect from you."

"You haven't been here twenty-four hours, yet you've changed everything we do," she said. Looking up at him, she felt lost in the depths of his green-gold eyes, a feeling she did not welcome and a reaction that perplexed her. His eyes were thickly lashed, adding to his sexy appeal, yet there was a sharpness to his gaze that made her feel he could see far too much.

"It's for your own good. Give it a try."

"I'd feel better with a schedule."

"That schedule of yours is damn dangerous."

She wanted to protest, to stop him from changing her life, but she knew she should go along with him. "All right, I'll go to the shop at nine."

"Rebecca," he drawled softly, and the word seemed to ripple over her like a feathery caress, even more than the first time he had called her by her given name. "You're not going to the shop tomorrow. I'll move things out here. You can tell me what you need and where to find it."

"I'll have to get my tools!"

Jake shook his head, fighting the urge to touch a silky curl that lay on her shoulder. "No, you don't. If we have to make twenty trips back and forth, the department will get your things moved here without you jeopardizing yourself by going to town."

He succumbed to temptation slightly and tapped her wrist, feeling the slender bone beneath his fingers. "Things will fall into place tomorrow. You might be surprised how much you like the change of pace," he drawled, and saw a flicker in the depths of her blue eyes and knew the moment her attention shifted from the schedule to the pull between them. "I'll bet the girls will like it, too."

"You've already charmed them completely," Rebecca said, aware he had been standing so close to her that their shoulders touched. He turned to look directly at her.

"But I haven't you," he remarked in that husky tone that set her nerves quivering.

"That isn't why you're here," she answered, and wished she sounded brisk instead of breathless, praying he couldn't hear her heart pound. Why had she had to draw a detective with charisma and an imperious manner?

"I don't usually annoy women," he remarked dryly.

"You've had a charming moment or two, but most of the time you keep the charm extremely well hidden," she remarked with a faint smile.

"Unfortunately, it better stay that way, for both our sakes," he said quietly.

"We're ready," the girls said behind her, and she turned with relief. She didn't want to feel breathless around him, didn't want to go all tingly and weak-kneed when he started studying her. This wild chemistry that was working between them—she knew he felt it, too. Maybe it was the tension of the situation that triggered it. And she knew he wasn't any happier about it than she was.

"We'll go in my car," Jake said. "I'll pull up as close as possible to the door," he added. "Wait until I get out and come around to the door."

As he closed the drapes and switched on a light, Rebecca wondered how much it would add to her electric bill. "I'll leave the window units on while we're gone, and then cut them off when we get back. They muffle a lot of sounds."

Frowning, she nodded reluctantly. As she followed him down the hall, he pointed to each bedroom. "Go pull shades, or whatever you do."

When she went to the kitchen, the shades were down and the stove light was burning. Jake was waiting at the back door.

He took Tara's arm. "Hold your sister's hand. You wait here, Rebecca." He led the girls along the short gravel path to the car quickly, helped buckle Sissy into the seat while Tara quickly fastened her own seat belt, and then returned to take Rebecca's arm.

She was aware of his height as he stood close to her, his arm going around her. "Keep your head down, and we'll run."

She nodded and he stepped closer, draping his arm across her shoulders. Rebecca inhaled, feeling her breasts tighten. The slightest contact with him set her pulse racing. His arm across her shoulders felt too good.

"Let's go," he said, and they dashed to the plain black car with tinted windows. Jake almost shoved her into the seat, and slammed the door behind her. He sprinted back to the house to lock the door.

While she waited, she saw a uniformed man come from the direction of the barn, and for the first time she noticed the police car parked in front of the barn. Jake spoke to the policeman briefly and climbed into the car.

"That's McCauley. He'll watch the house and grounds while we're gone. I'll introduce you next time."

"I'm glad he's there."

"Where are we going?" Sissy asked.

"We're going to my brother's house. His name is Zach, and his wife is Sally," Jake answered patiently, checking the rearview mirror.

Watching the countryside flash past, seeing the hills dotted with wildflowers, Rebecca was quiet and thoughtful. "You look gorgeous," he had said. Had he really meant it, or was he one of those men who gave out compliments as easily as they exhaled? She suspected he wasn't, and she felt annoyed at herself for even wondering about it. She didn't want to feel pleased by his compliments. He would disrupt their lives and then disappear, and she didn't want to feel anything except relief when he was gone.

The girls finally settled in the back, talking to each other, Jake becoming quiet.

"Besides your brother, do you have other family here?" Rebecca asked, curious about him.

"Yes. Another brother lives in the area."

"I was an only child. How many brothers do you have?" she persisted, aware he probably had a file of information about her. His terse orders and brief answers mildly annoyed her, and she was determined to know more about him.

"Three younger brothers."

"That's nice. One is in the FBI. What do the others do?"

"One works for a bank in Austin."

"Are they married?"

"Oh, Lord, yes."

"You don't sound happy about it."

"They all married too young."

"Are they still married?"

"Yes. All married and employed."

"That doesn't sound so dreadful, if they're employed and happily married."

When he arched his brows, she sensed his disapproval.

"They've had a tough time financially, and if they had just waited awhile, they would have been better off."

Amused by his answer, she laughed.

"I don't believe you've ever really been in love, Detective," she said. His frown vanished, and his head turned. He focused on her with a speculative look.

"You think I don't know anything about love," Jake said, his voice dropping and sliding over her with a warmth that made her pulse jump. His gaze lowered to her mouth, and she couldn't get her breath.

"You must think I'm cold and crusty as hell," he said, still studying her. "And I suppose I better be, for this job." He shifted his attention back to the road.

She kept quiet, not wanting to answer his accusation, but *cold* and *crusty* were not terms she'd use to describe him.

Jake drove across the northern edge of the city to take I-35 to Round Rock. Finally he drove into a housing area and turned into the driveway at his brother's house. It was in a new addition, and the neighboring yards were filled with children playing.

The house had a high stockade fence surrounding the backyard that made Rebecca feel better about leaving the girls.

"Sally's great with kids," Jake said as he stepped out of the car.

So are you, Rebecca thought, watching him come around the car.

A short woman with a big smile and a mop of red curls came outside to greet them and a man almost as tall as Jake appeared behind her. He had a ready grin, a smattering of freckles, hair not quite as dark as Jake's, but the same sexy hazel eyes.

Rebecca had an immediate liking for Jake's brother and sister-in-law who were warm and friendly, and in minutes the girls were happily playing. As Rebecca kissed them goodbye, Sissy barely looked up from the doll Sally had given her.

"They're wonderful with children," Rebecca said when she and Jake were back in the car. "I can tell that in just a short time."

"Yep, that they are. And they want their own, but so far, Sally hasn't gotten pregnant. I keep telling them they have a lot of time," he said.

As they drove away, Rebecca twisted in the seat to study him. "If I hadn't seen you with the girls and how much they already like you, I'd think you don't like children."

"It isn't that. None of my brothers can afford families yet. I helped put them all through college, and I'm still helping financially with my brother Bill. I just think they ought to wait."

"Is that what you're doing—waiting?"

He turned to give her another speculative look, and instantly she regretted her question. "Never mind. We should keep things impersonal, and we'll get along better. I keep asking you very personal questions."

"Damn straight we should keep things impersonal," he answered with amusement. "I can do my job much better if we do. And yes, I am waiting. I'm not married, so there's no question of starting a family. And I'm damn sure not ready to settle down. Not with my occupation." He wondered if he was telling her all this or reminding himself what he should do.

"What did your folks think about you becoming a policeman?"

"My dad was a cop, and he was killed trying to stop an armed robbery," Jake answered abruptly.

"Why in heaven's name did you go into law enforcement if you lost a father that way?" Stunned to learn about his father, Rebecca was unable to comprehend why he chose such a life under the circumstances.

"I suppose Dad instilled a love of police work in me in my early years. I always wanted to be a cop." Jake tried to keep the emotion out of his voice. "And every time I apprehend someone, I feel as if I'm catching the son of a bitch who gunned down my father."

She was quiet, and Jake wondered what she was thinking, but he kept silent, telling himself it was better to keep barriers between them, to remember that this was a job and when it was over he would never see her again.

He drove toward the state capitol, passing the broad, shady lawn surrounding it, going to the area of older homes and renovated warehouses that were now apartments west of the capitol. Soon he entered the drive to his condo, punched in numbers and waited for the iron gates to swing open. He drove behind the building, parking in a carport, beside a shiny red pickup.

"The pickup is mine, too. I think when we return tonight, we might take the truck. There's a backseat for the girls, and the pickup would draw less attention at your place than my car."

"We can just ride to the banquet in it."

"You don't mind going in a pickup?"

"Of course not," she said as they entered the building and he nodded at a man behind a desk in the lobby.

"It won't take me long to shower and change."

"Do you worry about Meskell following us?"

"I don't worry about it, and he didn't follow us tonight."

"How can you be sure?"

He shrugged. "I've been a cop a long time. And don't worry about the girls. Zach has a high fence, and he and Sally won't let the girls out of their sight or out of their house or backyard. Zach's tougher than he looks."

She smiled as they stepped into an elevator, and he punched the button for the tenth floor. "What's funny?"

"Zach looks very tough, but maybe the family resemblance gave me that impression," she said, recalling Jake's brother.

They were shut into the small elevator, the fragrance of her perfume tempting him. She was smiling at him, her blue eyes wide, the dimple showing, and he longed to cross the short distance between them and take her in his arms and see if her mouth was as soft as it looked. Just thinking about kissing her made his blood pump faster, and he knew he'd better cool down fast.

If only— He caught himself and realized the direction of his thoughts. Even if Meskell didn't exist, Jake knew, he wouldn't date a woman like Rebecca Bolen. He had shouldered responsibility since he was nine years old and his youngest brother was finally employed and on his own. Freedom was a heady luxury he didn't want to give up. *The pretty lady is off-limits,* he told himself. *She comes with wedding bells and two kids and a truckload of responsibility.*

The elevator doors opened and he crossed the hall, then suddenly stopped, his breath going out in a hiss. Rebecca glanced at him, saw his frown and followed his gaze.

The door to his condo was splintered, pried off the hinges, the doorframe as hacked up as the door, which was pushed ajar.

"Dammit." Jake drew his pistol. His hazel eyes changed, becoming glacial, chilling her while he motioned with his head and pushed her against the wall, leaning close to her.

"Meskell could be inside," he whispered, his breath fanning her ear, and in spite of her terror, she became aware of Jake's body, so close to hers, his hand on her shoulder, his mouth at her ear. "If you hear a fight," Jake said, pointing down the hall to the exit, "get out of here. Go downstairs and get security."

Rebecca nodded, her heart pounding, while she wondered if Lenny Meskell was listening and waiting.

Jake turned and flattened against the wall. Then, suddenly, he kicked the door in and disappeared inside the room.

Chapter 5

"Rebecca, it's all right. Come in," he called.

Feeling the tension ease, she went to the doorway and paused in shock. The door had fallen across an overturned table. The room was in complete disarray, with books pulled off shelves, furniture upended, lamps knocked to the floor. Jake held a phone and motioned to her to come inside.

Carefully she stepped over the debris through a tiny entryway that opened onto a living room with a kitchen and a bedroom to one side. Through the door she could see that kitchen drawers were tossed to the floor, their contents strewn over the room.

Across the living room was a balcony with a high wall and a spectacular view of the city.

"Delancy here. Who's on burglary tonight? Give me Werner."

Rebecca turned away, moving toward the balcony, hearing Jake discussing the break-in. His voice was calm, but one look in his hazel eyes and she could see the fires of rage.

"I have to accompany her to the banquet, and I have to shower. I won't be back tonight, so you guys close it up. I want to know how he got past security here, because it's tight. Yeah." He replaced the phone, and she turned around.

"Was this Lenny Meskell?"

"He might as well have signed his name on the door."

"What would he gain from this?"

"It's a message. He's not happy with me."

"Do you think he knows you're guarding me?"

Jake shrugged. "I don't know. I'll check to see if anything is missing."

"Jake, you can stay here. Get someone else to go with me to the banquet, if you need to see about your things."

He shook his head. "This mess isn't going anywhere, and one of the burglary detectives is a close friend. He'll take charge, and building maintenance will get the door fixed promptly." He paused, studying her. "Are you okay, Rebecca?"

She glanced at the trashed room and nodded. "I'm all right. It just is a reminder that my life has been threatened."

"It would be better if you touched as few things as possible. Here," he said, picking up a wingback chair. "Sit down here."

"I'll be fine, Jake."

He nodded and moved across the room, kneeling in front of the fireplace to run his hand up inside it. As he moved from place to place, she realized he was checking to see if things had been stolen.

"Did he take anything?"

"Nothing so far. I'll shower," he said, checking his watch.

She stood looking across the balcony at the lights of the city, twinkling in the darkness. "What a view you have!"

"It's pretty," Jake said from the bedroom doorway, studying her profile, his gaze sliding over her as his thoughts shifted from Meskell to Rebecca.

He went into the bedroom and closed the door, stripping to shower, turning the water to cold, wishing he could get his hands on Meskell.

Standing in the center of the room, wanting to disturb things as little as possible, Rebecca noticed books strewn over the floor. Judging from the titles, Jake was an old-West history buff, but she spotted books on law and criminals, too. Unopened mail was on the floor.

Mud-caked Western boots were by the overturned maroon leather sofa. Books, pillows, papers, compact discs and an empty beer bottle lay on the floor. She spotted a picture that looked old, guessing it must be his family when Jake was young. Leaning down to look closer, she saw that Jake bore a close resemblance to his smiling father. His slender mother was pretty. Rebecca wasn't certain which boy was Zach, but Jake was the tallest and looked like the oldest.

"I'm ready now," Jake said, and she turned around. Her pulse quickened. He looked incredibly handsome, with that same air of danger and toughness about him, his sexy aura heightened by his navy suit and conservative dark tie, the white shirt that was a stark contrast to his tan skin.

"My goodness, the ladies will be happy to see you," she said, and he grinned.

Someone knocked, and two men stood in the open doorway, one in uniform and one in a brown suit. "C'mon in. Rebecca, meet Detective Werner and Officer Tarkington. This is Mrs. Bolen."

She shook hands briefly with the tall, sandy-haired man who was the detective and the stocky blonde who was in uniform. She motioned to Jake, waving her hand toward the door. "I'll wait in the hall, out of everyone's way."

"You stay with me," Jake said, turning away to talk to the men, and she realized he didn't want her to wait outside. Even though she couldn't imagine that Meskell was anywhere close, she waited inside while Jake talked with the men.

When Jake finished discussing the break-in, he took her arm and they entered the paneled elevator.

As they rode down in silence, she was more aware of him than before. In the close confines of the elevator, she wondered whether the real danger to her wasn't riding only a few feet away. Meskell would be caught and locked up and forgotten. If she wasn't careful, the time spent with Jake Delancy might be unforgettable. She wasn't ready for a relationship, and she would never want one with a man who lived dangerously.

Handing over the keys for valet parking at the hotel, Jake held the glass door. When they stepped into the busy hotel lobby, he moved beside her.

"The party's on the second floor. We might as well just walk up the stairs," she said, motioning toward the curving red-carpeted stairway. When they started toward the stairs, his fingers laced through hers.

Startled, she glanced up at him, because she wouldn't have guessed Jake Delancy was the kind of man to simply hold hands even in the most casual way. And the slight gesture also caught her off guard because it was the first time since Dan that a man had held her hand.

For just a moment, she thought how nice it was even when it held no meaning. She was beside a handsome man, going to a party, and he was holding her hand. His fingers were a warm pressure against her hand, a physical contact with another adult, something she had seldom had in the past two years of her life.

As if he realized she was studying him, he glanced at her, squeezed her hand lightly and winked. She drew a deep breath, cautioning herself to be careful around Detective Delancy.

Together they climbed the stairs to the second floor, where the cocktail party was. Voices came from a room beyond open double doors. "I need to mix and mingle, and I'll introduce you to the few people I know," Rebecca said as they entered the crowded room.

Jake released her hand. "Don't worry about me," he said. "You go talk to people and I'll wander around."

"Are you concerned about Meskell?"

"No. We've beefed up hotel security tonight with undercover men, and there were two guards outside the door of this room. They're not hotel security. They're from the force. Just keep your eyes open."

"I feel ridiculous to be causing so much trouble."

"You're worth it," he said in a low voice. Something flickered in the depths of her eyes, and she seemed to relax slightly. She winked at him. "That's nice to hear, Detective Delancy," she replied in a voice that made his temperature jump. She studied him. "Sure you don't want me to introduce you?"

"Maybe in a little while," he said. "Just don't leave the room without letting me know."

Nodding, she walked away, and he watched the slight pull of her dress across her bottom. He wondered if she had any idea what an appealing woman she was. Knowing he was staring, he turned reluctantly, catching the eye of two of the undercover cops here in suits, aware security arrangements had been made swiftly this afternoon.

"Hi," said a feminine voice, as a voluptuous blonde approached in a black sequined dress that fit like a second skin. "I'm Melody Farrar. Is your wife one of the members of our group?"

Idly, Jake wondered what business Melody was in as he shook his head. "No, I came with a friend."

"Oh, and she's left you all on your own. Come have a drink."

"Sure," he said, moving across the room toward the bar with her. They talked for fifteen minutes, and when Jake finally extricated himself, he felt a stab of alarm. He had chalked up his earlier reaction to Rebecca to not having had a date in a while, but he had no such reaction to the luscious Melody. Far from it. All the time he talked to her, he had continued to watch for Rebecca's blond head or her green dress as she talked to people.

He glimpsed Melody chatting with three men. She was a good-looking woman, but he knew he wasn't interested.

Finally Rebecca appeared at his side, linking her arm in his. "It's almost time to go eat," she said, leading him away from a cluster of people. "They'll open the doors to the banquet room where we have arranged seating."

He already knew that and knew he would sit where he could see the doors and the stage. An undercover cop would sit at their table to watch the other half of the room.

All through dinner, Jake listened and responded to the conversation as he kept his gaze roaming over the crowd. The doors to the hall were closed, and while he felt the danger was minimal at the banquet, he didn't want to take chances.

Finally, Rebecca was introduced, and everyone applauded as she made her way to the stage. She moved with a graceful, yet sexy walk, the green dress pulling slightly across her hips, her hair bouncing gently. She climbed the steps to the stage and began to talk, her gaze meeting his and then moving over the audience.

When she finished her speech, she received resounding applause before she returned to her seat. Her face was flushed and her eyes sparkled, and he inwardly cursed Richard Vance for sending him on this assignment. It was like sending a starving man to guard a banquet. When the evening was finally over, people came up to Rebecca to thank her for her speech.

"Rebecca, introduce me," a tall, black-haired woman said. A balding, broad-shouldered man stood slightly behind the woman, and Rebecca smiled at them.

"Camilla, this is Jake Delancy. Jake, this is my friend Camilla and her husband, Larry Quinton."

Jake shook hands with Larry while Camilla smiled at him. "Rebecca, I'm glad you're finally dating! There's a band in the bar on the top floor. Come dancing with us."

For just an instant, a wistful look crossed Rebecca's face, and then it was gone. "I'm sorry, Camilla, but it's time I get the girls."

"You have to! Talk her into it, Jake. It's a great band, and we haven't gotten to know Jake yet. I haven't seen you since last month."

"Camilla, we have to go—"

On impulse, Jake squeezed her arm lightly. "We'll go upstairs for a little while."

"Great!" Camilla exclaimed, and Larry shrugged.

"I saw Valerie and Rob, and I'll ask them to join us," Camilla said. "See you in a few minutes."

As they left, Rebecca turned to stare at Jake, her brows drawn together in such a frown that he had to bite back a smile. "Why on earth did you do that? We said we should keep everything impersonal, and your brother and sister-in-law are waiting for us."

"It will be impersonal. We won't stay long, and Zach and Sally are probably having more fun than Tara and Sissy. How long since you last went dancing?"

She blinked and stared at him. "I won't be very good company. I can't handle some things yet, and dancing is one thing I haven't had to handle."

"You don't have to be good company at all," he replied easily, feeling a stab of sympathy for her even while becoming more determined that they go dancing. "This is as safe as walking around your hallway, because it won't mean a thing to either one of us. You can just enjoy a dance or two and then we'll go. It'll be good for you."

"You're getting mighty charitable," she said suddenly, amusement replacing her frown.

He laughed. "Okay, this isn't the smartest thing I've ever done, but I think it's time you enjoyed yourself, and maybe I want to dance with you once or twice, in spite of good judgment. We're not going to fall in love during one dance." The words seemed to hover in the air between them like a chant, and he wondered if he would remember them for the rest of his life. He tried to ignore the prickles that ran across his skin. He winked at her. "Come on. We'll both live dangerously."

She laughed softly, and he silently called himself every kind of fool as he followed her out of the banquet room, his gaze on the sexy sway of her bottom and long legs.

When they emerged from the elevator, he could hear the deep beat of the drums and the wail of a trumpet. They entered the crowded, darkened room, and in minutes he spotted the undercover guys, giving each of them a nod. Music throbbed, and the clink of glasses and bottles added to the clamor of talk and music. They sat at a long table and were introduced to four other couples, and then he stood and held out his hand. "Shall we dance?"

She placed her hand in his, her fingers feeling cool and slender, and he wanted to draw her close and wrap his arms around her and slow-dance her into lovemaking. Instead, he tried to avoid holding her close, aware of her blue eyes watching him solemnly.

"I may be rusty."

He shook his head. "Absolutely impossible."

"Up here it's easy to forget about danger and threats. I feel far above the city and all its problems."

He didn't answer, because he couldn't forget the danger and he was fighting the urge to pull her closer and feel her body moving with his. She followed him easily, as if she had been dancing with him forever. They moved in silence, her head turned as she gazed through the darkened windows at the myriad twinkling city lights.

The last time she had gone dancing, Rebecca had been with Dan. The hurt came, hitting her hard, like a sudden surging wave. She missed him incredibly, and it was easier to stay shut away at the house on the edge of town than to get out in crowds and do things that brought the memories tumbling back.

Hurting, she inhaled, fighting back tears while Jake tilted her head up. Rebecca closed her eyes. "I told you I couldn't handle this. It's the first time—"

"Shh..." he said quietly, drawing her closer, his arm sliding around her waist. "It's only natural," he said. "I don't care if you cry. There has to be a first time to dance again, and this is it. Now you've leaped over that hurdle. No one else here knows you're hurting, and it wouldn't matter if they did. You have a damned good reason to hurt."

Struggling to control her emotions, Rebecca was surprised at his concern, because she would have guessed there was not a gentle side to Jake Delancy.

Lost in memories, she closed her eyes and knew all the tears wouldn't change anything. Detective Delancy handed her his handkerchief and she wiped her eyes, moving with him and gradually regaining her composure.

He took the handkerchief from her and stuffed it into his pocket, and she was thankful for his silence while she got herself together.

"Of course, we're making the undercover guys angry," Jake said after a time.

Feeling in control, she glanced up at him. "How's that?"

"They're watching us and turning green with envy over my assignment."

She smiled, feeling better. And she would have been fine if she hadn't looked up into his hazel eyes. Their green-gold depths made her pulse skitter and melted some of the barriers around her heart.

Yet, she knew Jake Delancy was dangerous to her well-being, knew it to the depths of her soul, even though she hadn't been around him a full twenty-four hours yet. And the biggest part of that danger was her own attraction to him.

She missed Dan, longed for him, hurt over the loss. It had been two years now since his death. Her reactions to Jake bothered her. She was too aware of everything he did. Right now, she knew his hand was on her hip and his other hand was holding hers, and that slight, innocuous contact was unsettling.

She should be thankful he was not the marrying kind, but that was not reassurance enough when she couldn't stop her racing pulse.

When the song ended, they applauded, and then Jake took her hand. "We'll wait for the next one. That was just a warm-up," he said with a wink.

The next number was fast; as she danced around him, Jake wished she had worn something clinging, because he suspected her moves were half-hidden by the linen dress. It's a good thing they are, he told himself. She was setting him on fire, her eyes half-closed, her head thrown back as if she were being made love to, her lips slightly parted, while she drifted around him like a dancing flame. And then she turned, looking at him, her blue eyes taunting, filled with desire.

He loosened his tie, feeling hot and knowing it was only partially from dancing. He wanted to yank her into his arms and bury his tongue in her mouth. The chemistry that had sparked between them all day seemed ready to burst into a blaze.

Rebecca's gaze was caught, held by Jake's. His eyes were dark with smoldering desire as they moved around each other. For the first time in so long, she felt like a desirable woman, and she gave herself over to the feelings.

And then she realized that this was dangerous, that in minutes the sparks between them might become a blaze neither of them could ignore. She gave a shake of her shoulders and stood still.

"We should stop, Detective. It's hot in here," she said brusquely, knowing her anger probably showed, wondering if he would ever guess it was directed at herself for being attracted to him.

She turned to walk away, and he caught her arm, his fingers on her bare skin sending a current shooting through her. Before she could speak, the band started another old, familiar ballad, and he pulled her into his arms. And in spite of all good sense, she acquiesced.

This time Jake threw caution away and held her close, wrapping his arm around her waist. She moved with him, their steps together, her soft body pressed against him, the lilac scent enticing him while her silky hair touched his cheek.

He wanted to tighten his arms, dance into a dark corner and kiss her. He was acting like an adolescent. Melody danced past and winked at him, and he smiled in return. Now why couldn't she stir any reaction in him? He didn't want to think about the reasons. And then he was lost to the music, Rebecca's body against his, and they were moving together as if they had done this a thousand times over. His arm tightened around her narrow waist.

As soon as the dance ended, he followed Rebecca from the dance floor. Near the table, she glanced over her shoulder at him. "We should go now."

Having been about to suggest the same thing himself, he nodded. They said their goodbyes and rode down in the elevator in silence, standing far apart, as if trying to get back the distance that had been between them this afternoon.

Downstairs, he carefully surveyed the bright lobby. He hadn't seen any sign of Meskell, but the public place made him edgy.

At the door, Jake told Rebecca to wait, and she watched while he talked to the doorman, who stepped outside and motioned to one of the valets. In minutes Jake's pickup was at the door, the hotel lights shining on the bright red metal. He tipped the men and held the door for her, going around the pickup.

As Jake hurried to slide behind the wheel, his instincts told him Meskell was not far away. "Rebecca, there are too damn many cars and trees. Get down until we're out of this lot."

Instantly she unbuckled her seat belt and tried to lean down without touching him—an impossible feat in the pickup. "Put your head down. I'll know you're not coming on to me," he said with amusement, pushing her down.

She placed her head on his thigh and instantly his amusement was gone. He inhaled deeply, trying to keep his mind on his driving and Meskell.

"You can get up now," he said in minutes, his voice husky. He wiped his brow, then yanked off his tie and tossed it over the seat between them. She buckled up, and they rode in silence.

As soon as they pulled into the drive at his brother's house, he switched off the ignition. "Zach and Sally would keep the girls for a week or two if you'd like."

Giving it a moment's thought, Rebecca shook her head slowly. "Sissy can't cope with it. I'm sure she's had a good time tonight, but since she lost her father, she needs the reassurance that I'm there. She has bad dreams—she wakes up screaming for me, and I think she's afraid she'll suddenly lose me the way she lost her father."

Jake squeezed her hand. "Sorry. She'll get over that as time goes by."

"I hope so. Right now there isn't any other solution except to keep them with me."

He nodded and stepped out of the pickup. He spoke to
Zach and returned to wait until the garage door opened.
Jake pulled into the brightly lighted two-car garage and
stopped.

Both girls were asleep as Jake and Zach carried them to
the pickup. "Thanks again," Rebecca said, stepping out of
the pickup to speak to Zach and Sally.

Zach put his arm across Sally's shoulders, and he held her
close against him. Both of them smiled at her.

"Bring them again, Rebecca. And you come over, too,"
Sally said with a warm smile, while Zach kept his arm across
her shoulders.

"Thank you," Rebecca replied, sitting down and closing
the door quietly as Jake buckled up. Looking at Zach and
Sally, Rebecca was reminded again of Dan, because they
had had a good marriage and had been so much in love.

Jake backed out and they drove away. When the number
of houses thinned and the lights faded behind them, she felt
danger close in around her like the enveloping darkness. The
orange glow from the dash highlighted Jake's strong cheekbones and left the hollows of his cheeks in shadow. He
looked solemn, almost angry, and she wondered if he was
thinking about Meskell or about what they had felt when
they were dancing.

In the close confines of the pickup, she was conscious of
Jake all through the drive, remembering dancing with him,
her skin still tingling from his touch. What was it about him
that made the air seem to sizzle?

When they arrived home, he wouldn't let her carry either
girl inside. The tall policeman came out and stopped beside
her window, while Jake carried first Tara and then Sissy into
the house.

"I'm McCauley, Mrs. Bolen," he said in a raspy, friendly voice. Thick curls showed beneath his cap. "There were no calls, and everything was quiet. I'll be parked by the garage tonight."

"Thank you," she answered, feeling secure with McCauley outside, yet on edge at the thought of Jake and her under the same roof all night.

"Rebecca," Jake said, sliding onto the seat beside her and placing his arm across her shoulders, "we'll hurry inside." Her pulse raced and she was aware of him pressed against her side.

"Ready?" he said, looking down at her, and she prayed he couldn't hear her heartbeat.

"Yes. We only have a few feet to cross to reach the door."

"No need to take chances. Let's go," he said, sliding out and pulling her out. McCauley fell in step on her other side, and they all rushed to the back door. As she entered the kitchen, Jake stepped back outside to talk with McCauley for a moment, and then he entered the kitchen and closed and locked the door.

Only the small light above the stove was on, and it cast Jake's cheeks into shadow, highlighting his cheekbones, emphasizing the rugged angles and planes of his face and making her think of danger again. The tiny kitchen seemed to shrink, to be dominated by his broad shoulders and lean frame. Her heart was pounding, and she knew she needed to put more space between them than the small kitchen allowed.

"I'll see about the girls," she said, hurrying down the hall, feeling as if she were running from a demon instead of a man sent to protect her.

How could she stay with him night after night in the close confines of the house? Could she request a different detective? And how would she explain that? Tell Detective Captain Vance to please send someone who didn't give off sparks and ignite the fires of desire that had long been dormant. She shook her head, wondering if she had waited too long to start dating now, but she knew that wasn't the answer at all.

Rebecca went to the girls' room to undress them and get them into bed. Tara and Sissy went back to sleep immediately, and Rebecca paused before she left their room.

Sissy lay curled on her side, her thumb in her mouth, golden locks surrounding her face. Tara was on her back, her arms outflung. Both of them looked beautiful, so innocent, and she prayed the police caught Meskell soon. She kissed Tara's soft cheek lightly and brushed a lock of hair away from her eyes and then turned to kiss Sissy.

A few minutes later, as Rebecca entered the darkened living room, she found Jake standing in front of the window; he was holding the drape aside a few inches while he looked out.

"Hit the light in the hall," he ordered without turning from the window, and she felt the hairs on the nape of her neck rise as she switched off the light. She crossed the living room to stand behind him. "Do you see something?"

When he didn't answer, she studied him. He had shed his coat and she noticed a shoulder holster and pistol beneath his left arm. He dropped the drape into place and turned around, almost colliding with her.

"You wore a gun tonight."

"I usually do."

Aware she was standing too close, she turned, bumping a chair. His hands went out to steady her. "I seem to have a knack for running into things since your arri—"

The words died when she looked up at him. His hand was still on her waist, and his gaze had that intense quality a man has when he looks at a woman he wants. Her pulse jumped; she knew she should move, but she was immobilized, unable to do anything.

"Rebecca," he said in a husky voice that was like a caress, and her body responded, her stomach clenching, heat diffusing in her. He stepped closer, his arm sliding around her waist as he drew her toward him.

Chapter 6

Her heart thudded as he lowered his head, brushing her lips so lightly that the tantalizing, erotic contact took her breath. His lips felt warm and full against hers, his breath holding a faint touch of mint.

For a moment, memories of Dan threatened to overwhelm her. She didn't belong in another man's arms. "No," she whispered. "Jake, I can't. It hurts so badly. I miss him—"

"Shh, Rebecca. It's just a kiss," Jake whispered against her ear, his lips trailing to her mouth, brushing her lips again.

It had been so long since she had been kissed or touched. A tightening ran through her body, heat streaking in her as she felt barriers shatter like fragile glass.

Sensations bombarded her; the heat of need and desire, the tingling of her mouth, the strength of his arms around her. Her hesitation diminished as Jake leaned over her, and she let the memories go.

With a shudder, she placed her hands against Jake's solid chest, feeling the smooth crispness of his cotton shirt, the leather strap of the shoulder holster, his warm body beneath the cotton.

She intended to push him away, but his mouth opened on hers, his tongue slid over her lower lip, thrusting against her tongue, and her reluctance vanished.

His arm tightened around her, pulling her up against him, and Rebecca felt lost in a dizzying spiral. She should stop him. She didn't want his kisses, didn't want to respond hungrily. He was the wrong man, as well as the wrong *kind* of man. Yet her body quivered.

"No," she whispered again, turning her head. "You're a threat to me."

She shifted slightly, felt the shoulder holster that was a reminder of the danger of the man. She pulled away, sliding her hands down to push lightly against his chest. She felt as if she were coming up from the depths of a dream, opening her eyes to find Jake watching her. It was too dark to read his expression, but his breathing seemed as ragged as hers.

He ran his forefinger along her jaw. "A few kisses won't hurt."

She looked away, realizing that he probably dated quite often, was probably casual about kissing and dancing. But she wasn't. Even now, her heartbeat hadn't slowed and her breathing was erratic and words wouldn't come. Her hand still lay against his chest, and she noticed with surprise that his heartbeat was racing like hers.

"We're playing with fire, Jake, or at least I am. You may take all this lightly, but this is the first time for me since my husband. I just can—"

His finger brushed her lips, the faintest touch, yet it stopped her words and took her breath and made her mouth tingle for more of his kisses.

"You feel my heart," he said gruffly in a low voice. "I know you won't take things lightly. And I know too damned well we're playing with fire. I've never—not one time—mixed business and my personal life. I don't date any policewomen, nothing," he said emphatically. "But you and I are not yet at the point where we can't smile and say goodbye and walk away without heartbreak. Right?" Jake wondered if he were arguing with her or with himself. Her eyes were huge as she looked up at him with parted lips.

"I'm more vulnerable. That was my first kiss in so long. Since Dan."

He knew she was hurting, and he wanted just to hold her, to try to comfort her. He had to lean closer to hear her. "I can't take risks," she said solemnly. "Let's keep everything platonic from now on. I have to."

"Sure," he answered, fighting the impulse to brush a tendril of golden hair away from her cheek. He yearned to lean the few inches it would take to touch her and kiss her hard and long. Her mouth had been hot and sweet and tantalizing, making him want more. A lot more.

She nodded and turned away to head toward the hall, then paused. "I had a good time tonight."

"It was the best banquet I ever attended," he remarked dryly, and she laughed.

"I'll get some sheets and a pillow for you."

"I won't need them. I'll sleep on a chair, if I sleep at all."

"I'll get them," she insisted, and disappeared into the hall. He rubbed the back of his neck and mentally called himself a fool for dancing with her and kissing her. Leave the lady alone. Even if he was a marrying man, and he was not, they would mix like fire and water. She hated his job and he knew how disastrously some cop marriages ended up. And even as he argued with himself, his body burned from her kisses.

If Vance got wind of Jake's romancing the widow on the job, he'd be so far out in the boonies doing oil-field burglary duty that no one would ever find him. "Damn," Jake whispered, raking his fingers through his hair.

Trying to get his thoughts elsewhere, he turned to move the drape a fraction and peer outside. "Come on, Lenny," he said softly. "Get me out of this."

Jake stood quietly watching shadows shift and change as the wind blew. A car passed on the highway. Leaves fluttered in the mesquite trees. He heard Rebecca moving around in the house.

Rebecca closed her bedroom door and crossed the room, suddenly swamped with loss, covering her face and trying to cry silently, so that no one would hear her. She missed Dan. It should have been Dan holding her and kissing her. She sat on the edge of the bed and picked up his picture, looking at it with longing and knowing she had to let go of the past.

"I loved you and I still love you," she whispered. The image smiled at her and she knew she had to go on with life. She kissed the picture, feeling the cold glass against her lips. Carefully she set the picture on the table and glanced at the door, her body tingling and longing filling her.

The evening had been a series of ups and downs, moments of such hurt when things had reminded her of Dan. Yet, she had danced again and kissed again, and maybe next time it wouldn't be so difficult.

She stared at the door, too aware of Jake Delancy on the other side of it, sitting down the hall in the darkened living room. She didn't want to be attracted to him. He possessed too many qualities that she didn't like in a man—dangerous, reckless, a confirmed bachelor. When this was over, they would part ways and never see each other again.

She moved restlessly, unfastening the tiny buttons on her dress, reminding herself that Captain Vance thought they would catch Meskell within a week or two. She stepped out of the linen, feeling it slide down over her sensitized skin, the dress warm from her body.

She removed her underclothes, then pulled on the chambray shirt and buttoned it to her chin. She pulled on cutoffs beneath it.

She slipped her feet into moccasins and went to get pillows and sheets for him.

Jake heard a board creak and turned from the windows. Rebecca had changed and now wore a man's chambray shirt, and he wondered if she had any idea how sexy she looked in it.

His gaze raked down the length of it, his eyes accustomed enough to the darkness to make out her long, pale legs. As if she realized he was looking at her, she pulled the shirt collar high beneath her chin. "I couldn't find my robe today."

"I'm not complaining," he answered with amusement.

"I know you're not, but I didn't want you to think that—Never mind. Here are the sheets and a pillow," she said briskly. "Do you want me to sit up for a spell so you can sleep?"

"No thanks," he answered, his voice husky. He jammed his hands into his pockets and fought the urge to cross the room to her. "I won't invade your privacy, but if you'll leave your door and the door to the girls' room slightly ajar, I can hear sounds better. And I'm going to have to switch off the window units. They would muffle the sound of an army coming in through a window."

"Sure. I'm going to bed now," she said quietly, and turned away. He watched her long legs as she left the room, fantasizing about having them wrapped around him.

"Dammit," he muttered under his breath, wondering why he was so attracted to Rebecca Bolen. There wasn't any logical reason. Not one. He'd had a good time with her tonight, he respected what she had done with her business, and she was obviously a good mother. But the sparks between them had been there that first moment he stood in the hot sun in her driveway and introduced himself.

Jake switched off the window unit. With a noisy rattle, the motor died, and he shook his head. It was going to be a hot night.

Hours later, feeling hot and rumpled, Rebecca glanced at the clock on the small bedside table and saw that it was a quarter to four in the morning. She'd been unable to sleep since she shut off the light. She sat up and ran her fingers through her hair and across her damp nape. The house was warm, and she wanted a drink of water. If she moved through the house, would he think it was a prowler?

For another ten minutes she flounced and turned in bed, finally getting up. She pulled the cutoffs beneath the chambray shirt and stepped into the hall. She glanced toward the darkened living room. A tiny night-light burned in the bathroom, shedding a faint glow in the hallway.

"Jake," she whispered. "Jake?"

"I'm here," he said from the kitchen, and she jumped, whirling around. He stood in the kitchen doorway, his hand upraised against the jamb, his silhouette dark against a moonlit window behind him.

"I can't sleep. I just didn't want to startle you or have you think someone had gotten into the house. I just want a cold drink."

"Come on. We can sit and talk a minute."

When she entered the kitchen, he hit the light switch as she crossed the room to get glasses. "Want tea, or a cola?" she asked.

"You don't have tonic water, do you?"

Shaking her head, she turned to look at him. Now, in the light, she saw that he was bare-chested, and she was unable to keep from looking at him. He was sculpted with muscle and deeply tanned. Low on his left side, a jagged white scar cut across his ribs, and another was high on his right shoulder. Faded jeans hung low on his narrow hips. Her mouth went dry. His flat stomach was a washboard of muscle.

Realizing she was staring at him, she looked up to find his gaze drifting slowly over her. Her legs tingled, her body burned, in the wake of his perusal. His hazel eyes met hers, and she felt as if she couldn't take another breath.

"No tonic water," she said unsteadily, turning blindly to the counter, too aware of him and of herself. She knocked over an empty glass and caught it up instantly.

"I'll take a cola," he said, crossing the room to take the glass from her hand. As soon as the drinks were poured, Jake jerked his head toward the living room. "Let's sit in there. It's dark and I can watch the yard."

She felt skimpily dressed in the long chambray shirt and cutoffs. She didn't hear him behind her, but as she settled in a corner of the sofa in the darkened living room, Jake crossed the room to sit in a chair and stretch out his long legs. He looked long, lean and powerful, overwhelming in the tiny space.

If she was reacting this strongly to nothing more than seeing him bare-chested—what would the next week be like, when they would be together constantly?

And she knew she should get up and go right back to bed. Better to flounce in the heat then to flirt with temptation, yet she couldn't get up and go.

His profile was to her as he studied the grounds outside. He had pulled the drapes open and moonlight bathed the yard, spilling through the windows, and faintly illuminating the living room. The silvery light played over his strong shoulders, splashing across his long, jean-clad legs, which were propped on another chair.

His attention shifted to her. "Too scared to sleep?"

"No," she answered. "I'm not frightened with you here and McCauley in the yard. Just restless," she admitted, blushing because she knew exactly why she was restless.

Jake wondered if their kisses had caused her sleeplessness. Even if he'd had the chance to sleep, he knew, he wouldn't have been able to. He had difficulty keeping his thoughts on Meskell. All he had to do was be in the same room with Rebecca and the blaze started. Under any other circumstances he would pursue that reaction, but now it worried him. At the same time he was trying to convince himself he didn't want to feel any attraction to her, his gaze was drifting slowly over her long legs—until he realized what he was doing.

"If you're with us, Meskell could shoot you by mistake," she said.

Jake shook his head. "If he does, it won't be by mistake. If we're together, he'll go for me first."

Startled, Rebecca stared at him. "Why?"

"If he takes me out, you'll be easier to get. If he uses the first shot on you, he knows I'll nail him."

"That's dreadful," she said, aghast. Dismayed by what he said, she couldn't understand how he could enjoy his work. "That makes this assignment doubly dangerous for you. Isn't your supervisor aware of that?"

"Yes. He knows I'm willing to take chances to get Lenny. I don't intend to let Meskell get me."

"I'm glad I don't date you," she said, horrified by the risks Jake took, by his eagerness about going after an armed and dangerous man.

Jake Delancy's white teeth flashed, and she realized what she had said about dating him. "I'm sorry!" she exclaimed, burning with embarrassment. "That remark wasn't personal. I just wasn't thinking! I'll never understand men like you who are willing to live dangerously all the time." She looked away, knowing they should get away from such a personal topic.

"You married one," Jake remarked dryly. "Were you unhappy with the marriage?"

"No," she answered, feeling a stirring of anger. "You know I wasn't unhappy, or I wouldn't still be grieving after two years. I loved Dan terribly, but I hated his work, and it finally took him from me."

Jake stood, becoming a dark silhouette against the dark windows. As he crossed the room to her, Rebecca's pulse jumped and raced. He leaned down to catch her chin in his warm fingers. She couldn't see him because his face was in shadow.

"You loved a man who liked an exciting job that involved taking risks," he said quietly. "You're hurt because you lost him, but you're drawn to that kind of man, Rebecca. And you're willing to take some risks yourself. You were ready to defend yourself against Meskell that day in the courtroom."

She jerked her chin from his hands and clamped her lips closed, her pulse drumming. "Get away from me, Detective Delancy, for your sake and mine. I can't get involved in a light fling."

When he didn't answer, she looked around and saw him sit down on the chair again and prop his feet up. "I know you can't. Honey, you have vine-covered cottage and white picket fence written all over you, and that's even if you didn't have the girls to think about. Let's get on a safer topic."

"Amen," she exclaimed. *Honey.* He had meant it in the most casual way, yet it had sounded special and brought a quick response from her heart.

"The girls get up early. I'll warn you now. Sissy doesn't know to leave sleeping people alone, and there's never been a man here before who wasn't a relative. She misses her father terribly, so sometimes she's very friendly with men."

"After this is over, you ought to date, Rebecca. You can marry again, and then the girls would have a father."

"Maybe someday," she answered, thinking about the evening. "I enjoyed dancing tonight, but it's difficult to imagine dating again." She was curious about his life when he was away from work. "When do you catch up on your rest?"

"I'll take some time off after this case—a weekend—and do nothing but relax and sleep," Jake answered perfunctorily, barely aware of what he said to her. He had called her *honey,* and he was appalled. She was *business,* and he'd damned well better start remembering it and stop making passes and addressing her with terms of endearment. He did not use the term loosely. As a matter of fact, he was trying to think of the last time he had called anyone *honey,* and he couldn't.

"What do you do to relax? Play golf? Fish?"

Stretching out his arm to pick up his drink, he took another long gulp of cola and rubbed the can against his temple as he turned to look at her. "I own some land west of town. I stay out there some weekends. I have some cattle."

"A ranch?"

"Of sorts."

"You want to ranch and be a cop?"

"Maybe someday, when I have to retire, I'll switch from being a cop to becoming a rancher. I can't do this forever. The department won't let me."

"But you'll do it until they retire you?"

"Yes, I will."

"You don't get bored or restless with ranching?"

"Nope. I like the change. And then I go back to the cop routine."

"I didn't know police work involved a routine."

"Sure. There's paperwork, monthly reports, ordinary desk work that has to be done. I hate that part of it." He sipped the cola and was silent for a few minutes.

"What's the worst part?"

"The desk duty, oil-field crime—that's a filthy mess."

"What's the best?"

"Undercover work."

"I should have guessed," she remarked, and he glanced at her.

"How did you get into the glass business?" he asked her.

"I only attended college two years, but I majored in graphic art and went to work for an advertising agency. An etched-glass business became a client of mine and I did work for them. They liked my work and asked me about doing some designs. One thing led to another and I started working there on Saturdays.

"I had Tara the year after Dan and I married, but we had juggled schedules so he could stay with her part of the time, and the other part my mom kept her when she was alive. Dan carried insurance, and after his death I took some of the money to open my own shop. I prefer working with etched glass to graphic art, but if the shop doesn't succeed, I'll go back to the other. I'm saving as much as I can for a college fund for the girls." She slanted him a look. "Actually, I would have guessed that you already knew everything I just told you."

"I knew some of it, but not how you got into the glass business." He stood and moved toward the window again.

She felt a sudden chill as she watched him; he seemed to be studying something outside. "Do you see someone?"

"I don't know. All the damned mesquite you have growing around this place makes it tricky to see what's out there, yet it doesn't hide your house from the road."

"The oaks were here, but the others, the pines behind the house, were part of a tree farm at one time. We love walking through the woods."

He sat down again. "A shadow moved, but it's low to the ground. Maybe it's a dog." He glanced at her. "Where did you meet your husband?"

"We both went to high school in Austin. We grew up knowing each other. We married when I was eighteen, so I was nineteen when Tara was born. Dan loved being a fireman. He did carpentry work, too, to add to our income." She looked down, tucking her legs beneath her and smoothing the shirt on her knees. "I miss him."

"I'm sorry." Jake shifted, propping his bare feet on another chair, his long legs stretched out. Now her eyes had adjusted and she could see him easily in the moonlit room.

"Have you ever been hurt because of your work?"

"I'm surprised you didn't notice the scars when we were in the kitchen."

"I did notice," she said quietly, remembering exactly how he looked.

"I've been stabbed and slashed and shot. The gunshot took the longest to heal."

"How'd you get shot?" She listened to the rumble of his deep voice as he briefly told her about the case from five years earlier, yet even the intimacy of the small, darkened room and the deep rumble of his voice couldn't stop the chill that enveloped her as he talked about the danger he had been in.

"It's a good thing you don't have a wife," she said solemnly. "But I'd think your brothers would worry."

"They've grown up with a father who was a cop and then their oldest brother. They accept police work as part of life."

She was quiet, thinking about his recklessness. "Didn't you worry that something would happen to you and then they'd be alone?"

His muscled shoulder lifted in a shrug. "I was younger then and felt invincible."

She drew a deep breath, knowing Dan had felt the same way. "And you don't feel invincible now?"

"No. I don't take the chances I used to. I'm doing my job and I'm careful. I have a bulletproof vest," he added, and there was a note of amusement in the last statement.

She studied him, knowing that in so many ways he was like Dan. "You testified at the trial," she said, wondering if he was bothered by her questions, feeling on occasion that she was pulling the answers from him.

"Yes, I did. I'm glad the jury came back with the guilty verdict so quickly. Meskell still has to stand trial for the other killing."

"The policeman? Were you friends?"

"Yes," Jake answered, and Rebecca could detect the anger in his voice.

"You said he was a co-worker."

"He went to college when I did. He was four years younger than I was, but I talked Dusty into becoming a cop. And I was with him that night. We got a call about the convenience-store robbery. When I drove up, Dusty was in the car ahead of me. He stepped out of the car and then Meskell drove out from behind the building. Dusty pulled his gun and aimed at him. Meskell leaned out and shot him," Jake said in a tight voice. "He went down, and another squad car came along to chase Meskell. I stayed with Dusty, and he died while I was with him."

There was no mistaking the pain and anger in his voice, and Rebecca felt a strange mixture of sympathy and dislike. "I'm sorry, but it seems like that's all the more reason to hate the kind of work you do."

He shook his head. "When we finally caught Meskell and I arrested him, he fought me. But I got in one good punch—that was for Dusty."

"You got in another good punch in the courtroom at his trial, thank heavens."

"I enjoyed it, and I know Meskell hasn't forgotten. We'll get him," Jake said with a quiet determination that sent a shiver down her spine.

"You'll risk your life if you do. You're risking it to stay with me."

"It's my job. It doesn't matter that you don't like what I do. I'll be gone before long. Did you fight with your husband over his work?" The moment the question was out, Jake turned to her. "Forget that I asked you. That's none of my damn business."

"It's all right. No, I didn't. I always thought he'd come home to me. I just never believed he could get hurt. I guess he had me convinced of that because that's the way he felt. I suppose you do, too."

"I know I can get hurt. I've been hurt, and I'm thirty-four, old enough to lose any illusions."

"Yet you like your job anyway."

"Yes, I do. Someone has to do it, Rebecca," he said, and his use of her name was like a feathery touch on raw nerves. "Be thankful I'm willing."

"I suppose I am."

Jake turned away, knowing she had been hurt badly, understanding her loss and her feelings, remembering how angry and hurt he had been when he lost his father. It had been a nightmarish time for the family.

Rebecca needed to come out of her shell, though, and go out again. There were plenty of men who had safe careers. He remembered her quick, intense response to his kisses and tried to think about something else as his body responded to the memories.

After a few moments of silence, she said, "You have a nice family."

"Sally and Zach?"

He stood again, and this time moonlight slanted through the window, splashing across his bare chest and over his long legs. She drew her breath; Jake Delancy was too handsome and virile, and this house was too small.

"What's wrong?" she asked.

"Shadows keep moving. Nothing important, except I know Meskell could be around. I'll be back." Picking up his pistol, Jake moved soundlessly out of the room.

She went to the window to look outside. Moonlight spilled across the yard. The low mesquite trees were dark shadows. Beyond them the highway was empty, and the trees on the opposite side were a mass of black shadow.

Feeling the heat, she lifted her hair off her neck, brushing strands back from her face.

After a time, she realized Jake hadn't returned and she frowned, glancing over her shoulder. The house was too small for him to take this long looking through it. Why was he in the kitchen so long?

Another chill ran across her nape. At night the situation seemed more threatening than it had during the sunny day. She went to the hall. "Jake?" she whispered, and listened to a silence broken only by the hum of the refrigerator in the kitchen.

Worried, Rebecca stepped into the girls' room to make sure they were safe. They slept peacefully, Sissy still curled into a ball with her thumb in her mouth. Tara had turned over on her stomach. Rebecca walked down the hall toward the kitchen. Her nerves felt on edge, and she wondered what had happened to Jake.

"Jake?"

Still only silence. Why didn't he answer? She paused before the kitchen door.

"Jake?" When he didn't answer, she stepped inside. The back door was slightly ajar, and her heart seemed to lurch. Where was he? Why had he left the house?

She went to the door and stood uncertainly, looking down at the moonlight spilling over her blue shirt. If she stepped outside, the chambray would probably show as clearly as if it were day.

Suddenly a shadow moved, and a man slid through the open door. She gasped, jumping back.

Chapter 7

"**H**ey!" Jake caught her up against him. Her hands went against his bare chest and desire burst like a flame inside her.

"I didn't mean to frighten you," he said in a husky voice. He reached out and placed his pistol on the table, pushing the door closed with his foot while still keeping his arm around her. She heard the faint click of the door shutting, the intake of Jake's breath. She was aware of the warm, solid feeling of his chest. Her pulse raced, and she couldn't catch her breath or say a word.

His left hand slipped behind her head to wind in her hair and tilt her face upward. Torn between wanting his kisses and knowing she should resist them, Rebecca fought an inner battle. While they stared at each other, her pulse roared, and beneath her palm she could feel his heart racing as rapidly as her own.

"I went outside to look around," he whispered, and she barely heard what he said.

She tingled, her breasts grew taut, her body heated. She

looked at his full underlip, remembering how it had felt to have him brush his mouth over hers, to kiss her.

"No," she whispered in desperation, and twisted away from him. "We agreed—"

"I know what we agreed," he said in a low, husky voice, wondering why he couldn't keep his hands to himself around her. He didn't have that problem with other women. The one brief moment when his arm was around her had scalded him. He had meant only to steady her, and then she'd pressed against him with only the worn chambray between her breasts and his chest. He'd felt her softness and her warmth and he had wanted to lean down and kiss her protests away. Yet she was right. It would be like placing dynamite close to a fire. He didn't want commitment or marriage.

And he had never been tempted to mix pleasure and his professional life. To do his job, he needed to keep a cool head. And he knew they would say goodbye as suddenly as they had gotten together. Yet, damn, she was fiery and sweet at the same time!

In spite of her marriage and two children, there was an air of innocence about her. Maybe it was her big blue eyes. And yet she had a sensual side. The sexy sway of her hips and her blazing response to him were a heady combination.

"Don't look so stricken. We didn't hurt anything or anyone," he said, trailing his finger along her cheek.

"I don't even know you," she whispered, fastening the top button of her shirt.

He reached out to release the high top button, watching her eyes widen, seeing that she wasn't going to stop him. For a fleeting second, his imagination ran wild as he fantasized about unbuttoning all the small white buttons down the front of her shirt and pushing it open. His hand still tingled from holding her, the softness of her body etched in his mind and on his nerves. His knuckles brushed her throat.

"Relax and enjoy yourself, Rebecca."

"I don't know how to relax about some things. I've never known many men, because I married young. I've really never dated anyone except Dan."

Maybe that explained part of the air of innocence she still retained. Jake thrust his hands into his pockets, something he seemed to have to do repeatedly with her.

"When I came in here, I was worried about you. Where were you?" she asked, her voice still low and breathless.

"I told you, I walked around outside," he replied, wondering if she didn't remember.

"I'd think you'd make a good target."

"I was careful." He reached back to turn the lock, and she abruptly moved away. He watched the shirt pull slightly over her bottom as she walked, and the unbidden vision of her minus the shirt taunted him.

At the kitchen door, she paused. "Good night, Jake."

"Night," he said, still standing by the door. He waited until she left the room before he looked outside once more and then headed toward the living room. As he passed her room, he saw that her door was closed.

Damned good thing. Next thing you know, Delancy, you'll be thinking of some excuse to go into her bedroom, he thought. He swore under his breath. Why was he so drawn to her? He remembered Melody Farrar at the banquet. She had come on to him like a fire truck roaring to a three-alarm blaze, yet he couldn't keep his mind off Rebecca. He wiped his damp brow and walked to the living room window to gaze into the darkness, knowing it was just as well he wasn't trying to sleep because he knew he wouldn't be able to do so.

He thought about his past relationship with Genny Smith, who was dark-haired, earnest about her career, going to law school and working part-time in a law office. There was nothing serious between them. Genny was ambitious, all her energy and thoughts focused on her job. They had fun together and were good companions and the sex was nice.

Or it had been. He hadn't seen her for two months now. And he suspected that even if this job ended tomorrow, he wouldn't give Genny another call.

His thoughts drifted back to Rebecca like a magnet to metal. Rebecca Bolen's kisses were hot enough to melt his bones. She had a funny sense of humor that surfaced unexpectedly, revealing a warmth and capacity for fun. And she was more exciting than any other woman he had known.

Forget it, Delancy, he told himself. She was far more vulnerable than she realized. He intended to protect her and then to get out of her life.

He moved restlessly through the house again, standing at the kitchen window and staring at the dark shadow of the forest of pines. Beyond them was an open field and then one of the roads that were under surveillance.

His thoughts went back to Rebecca and the hurt in her voice when she had explained that the kiss they'd shared had been her first since her husband. Jake felt a strange twist of pain for her. Was she scared to love again, afraid of getting hurt again, or still grieving over her loss?

Forget it, he told himself, annoyed at the stirring of sympathy. The lady is doing what she wants to do. If she wants to live out here like a hermit, that's her choice. Yet what a waste it was. He moved impatiently, rubbing the back of his neck, memories of holding her, dancing with her, swirling in his mind like fascinating bits of glass in a kaleidoscope. The images taunted him, and he was hard again, aching and thinking about her fiery kisses. He swore and strode through the house, feeling as if he were in a cage.

For the next hour, Jake prowled around the house. He was restless, but gradually exhaustion overcame him. As dawn broke, he put his pistol in the holster and placed it on a high shelf where the girls couldn't reach it. Sinking back on the lumpy chair, he stretched out his legs and closed his eyes.

* * *

Less than two hours later, something tickled his nose. Jake batted at it and felt it again, on his cheek. Something warm wriggled on his lap. He opened his eyes to look down into big blue eyes and a dimpled smile. Dressed in a fresh blue T-shirt and blue shorts, Sissy trailed a large white feather along his jaw. She was a warm bundle, her eyes sparkling with mischief. She smelled sweet and soapy, and tendrils of her hair were wet.

"Did I wake you?"

"What did you expect to do, tickling me with that feather?" he asked with amusement.

She shrugged and grinned. "You're sleeping late. Mommy is in the kitchen. Do you like to feel a feather on your face?"

She looked hopeful, expectant, and suddenly he wondered if this was something she had done with her father. He didn't know anything about what would please her. Standing, he caught her around the waist and swung her over his head. She squealed and giggled and he laughed in return.

"That's what you get when you wake a sleeping man with feather tickles!"

"Sissy!"

He heard Rebecca's voice and swung Sissy to the floor. Wearing a pink T-shirt and cutoffs, Rebecca stood in the doorway. Her face had drained of color, and she was staring at them both. "Sissy, you shouldn't have awakened Mr. Delancy."

"He was almost awake."

"Now I'm completely awake, so it doesn't matter," he said. Sissy laughed up at him and then ran for the kitchen.

"Breakfast!" she called, and then she was gone, leaving him with Rebecca. Raising his arms over his head, he stretched.

"I'm sorry she woke you. You couldn't have slept very long," she said, and suddenly her voice sounded different.

He lowered his arms and caught her looking at his chest. Her gaze flicked up and met his, and she blushed. He wondered what was running through her mind to make her blush. He would have been willing to give a month's pay to find out.

"She used to do that with her father, didn't she?"

"How'd you know that?" Rebecca asked, frowning at him as he moved closer to her. He wanted to tilt her chin up and kiss her lips, which were pursed. Mother and daughter were both irresistible.

"Just a guess."

"I hope she wasn't sticky."

"Not at all. She smelled sweet. Maybe it's just little boys like my rowdy nephews who are noisy and sticky. Little girls are nice. So are big girls," he added softly, unable to stop. Something flickered in her gaze and she drew a deep breath, making her shirt strain over her full breasts.

"Come eat breakfast," she said abruptly, turning for the kitchen.

"I'll be there in a few minutes. I'll shower first." He watched her walk away down the hall and then he strode outside to the pickup to get his things, coming back to step into the shower.

Twenty minutes later he was dressed in jeans and a navy T-shirt and cowhide Western boots. When he entered the kitchen, he glanced at the girls.

"Good morning."

"Morning," Tara said, bending her head over a small object in her lap, her long brown braid over her shoulder, a bright blue ribbon tied around it. Sissy played with a small stuffed rabbit. Patches of its fur were worn away, and one ear was patched. She gave him a wide grin while Rebecca glanced at him and handed him a glass of orange juice and placed slices of bread in the toaster.

They sat at the table, and she pulled a tablet in front of her. "I've made a list of things I want brought home from my shop, and I've tried to think of everything." She raised her head to look at him, and Jake could see the annoyance in her eyes. "It seems to me that we should be able to go into town and gather everything that needs to be moved out here. It would be so much simpler."

"You're moving your work here?" Tara asked, raising her head.

"My department is going to move your mom's shop to the barn so she can work at home," Jake answered.

"Awesome!" Tara exclaimed.

"Here at home?" Sissy's eyes sparkled while Tara continued to stare at Rebecca.

"You're going to work here? All the time, or until that man is caught?" Tara persisted.

"Just until they catch him," Rebecca replied with a note of exasperation.

"As soon as he's caught," Jake added, "we'll move all her work back to town."

"You're certain this is necessary? It's going to cause a dreadful disruption to my business."

"It's important," he replied quietly, aware that the girls were looking back and forth between their mother and him.

Sighing in resignation, she turned to look at her girls.

"This also means that for the coming week, Tara, you and Sissy will have to stay home and miss your lessons in town."

A howl of protests rose in the air, and Jake wished they had settled this issue before he joined them. Rebecca looked unruffled as she gazed at her girls. She reached out to touch Sissy's curls.

"I don't like it, either," she said gently, "but hopefully, it'll be for a very short time and then we'll go back to the way we've always lived. Right now we're in some danger until they catch the bad man, so we just have to be careful. It won't last long. Okay?"

"Sure," Tara said with a sigh, and Sissy's lower lip thrust out, but she nodded.

"Maybe there's some special thing you'd like to have added to this list," Rebecca suggested. "Maybe that Disney video you two have been wanting—you could watch it this week."

"Right! Super!" Their frowns melted into smiles, and Tara wiggled with eagerness. "And what about another tablet for my paints?" she asked.

Rebecca laughed. "Whoa. Not too many requests. But I think we can add the tablet, and maybe a coloring book for Sissy."

"Yeah!" Sissy exclaimed. Both girls seemed content and the problem resolved, and Jake wished their mother was that easy to placate.

Tara turned her attention back to the bits and pieces of plastic on the table. "What do you have there, Tara?" Jake asked.

She glanced up at him, holding a black object. "It's the remote control for the television in the living room. It doesn't work because it's been dropped. I found some of the pieces to it this morning."

"Want some help?" he asked.

She climbed down and came over to hand him all the pieces of the remote. He placed them on his knee and began to put them back together, concentrating on them, aware that Rebecca was bent over her list, writing furiously.

She got up to pass out the toast that had popped up. His gaze drifted down over her shirt and trim, faded cutoffs, her long shapely legs, which looked smooth as silk. With an effort, he returned his attention to the remote as Sissy came to stand beside him. He fit another pin in the control.

"Why don't you have whiskers?" Sissy asked.

"I just shaved them off. I'll have whiskers by tonight, if you want to see some."

"You have a lot of hair, but it's not as long as my daddy's was."

"Is that right? You have very pretty hair," he remarked easily, and she smiled at him.

"Do you like curly hair or straight hair?"

"I like both," he answered, aware of Tara's straight brown hair.

"Do you like orange juice?"

"Yes. Do you?" he asked, and she shook her head and wrinkled her nose.

"Do you like strawberry jam?"

"Sissy, stop asking Mr. Delancy so many questions," Rebecca said.

He shook his head. "I don't mind questions, and yes, I like strawberry jam, and I'll bet you do, too."

Sissy nodded. "I like strawberry jam and bread and butter. Do you have a sister?"

"No, I have three younger brothers, but they are all grown up now and married. Now, Tara," he said, closing the remote. "Take this into the front room and see if it works."

"Thanks." She took the box and ran out of the room with Sissy trailing after her, while he turned to take a drink of cold orange juice.

"She never runs out of questions. They've had their breakfasts, so this is for us. Would you like coffee?"

"Have any made?" he asked, thinking she looked as refreshed and bright-eyed as if she slept the whole night, instead of only a few hours.

She stood and moved around the kitchen. "I will in just a minute. I don't drink coffee, and I just didn't think about it. And don't protest. It's no trouble to make."

"You win."

She glanced over her shoulder at him, a sudden twinkle in her eyes. For an instant he wished things were different between them. But then logic set in and he realized it was a good thing that their relationship remained strictly business.

He passed the plate of toast to Rebecca, who was placing a sugar bowl and cream pitcher on the table.

"It works!" Tara called from the living room. With her pigtail bouncing, she came running to the door. "The remote works! I can change the channels!"

"Good."

"Thank you for fixing it." She turned to race back to the living room.

"She'll be happy now," Rebecca said, sitting down to butter her toast, giving him one of her dazzling smiles. "Tara loves the remote. I don't know why, because she never sits down. I think she likes to watch the channels flash past."

"You should smile more often," he said quietly, and something flickered in the depths of her eyes.

"I will when Meskell is caught," she replied solemnly. The only reaction to his compliment that he could detect was the breathlessness of her voice.

"When he's caught and this is over, Rebecca, you should get out more. Get back into life and start dating."

"I'll remember that bit of advice."

He gave a rueful grin and shook his head, raking his fingers through his hair. "Sorry. None of my business again."

"I'll bet you gave your brothers fits with your 'advice.'"

He smiled and shrugged. "They gave *me* fits, so we're even."

"Considering your line of work," she said, "I suppose it's a good thing you can take charge of situations."

"Considering my line of work... You sound as if you view me as Count Dracula."

"No, you're just a tough, hard man. It surprises me when you show another side."

He was a hard man, all right. She could turn him on with the slightest bit of teasing or one of her dimpled smiles.

"You don't really know me," he said quietly. "Don't be so quick to judge."

"I know that you're accustomed to taking charge, giving orders and having people do what you want," she said, and suddenly all the lightness was gone from her voice and the chilling dislike was back. "And you thrive on peril."

"Rebecca, you loved a guy who wasn't afraid to get out and do a dangerous job. Someone has to do those jobs, but your loss is influencing your opinion of other men."

"That's right, it is," she said firmly. She finished her toast and orange juice quickly and moved away from the table. He stood to get some coffee and carry his plate to the sink. Rebecca turned abruptly, and he went up on his toes, curving his body and pulling his dish close against his middle to avoid her smashing into him.

"I'm sorry. We can't seem to keep from colliding!"

"I haven't objected once," he said with amusement.

"Are you really ready for that kind of collision in your life?" she asked, and then wanted to bite it back. His brows arched, and he leaned down. "Never mind," she added quickly.

"I'm more ready than you could possibly want me to be," he said.

She ran her hand across her brow. "I don't know why I say things like that to you!"

"I do," he answered solemnly. "Because beneath all that nonsense about disliking my profession, there's a friendly, warm woman who enjoys flirting on occasion." His voice became husky as he looked at her, and he wanted to reach out and pull her into his arms, but he knew he shouldn't.

She tilted her head to study him. "Are all your jobs like this?"

He held up his hand. "I told you last night and I'll say it again, I swear to you, and may lightning strike if I'm not being truthful, never—not once—has a job been like this."

He leaned slightly closer, and his voice dropped another notch as he answered her. Rebecca felt as if she were on fire, feeling pleasure shoot through her at his answer, yet knowing that she should not be pleased.

Flustered by his answer, feeling hot beneath his steady, smoldering gaze, she moved past him and sat down, staring blankly at her writing tablet. She listened as he moved around behind her.

"Want some coffee?" he asked.

"No thanks."

He poured a cup and came to sit down, pulling a chair around beside her, and her attempts at calming down were for nothing. Her pulse jumped as he moved close.

She twisted around to study him. "Didn't your supervisor give a thought to sending a single guy out here to stay with us?"

"Vance thinks I'm such a confirmed bachelor, he probably gave it little thought," Jake answered dryly. "If he knew what's going on out here, I'd be in deep trouble."

"There's nothing going on out here!" she snapped, wanting to get up and move across the table from him.

"Like hell there isn't," he said softly. He ran his finger along her cheek, and Rebecca's pulse skittered. "And you're bringing it out in me."

"Well, I'm not doing it deliberately!" she snapped, and the smoldering look in his hazel eyes deepened. He leaned closer to her, and Rebecca felt as if all the air were gone from the room. Her heart was pounding, and she wondered if he could hear it.

"You didn't accidentally kiss me last night," he said softly. "We're both responding in ways that neither one of us wants, but I'm not taking sole responsibility, lady."

His words played over her quivering nerves, shaking her because she knew he was right. She had flirted with him, responded to him, returned his kisses. She twisted away, pushing back the chair and moving to the window to gaze outside.

Jake watched her, his gaze running down over her derriere and long legs, feeling his body respond to the sight of her while he silently swore at himself. He should be able to exercise more control over himself and keep his damned mouth shut.

"All right," she exclaimed, her voice low and tense, as she turned around. Her eyes blazed with anger, and he wondered if it was all directed at him, or a little of it at herself. "I admit I kissed you, but I knew better and I didn't want to on one level. I'm vulnerable—"

Jake stood up and crossed the room, stopping a few feet from her. "Don't cry."

"I am not about to cry! I'd like to pick up one of those chairs and slam it over your head!"

If it had been under other circumstances, Jake would have been amused, but he wasn't, because he knew she was hurting and angry.

"Rebecca," he said softly. "Truce. Let's both resolve right now to try to avoid letting anything get out of hand between us. I'm not a marrying man. You don't like cops. Those are big enough barriers, if we'll just remember them. Let's get back to work and stick to business."

Jake knew his words were as false as a six-dollar bill, but he was going to give it a try.

She tilted her head, pursed her rosy lips. "You are full of it, Detective Delancy. That is the most blatant bunch of..." Her voice trailed off, and he suspected she would not say aloud the words that were in her mind at the moment. "But I agree. We'll stick to business."

He nodded and sat back in his chair, moving it around the table away from hers, deciding he could lean across the table and read her list upside down if he had to.

He kept his gaze riveted on the tablet, congratulating himself on gaining her cooperation, idly wondering how long it would be before his good intentions went out the window. Just think of marriage and responsibility and you'll cool down, he thought. Think about the expenses Bill accumulated during his last year in college.

"All right, here's the list. I don't know where some of the tools are—they'll be scattered all over the shop."

"Do you know anyone in the business we could call and have them meet us there and describe or pick out the tools you want?"

She ran her hand through her hair, letting long golden locks tumble back across her cheek and shoulder, and he forgot the question, wanting to reach out and feel the same silky curls slide across his hand.

She bent over the tablet and wrote a number. "A friend of mine is in this business, and he would probably help your men."

"Okay, let's see the list. How big is this table you need?"

"It's very big and heavy. About eight feet long and four or five feet wide, I'd guess. There are three tables in my shop. I can get along with just one."

Item by item, they went over the list. The last items were the video, tablet and coloring book for the girls. He glanced up at Rebecca.

"Add a few other things for the girls. It could get to be a long week."

Rebecca nodded and stared out the front windows while she thought about it.

Jake looked at her profile, her slender throat. "Also, while you're at it, give me a grocery list."

She groaned. "This is ridiculous."

"You saw what happened to my apartment. And I can tell you again how I watched Meskell gun down my friend."

She gave Jake a solemn look, nodded her head and wrote a list. As she did, Jake poured another cup of coffee and stood by the window to drink it.

"All right, here's the list."

She handed it to him and watched as he went to the telephone. As he talked, she moved around the kitchen, cleaning it and trying to ignore Jake, finally leaving the room to do some chores.

Within the hour, as she worked in the kitchen, he came into the room. "I want to look at the barn. Do all of you want to go with me or stay here?"

"I'll come along, and I know the girls would love it."

At the back door minutes later, Jake studied the woods directly across from him while he checked with Terry Woodson on the radio to make certain the area was secure. The morning sun was high and the sky the deep blue of a cloudless summer day that promised to be hot.

He heard footsteps as Rebecca and the girls entered the room. "Tara, you and your mother hold Sissy's hands. I'll stay beside you," he said to Rebecca. "Let's all go as fast as possible."

They nodded, and Jake opened the door, giving one more look to the woods in back. He was depending on the department to give a warning if Meskell came into the vicinity, but he still hated crossing the wide-open expanse of ground.

They went as fast as Sissy's short legs could go. Jake could have carried her and all of them gone faster, but he wanted his hand free if he needed to draw and fire. They rushed inside the barn the moment he had the door open.

"Think this will be all right?" Jake asked.

She looked around the barn. There was a wide center aisle with double doors opening to the north and south. Overhead, lofts ran along either side. The stalls were empty, and the place smelled of dust and hay, but she thought the wide center passage would give her all the room she needed. The barn was cluttered with things stored and forgotten.

"I never come out here, and we keep all our junk here," she said. "We'll have to clear this out to make room for my things."

"We can start on it, or I can get the men to do it when they arrive."

"I'd just as soon get started. It'll give me something to do to work off some energy."

Jake turned to look at her and she knew how he had taken her remark. Giving him a steady look in return, determined to stick with her morning's vow to keep things platonic, she tried to get her thoughts back to making the barn as bearable a workplace as possible.

"I'd like more light. Even with the doors open, I don't have the lighting I need."

"I'll rig something up," he said, studying the high ceiling fitted with dim bulbs far above them.

She smiled at him. "Ninety percent of the time you seem so much the tough cop, and then sometimes you seem like a regular guy," she said in a low voice that wouldn't carry to the girls.

He touched her collar lightly and then tucked a strand of hair behind her ear. "If circumstances were different, it wouldn't be just ten percent regular guy with you," he drawled quietly, and Rebecca felt her pulse flutter.

Tension vibrated between them, that magic chemistry that neither of them seemed able to control. Their surroundings faded away. Dimly, she heard Tara and Sissy talking, but she was lost in Jake's gaze, remembering standing in his arms last night. She drew a deep breath and saw his jaw clamp shut.

He turned abruptly, and she ran her hand across her brow, feeling as if she had just had a narrow escape, yet at the same time experiencing a pang of longing.

"Do you have an extension ladder?"

"No, I don't."

"We'll get one, and a couple of big electric fans," Jake said, striding through the barn to the double doors at the opposite end and sliding them open.

The girls scampered over the barn, climbing to the loft, squealing with delight, and Rebecca knew they loved being out of the confines of the house. She and Jake worked together, clearing boxes, Dan's old fishing tackle and golf clubs, things packed away and forgotten.

She watched as Jake hoisted a bag of fertilizer, his muscles bulging. He carried it to the back of the barn, dumped it and yanked his shirt off, wiping sweat from his forehead. Sunlight spilled through the open doors over his broad shoulders and muscled back. She inhaled, her resolutions forgotten as she stared at his shoulders and narrow waist, his jeans riding low across his narrow hips.

She turned around abruptly and picked up boxes to move, carrying them out of the way into an empty stall. Something rustled in the dark corner of the stall, and Rebecca froze.

She dropped the box and jumped out of the stall, whirling around and slamming into Jake, who caught her.

Chapter 8

"Hey!" Jake's hands on her arms steadied her.

"There's something in the stall," she said. "It must be a mouse or rat or snake, but it just startled me."

He pulled out his pistol and stepped past her, and she followed. A mouse scampered through the hay into a corner.

"I can shoot it, but it would frighten the girls."

"It would horrify them. I'm sorry. My nerves must be on edge. Just let it go. Maybe I can get them a kitten, and that will take care of more than one problem."

"Want me to get a kitten?"

She smiled at him. "You're like a genie."

"Not exactly," he drawled, and once more the tension between them sparked, and she realized they were still standing just inside the stall, close to each other in the dim light of the barn.

"We should get back to work," she said, stumbling away from him, hurrying to pick up another armload of boxes, as if to put some kind of physical barrier between them.

At midday, a flatbed truck arrived with three men, who piled out. Jake went forward to meet them, bringing them into the barn to introduce them to Rebecca and the girls.

"You'll need to direct us where you want things," Jake said, "but first the guys want to unload the groceries."

"Sure."

"You get in the truck and ride up to the house. Would the girls like a little ride in the back of the truck?"

"I'll ask."

In minutes both girls were settled in the back of the truck with boxes of supplies and sacks of groceries. After the ride ended, they went inside to help put away groceries. When they finished, Jake turned to Rebecca.

"The area around the house should be safe. McCauley's relief, Terry Woodson, is in the woods behind the house right now. Woodson has made the rounds, the surveillance teams haven't reported anything, and with the men here I think it'll be safe for the girls to play in the yard."

Rebecca leaned around Jake. "Hear that?"

Both girls nodded with eager grins. "All right. You must stay near the house—between here and the barn."

"If you want to ride back to the barn in the truck, you may," Jake said, and received more enthusiastic agreements as Sissy jumped up and down.

They drove to the barn and Rebecca directed where she wanted all her things as the men unloaded the truck. Rebecca showed the men where to set the scarred wooden table.

While they continued unloading the truck, she unpacked boxes and set up her work area. She watched as the men carefully uncrated her etched glass.

When it was finally in place, Jake walked around, looking at framed etched glass depicting a vase of lilies. He moved to a colorful stained-glass design of a mountain and blue sky and touched the frame lightly, glancing back at her.

"You're good at this."

"Thank you," she said, feeling pleased. "I'm doing that one, the mountain project, for a house," she explained, aware of Jake's solid bulk as he came to stand beside her.

"I'm doing a door and two windows for a house," she said. Jake looked at large shapes of clear beveled glass, knives, strips of lead, and pliers. The large table would not have fit into her house without the furniture being removed.

"I can see why you have to work in the barn."

"This is going to be fine for a workplace," she replied.

By late afternoon, the two men had gone and an electrician was working in the barn to run wiring and put in extra lights.

While she fixed a tuna salad for dinner, Jake entered the kitchen. "When I called the electrician, I had him pick up some motion-detector lights to put up outside your house and barn while he's here."

"I didn't know the police department did things like that," she said, studying him and guessing what his answer would be as he gave her a level look.

"I did it because I wanted to. It'll make my job easier, and those lights aren't expensive."

"You don't have to do that."

"Forget it," he said gruffly. "It's done."

"I'd like to pay you for the lights and wiring."

He shook his head. "I wanted to do it."

For a moment, Jake thought she would continue to argue, but then she smiled. "Thank you."

"I'll go see how he's coming and check on the girls," he said, and left, letting the screen slap shut behind him.

Feeling another strange mixture of emotions, she followed him to the door, watching through the screen as his long-legged stride covered the ground swiftly. In seconds the girls had jumped up and were trailing right behind him.

The electrician stood on a ladder outside the barn, and Rebecca shook her head. Jake shouldn't have bought the lights. Was he also paying the electrician for the extra wiring and to work on Sunday? He was so damnably cavalier, giving orders without hesitation, taking charge, yet at the same time, he could be considerate, gentle, and far more understanding than she was comfortable with.

During dinner that night, over sliced juicy red tomatoes, tuna salad and golden corn, Sissy stared at Jake, and he suspected a question was forthcoming.

"Can we ever ride in a police car?" she asked.

"Yes, you can," Jake said. "I promise that sometime I'll take you in one."

Sissy brightened, and he glanced at Rebecca, who smiled at him. Each smile made him warm, and he wished he could make her smile more often. She was an independent woman, he reminded himself, completely self-sufficient, and he knew she couldn't wait for him to get out of her life.

"Can you turn the siren on?"

"We can turn the siren on and the lights on if I'm out here where it won't startle people. I can't do it in town, because that means people have to get out of the way because I have an emergency."

"Like a fire," she said solemnly, and he remembered about their father.

"Do you ever go to fires?"

"Sissy, let Mr. Delancy eat his dinner," Rebecca said quietly.

"It's all right. Yes, sometimes policemen go to fires, as well as the fire department."

Sissy nodded as if satisfied, while Tara studied him.

"You can get hurt at work just like our daddy did, can't you?" Tara asked, and Jake felt a pang for her. He glanced at Rebecca and saw a stricken expression on her face, but only for a second, and then it was gone.

He realized how badly she must have hurt for the girls, besides what she had suffered herself.

"Yes, Tara," he answered carefully. "I am in danger. Policemen and firemen take chances, but we're doing a job to help people. Someone has to take those risks."

"Do you like being a policeman?" she asked.

"Yes, I do."

"Have you ever been shot?" Sissy asked.

"Yes, I have," he answered truthfully. "It wasn't a terrible wound and I recovered from it and that's all over now."

"And I have a question," Rebecca said, interrupting cheerfully. "Who is volunteering to clear the table tonight?"

Tara groaned, while Sissy studiously looked at her plate.

"I think I'll be your volunteer," Jake said. "If I don't keep in practice, by the time I get home, I'll forget how."

The girls grinned at him happily, and he was relieved the questions about his job were over.

After dinner he shooed Rebecca from the table and quickly cleaned the kitchen. Rebecca was settled in the living room, working a puzzle with the girls, while he moved through the house, checking windows. Finally he stepped out the back door to walk around the house, gazing off toward the barn and getting a wave from McCauley, who had come on duty again.

Jake went inside to watch Rebecca continue to work a puzzle with Tara and Sissy, and then sat in the living room and listened to a five-minute news announcement on television. When Rebecca left to draw a bath for Sissy, the child came over to stand beside his chair and study him. He smiled at her while her big blue eyes continued to stare at him.

"When you get married, do you want a little girl?" she finally asked.

"Yes, I do," he said. "Little girls are sweet."

"I like you here with us," she said shyly.

"Thank you, Sissy. I like being here." She was a charmer.

"Do you like Mommy?"

"Yes, I do," he said, wondering if Rebecca could hear her questions. Judging from the sounds of water splashing into the tub, she probably could not.

"Will you date Mommy someday?"

The question surprised him. What did Sissy know about dating? She couldn't have any idea what she was asking about, and he wondered what her concept of dating was. He looked down into wide, expectant blue eyes. For an instant, he thought of the empty condo that he did not miss, and the fact that he didn't miss it surprised him. He shook his head.

"No, Sissy, I don't think your mommy and I will date."

Sissy's lower lip turned down, and she looked so crestfallen that he was sorry he hadn't cushioned his answer.

"Sissy, bath time," Rebecca said from the doorway.

With relief, Jake watched Sissy run from the room, wondering what questions Rebecca would get now.

He glanced across the room at Tara, who seemed absorbed in a book and oblivious of the conversation.

"Tara, bedtime," Rebecca called.

"Yes, ma'am," she said reluctantly, sliding out of the chair while she continued to read. Amused, Jake watched her navigate a path across the room and down the hall as she seemed to continue looking at her book the entire time.

He stood and moved around, turning down the lights and finally standing near the front window to gaze at the trees across the road. Where was Meskell?

Lenny Meskell leaned back in the sleek black car and relaxed. How long until the car would be reported stolen? Not for a few hours, he thought. He had taken it only minutes after the dude left it and went into the movie. There was no one out here in the wilds looking for it, anyway.

He reached across the seat and ran his hand along the cool barrel of his rifle. *Tonight.* Tonight he could take out the cop, and the blond would be his. When he came back this way, she would be his.

He licked his lips, thinking about her. She'd beg him to let her go. He'd head down south, be across the border, stop first to get some money. Hit a couple of places. He glanced down at the duct tape. He had it all planned, been dreaming about it for the past few days. He would climb into her bedroom window tonight—and if the cop had it locked, he'd bust through the glass and get her before that cop ever got to her.

Lenny remembered her house. Her bed was close to the windows. Damn close. He'd get her in a flash.

Once he had her, the cop would have to lay down his gun. Lay down his gun and die. Meskell chuckled. What a pleasure it would be to gun down the bastard.

And she would go with him so willingly, because of her children.

Once they got back to the car, he'd take her before he bound her up. His breathing became fast. It had been too long since he'd had a woman. He'd haul her up to the car, rape her—that would calm her down—and then he'd bind her up and throw her into the trunk. They'd be off to Mexico, crossing the border, maybe taking a different car. It wouldn't matter. Whatever he could sell best in Mexico.

And when he tired of her, he'd put a bullet through her. He licked his lips, clenching and unclenching the steering wheel, anxious to get to his destination.

He topped a rise and saw pinpoints of twin red lights ahead. Who the devil was on this road at night? He seldom saw anyone. No one farmed out this way. It was the edge of the city. Farms were farther out, and there was no industry in this particular area.

He drove, watching the lights, wary of anything unusual. He had been out here only once before—the day the cop came to stay. He'd come back later, and a cop had passed him on the way out. Lenny had figured they had found the note and that the place was probably swarming with cops, so he had turned around and headed back into town.

He knew where the copper lived. It had been tricky to get past the guy at the desk. Meskell thought about how he had swiped a bouquet of flowers from a floral delivery truck and then waited until he saw two elderly ladies going inside the apartment house. He had fallen into step with them, holding up the flowers and conversing politely with them as they passed the security desk in the lobby. Then he had asked the talkiest biddy if she would mind asking at the desk which apartment belonged to J. Delancy, because he was supposed to deliver the flowers to him and he had lost the apartment number.

Lenny remembered standing around the corner in the lobby and listening when she stepped to the desk and the security guard greeted her politely and answered her question without hesitation.

"Do you want me to call Mr. Delancy and see if he's in?" the guard had asked.

Lenny laughed. He hadn't waited to hear the answer, but had taken the elevator and stepped out two floors above Delancy's and waited in the alcove by the cold-drink machine, giving enough time for security to check and make certain no one was trying to get into Delancy's place.

And then it had been sheer pleasure to tear the place apart. He laughed in the darkened car. Delancy would know who had done it. He would know the moment he saw his door kicked in, because Lenny had sworn to get him.

Lenny watched the red taillights ahead, wondering about the car's destination when suddenly they swung off the road and disappeared into the darkness.

He frowned and stared into the night as he sped along. There weren't any side roads leading into this one for another mile. They had just crossed a road, and there wouldn't be another one in sight yet.

He frowned and jammed his foot on the brake and slowed. The car hadn't pulled off to one side on the shoulder and then turned. It had just turned and disappeared into the night.

He continued another quarter of a mile, then slowed and pulled to the side of the road, debating whether to go back and try again another night. He cut his lights and sat in the darkness, letting his eyes adjust, estimating it must be another half mile where the car had turned. He could have sworn he hadn't seen roads leading off this one except the regular county road, and the car had already crossed that and then turned.

Could it have been farther along than he thought and turned onto the next county road? The lights had just disappeared into the night. He sat lost in thought, deciding to wait and think what he should do. Whoever had been in that car had pulled off and driven into the woods, just the way he himself had planned to do.

That bothered him. While he sat there and thought about it, he saw the beam of headlights splash over trees in the distance and then turn onto the road. The car was coming back!

He didn't want to be seen by anyone. He switched on the motor and turned into the brush without turning on his lights, rolling down a slight incline. He hoped to hell he could get back out of the place. He peered through the darkness, saw a tree looming dead ahead and jammed on the brake. He hit the tree, but it was only a slight bump. He cut the motor and waited, seeing the lights of the approaching car.

A car raced past. It was black, twin spots on it.

Lenny got a cold feeling in the pit of his stomach. Suppose the cops had staked out the place after his note?

He swore and hit the steering wheel with his fist. He picked up the rifle and fingered it, wanting to blast away. He had waited to get the bitch. He wanted her, and he wanted his freedom.

He replaced the rifle. It might not have been a cop, but he'd wait. And he'd come back earlier tomorrow night, back to this same spot, and see if a car passed him and turned off the highway.

He swore as he turned on the motor, jammed the car into reverse and backed onto the road, swinging around without turning on his lights. Glancing at the odometer, he made a note of the mileage, wanting to be able to come back to the same spot.

Lenny drove slowly, glad for the moonlight, looking at the gray ribbon of road while his thoughts churned. If that had been a cop, he was too far away to watch her house. Were the cops watching the damned road?

At the first intersection, he turned away from the city and sped away, switching on the lights and swearing. He needed to ditch this car, get something he could drive cross-country. He would be back tomorrow night.

Jake stared at the trees, wondering about Meskell and where he was, beyond the circle of light from the motion detector lights. He moved quietly, walking around the house, looking at Rebecca's drawn drapes. Some of them had little tears, and if someone got up close, he might be able to see into the house when the light was on. Meskell had better not ever get the chance.

The idea of his stalking Rebecca sent a charge of white-hot anger through Jake. He realized how tense he was; he relaxed, unclenching his fists. She has you tied in knots, he told himself. He'd better keep his emotions out of the way or get someone else out here to sit with Rebecca. He wouldn't be any good to her if he didn't keep a cool head.

He looked at Rebecca's windows. Her room was dark, and he knew she was in the bathroom with Sissy, or with the girls in their bedroom. He inhaled deeply, knowing he was

in full view, but counting on McCauley and the surveillance team to be doing their jobs.

The moon was white and full, shedding a silvery glow
over the countryside. Not a breath of air was stirring; it was
hot and heavy. How long since the last rain? He couldn't
remember.

He wiped his brow and moved on, treading carefully. He
turned the corner and listened to the air conditioner puffing away. Even after Meskell was caught, Rebecca needed
to consider moving closer to some neighbors. It wasn't safe
for her or the girls out here. He shook his head. Let the lady
live her own life, he thought. She's an adult, doing what she
wants to do. She's made it clear she doesn't want your
opinions. And you have no claim on her.

Annoyed with himself, he strode back to the house noisily, his thoughts on the beautiful widow, unaware of the
crunch of gravel and the swish of grass beneath his boots.
He entered the house and slammed the door.

When he stepped into the living room, Rebecca appeared
from the hall, her brows arched in question. "Anything
wrong? I heard a door slam."

She was flushed from helping Sissy with her bath, and her
cotton shirt was unbuttoned slightly, far enough for a
tempting show of flesh. Strands of blond hair curled damply
about her face and she looked disarrayed, approachable,
sexy. His gaze flicked over her and then met hers, seeing her
curiosity change to awareness.

"I was checking around outside."

"Oh?" Her brows arched higher. "You don't usually
slam doors."

"No, I don't," he answered evenly. "I was thinking about
your living out here after this is over."

"Oh," she said again, and a cool look came to her features. "I'm tucking the girls in." She turned and left, and
he looked at her long legs and the sexy sway of her fanny as
she walked down the hall.

"Good going," he told himself under his breath, knowing he had annoyed her. He didn't want to watch television, and he switched it off. He didn't want to sit still, either. He moved around the small room, wondering if tonight would be the night Meskell made his move. It was time. If he waited any longer, Meskell's nerves would be stretched thin.

Tonight should be the night. And it was a scorcher outside. The weather report on the news earlier had given the temperature in the city today at 111 degrees. Tonight should cool to a mere 88. In a small box of a house without central air-conditioning, it would be a furnace.

How early would Meskell try to come? Jake guessed about two or three in the morning. Maybe a little later. Make sure everyone was asleep. About four. Still dark enough for cover. Which way would Lenny come?

Jake guessed from the woods behind the house where he had been before. Jake clenched his fists. He wanted a chance at Meskell.

Rebecca's voice floated on the air as she sang a lullaby, and Jake paused to listen. She sang softly, yet he could catch the lilting phrases.

Rebecca leaned down to kiss Sissy good-night and Sissy touched her hair. "I like Mr. Delancy, and he can be my new daddy."

"Honey, we barely know him," Rebecca replied, startled by Sissy's remark.

"We know him," Sissy argued vehemently. "We know him real well."

Rebecca felt a rush of sympathy at the longing in Sissy's voice. "I don't think Jake wants to be a daddy," Rebecca replied carefully. "Getting married just isn't what he wants to do."

"He doesn't like children?" Tara asked, frowning.

"Yes, he likes children, but that's different from becoming a father."

"How?" Sissy asked.

"A father has some big responsibilities toward his children. That's different from just liking children."

"How's it different?" Sissy persisted. "What responsibilities?"

"A father has to take care of them?"

"Mr. Delancy would do that. He takes care of all of us."

"No, he doesn't. He's protecting us from a bad man, but that's different."

"I want him for my new daddy," Sissy said, her lower lip thrusting out.

"Sissy, this is his job. When they catch the bad man, Mr. Delancy will go to his next job, to protect another family or catch another bad man," Rebecca said, afraid that Jake was beginning to fill too many voids in their lives. And she hurt for Sissy and Tara, because Dan had been a wonderful, loving father.

"I don't want Mr. Delancy to go," Sissy said.

"Well, he isn't going now, so don't worry about it. He'll be right here to eat breakfast with you. Now sweet dreams."

Sissy smiled, seemingly satisfied again, and Rebecca kissed both girls again before leaving the room and switching off the light.

Her gaze went beyond them to the darkened windows, and she wondered how safe they were. When would Meskell do something? Jake said it would be soon. Rebecca felt threatened, and was glad to know Jake was only yards away.

Knowing she should stay to herself, yet aware that Jake would be gone all too soon, she went back to the living room and curled up on the sofa to talk to him. It had been a long time since she had had a man around to talk to, and soon enough she would go back to her solitary nights.

"The girls had a wonderful time riding in the truck today and getting to play outside and in the barn. You're good with children, Jake. It's too bad you aren't a marrying man, because you should have your own family."

He gave her a cynical glance. "I've had my family. I've been a dad since I was a little kid. I've supported my brothers, raised them, done everything a parent would do. I'll marry someday, after I retire to the ranch."

"You might be a little set in your ways by then," she said with amusement. "When is this retirement going to take place?"

"I'm thirty-four. I started so young that I can retire and draw a pension before too many more years. I figure after I'm forty, the department will retire me, and I'll move to the ranch and get married."

"And you accused me of being too regimented and scheduling my life."

She studied him. "Be careful, Jake. You might have to toss aside your planned future. It would serve you right, after demolishing my schedules."

"My future isn't set in concrete. I just have a general idea."

Her soft laugh was a taunting invitation, and Jake wanted to get up and go over to the sofa, yet he knew he'd better stay right where he was.

"How long have you had your ranch?"

"I bought the first parcel of land about seven years ago, and I've been adding to it steadily."

"Did you go to college in Austin?" she asked.

"Yes, with a major in criminal justice. I started with the department when I was eighteen and went to college at night. It took me so many years to get a degree, I thought all my brothers would have one before I did."

Rebecca wondered about him; all the responsibilities he'd had to shoulder at such a young age were probably part of the reason he took command of everything around him. He glanced at her and she looked away, as always feeling a strange flutter when he caught her staring at him.

They continued talking about his ranch and then about the girls. It was three in the morning before Rebecca went to bed. In her room she stared at the clock, amazed she had stayed up so late talking to him.

The time had flown past, and she felt another strange mixture of opposing emotions, because she liked talking to him. She had to admit to herself that she had enjoyed most of the day with him. At least she had enjoyed it since the volatile moments at breakfast.

She didn't want to lose her heart to Jake Delancy. Beneath his easygoing charm there was still the hard cop who lived with danger daily, and she must not forget that for a second. If she was tempted to forget, all she had to think about was the pain of losing Dan.

The house creaked and she became tense, looking at the windows, sitting up and glancing toward the hall. With Jake in the house, she slept with her door almost closed, but she was tempted to open it so that she could see into the girls' room and reassure herself about their safety.

She pushed aside the covers and scurried across the room to open the door. Jake would probably think she was hot and had opened it. No light came from the living room, the only illumination the small night-light that she usually kept in the bathroom.

She could see Sissy's and Tara's heads and knew they were sleeping peacefully. Reassured, Rebecca went back to bed, wiping her brow and picking up a piece of paper from the table to fan herself. Jake must have turned off the air conditioners. What did he think he needed to listen for if he expected the surveillance men and McCauley to catch Meskell before he ever reached the house?

As she closed her eyes, she prayed for their safety and for the police to catch Meskell quickly.

The next morning was Monday, and it was strange to change their routine completely, to know that she wouldn't go into town to work. Rebecca headed for the shower and emerged just as Jake was walking down the hall with his hand in Sissy's.

He was bare chested, locks of hair damp against his forehead. The air conditioners were turned on now, and she could feel the coolness in the hall after the steamy bath. He turned to smile at her.

"Good morning," he said in a deep voice, his gaze running over her, and she became aware of her blue T-shirt and cutoffs, suddenly feeling barer than she really was. And she was just as acutely conscious of his bare chest, having to fight the temptation to scrutinize him in return.

"Morning. Did you wake Mr. Delancy again?" she asked Sissy, who merely rolled her eyes and grinned, completely unabashed.

"It was time. She makes a good alarm clock. A much cuter one than I have," he said, but his voice deepened, and Rebecca's pulse quickened, because she suspected his thoughts were far from Sissy.

"I'll be right there to get breakfast," she said.

"No rush. I'm accustomed to doing that for myself, remember? And before that, I did it for my brothers."

"Oh, yes. Mr. Responsible Bossy Dad," she teased, and instantly wanted to bite back the words.

His brow arched, and Sissy tugged on his hand. "C'mon," she urged impatiently, and turned to run to the kitchen.

"I'm coming, Sissy," he said without taking his eyes from Rebecca. He moved closer and his voice lowered. "You're flirting, Rebecca."

"I didn't intend to," she said in a sudden panic. "I don't know what comes over me when I'm around you! If you'll move out of the way, I can—"

"No. I know what comes over you," he said softly, moving still closer. "You're all woman, Rebecca. Warm and full of life. You've capped it all up too long, and it's a volatile mixture."

"Don't you remember yesterday morning? We vowed we weren't going to do this."

"I didn't start it," he said lightly. Suddenly his eyes narrowed and he stepped aside, unblocking the doorway to her bedroom. "By damn, I can't resist you. You're right. We vowed we weren't going to do this."

He strode down the hall and she dashed into her bedroom and closed the door, crossing to hang the blue chambray shirt on the closet hook. Her hands trembled.

I can't resist you. The words echoed in her mind. And when she let down her defenses, forgot he was a cop, the flirting came naturally. She had never flirted with any other man except Dan. Never.

How long would it take to forget Jake when he left? He hadn't been here long enough to make a dent in their lives. And yet... Sissy was crazy about him. It was more difficult to tell with Tara, yet she followed him around the house, and yesterday she had followed him around the yard and barn.

She should be able to fall back into her old routine without a ripple. Yet the thought of the house being so quiet again didn't hold the appeal it once had.

She turned and glared at the door. Jake had come into their lives with all the force of a whirlwind. He was dynamic, macho, appealing!

She placed her hand on the doorknob and took a deep breath, feeling as if she were going forth to do battle.

Tempting smells came from the kitchen, and she entered to find coffee brewing. The orange juice had been poured, and Sissy was eating a bowl of cereal with slices of banana cut up in it. Slices of tart green kiwi and ripe, juicy cantaloupe were in a bowl on the table, and a bowl of cereal, minus the banana and milk, waited at Tara's place.

"My, you're efficient."

"I thought I better make myself useful. Maybe I'll be more appreciated," he said in such a humble voice that she laughed.

"Now sit down and I'll serve your breakfast."

"I can't imagine. I'll get my own," she said.

"Okay, but I offered."

She fixed a piece of toast, saw he had a bowl of cereal with banana, as well as a bowl with a slice of cantaloupe and some kiwi. He poured coffee and sat down.

By the time they had eaten, both girls were through and had gone to change to go to the barn with Rebecca and Jake.

Rebecca pulled her tablet in front of her and bent over it.

"Now what are you listing?"

"The customers I need to call today. I have customers to contact, suppliers to talk to. I need to let everyone know where they can find me."

"The phone in the barn is in working order."

"Good. How much longer do you think this will go on?"

Hazel eyes met hers, and she knew she would get an honest answer. "Anytime now. Meskell's nerves will be stretched thin before long. If he doesn't come soon, then something is wrong. He's on to the surveillance, or something happened to him."

Jake's cellular phone rang, and he crossed the room to pick it up from the counter.

Rebecca could barely hear him while he talked, and she went back to thinking about her work and her customers, planning out the day.

Jake came back to the table. "Some guy reported his car stolen last night about midnight. It was found abandoned this morning across town, but one of the prints they lifted matches Meskell's. He's mobile. The car had a lot more miles on it than the guy remembered."

She felt cold in spite of the warm morning. Jake's serious tone brought back too much of the threat. "Do you think he drove out this way?"

"No one knows. Your guess is as good as anyone's. The only thing we know is that he didn't try to come after you last night. They're checking any robberies in the area and nearby towns to see if any fit his M.O. He could be taking some time to get his hands on more cash."

"Why do you say more?"

"Because he'd stolen some before the night we caught him, and no one has ever found it."

"Was it very much?" she asked, wondering if Lenny Meskell had enough funds to enable him to get around easily.

"We figure he might have anywhere up to thirty thousand stashed from a robbery he pulled."

She closed her eyes. "He's smarter than I thought and if he has money he can do a lot of things."

"He's not that damned smart," Jake said roughly. "We caught him before and we'll catch him again."

"He must have had some foresight to have stashed stolen money."

"Not much. He planned to come right back and get it. We ruined his plans." Jake's radio beeped and he picked it up.

Rebecca tried to get her mind back on her work, but she kept thinking of Meskell driving somewhere near her house. Jake finally put away the radio.

"That was Woodson. He's come on duty and he and McCauley checked out the woods around the house and the barn. Woodson is at the barn now, but he's going in to the trees behind the house. Tell me when you're ready to go to the barn."

"I'll see about the girls."

She stood and left the room and Jake forgot about Meskell as he watched Rebecca walk away.

Two big fans were installed in the barn, circulating air that was still cool from the night. The lights were bright, and she began to get her things organized while the girls trailed around behind Jake as he looked the barn over.

She spent the first hour calling customers. By that time Sissy and Tara were playing in the loft with the dolls they had brought from the house. Jake sat on a bale of hay near the doors that opened toward the woods to the north.

She gathered her tools and placed the glass she needed on the table. In minutes she was concentrating on the glass.

At midmorning, Jake sauntered over to her. "What are you working on?"

"This is for a front door panel," she said, pointing to a fleur-de-lis pattern. "I lay out the cartoon—that's the pattern—and cut the pieces of glass." She pointed to the work in front of her.

"Now this is being leaded up," she said, pushing a piece of glass into the corner of a framework fastened to the table. "I work toward this corner to start."

He picked up a long, pliable piece of lead, holding it in his tanned, blunt fingers, and she glanced at him. "That's the way I buy the lead. Then, before I work with it, I stretch it."

While he replaced it on the table, she bent over her work. In seconds, she looked up to find him still watching her.

"It's interesting."

She bent over the glass again, but she was still aware of him, standing so close, watching her as she fitted small strips of lead between pieces of glass.

Jake moved away to glance at the woods again and then sat down on an overturned barrel, shifting to look at Rebecca. Her hair fell forward in a curtain of silky gold as she leaned over the table and concentrated on the design.

Jake's gaze ran over her round bottom, her long legs, and he wondered how easily he would forget the time spent with her and her girls. This morning Sissy had wakened him with a feather again, tickling his chin and giggling, her eyes sparkling with irresistible mischief.

Jake's radio beeped and he yanked it up. "Jake, this is Werner. A postal truck just turned into her drive," said the deep voice over the static. "I'm at the stakeout, watching the front road."

"I'll watch." He replaced his radio and moved toward the front. "What time does the mail usually come?"

"Midmorning," Rebecca said, glancing at the drive. The clatter of an engine could be heard.

Jake went forward, his hand sliding to his hip, not far from the pistol tucked into the back of his jeans. He stood just inside the barn and watched as the small mail truck stopped beside the box. The postman placed letters and papers inside and then swung the truck around, driving away with a plume of dust behind him.

"I suppose you'll go get the mail," Rebecca said dryly, and he looked down to see that she had come to stand beside him.

"Don't stand in the doorway when the mail comes."

"Yes, sir!" she snapped, her eyes getting the little pinpoints of fire that amused him. "I suppose you think the mailman might want to eliminate me, too."

"It would not be beyond Lenny to waylay your postman, either knock him unconscious or kill him, and dress in his postal uniform. That would get him past everyone. We don't need you running out to meet him."

"Oh!" Her mouth formed a round circle, and he fought the temptation to lean down and place his lips over hers. "I hadn't thought of that."

"You don't have a criminal mind."

"You do?"

"I'm accustomed to working with them and thinking like they do," he answered. "I'll get the mail."

He jogged out to the box, glad for the chance to get some exercise. The metal box was crammed with mail, and he scooped it out, jogging back to the barn to place it on the table beside her. "If you get a crank letter from him, let me see it. We'll want it for fingerprints, that sort of thing."

Frowning, she nodded, and he sighed because she hadn't thought of a letter from Meskell, either. But it turned out all her correspondence was legitimate.

At noon they took a break for lunch and dashed back to the house, which was cool from the air-conditioning.

Jake helped Rebecca fix sandwiches and fruit, and the moment they were through, the girls carried their dishes to the sink and ran off to watch television.

The phone rang shrilly and Rebecca crossed the room to answer it. "Bolens'," she answered, and Jake watched all color drain from her face.

Chapter 9

"**H**e's gone," she said, sounding dazed. Jake snatched the receiver from her hand and heard the buzz that indicated the line was clear. He punched a single digit, and a man answered.

"Get a trace?"

"We'll let you know."

Jake replaced the receiver. "What did he say?"

Rebecca's face was white, and Jake's fury mushroomed. "He said, 'The first shot takes out the cop. Then you're next.' And then he called me a name."

"Dammit." Feeling frustrated and helpless, Jake paced the room. The phone rang, and he reached out to yank up the receiver. "Yes?"

"No trace. Out of area. Sorry."

Jake slammed down the receiver and looked at her. "They couldn't trace it."

"Jake, I don't want the girls to pick up the phone and talk to him."

"Do they answer often?"

She bit her lip and seemed lost in thought. "I'm going to tell Sissy that I'm getting business calls here now and I want to answer."

"And Tara?"

"I'll tell her the truth. I can discuss some things with Tara as if she were another adult."

"I'll answer the phone if you want me to."

The fear and anger left her. Her mouth curved in a faint smile. "Suddenly I'm working at home and a male is answering my phone. Do you know what my customers will think? You let me answer, but thanks for the offer."

She was leaning against the kitchen counter, and he couldn't resist placing his hands on either side of her. "I can't imagine. Tell me what your customers will think?"

"The hell I will, Detective," she answered saucily. Her voice had become breathless. His gaze lowered to her mouth, which was only inches away.

"How can you make me forget all about my job and all the danger I'm in? You're standing too close, Jake," she said breathlessly, and all the lightness was gone from her voice.

"When you really let yourself go," he drawled in a husky voice that made Rebecca's heart thud, "I wish I could be there."

"No, you don't," she answered solemnly. "Just think of all your plans for years and years of bachelorhood."

"Sometimes I think you don't really need me. You know how to defend yourself damn well."

Rebecca knew they were sparring, both flirting, trying to stop, trying to keep their distance, yet as unable to resist temptation as moths near a flame. But most of the moths she had seen flitting around candlelight had gotten burned.

Jake couldn't resist. He leaned forward, brushing his mouth over hers, feeling everything inside him tighten. He was hard instantly and painfully. He wanted to wrap his arms around her and kiss her, to taste her mouth and feel her softness crushed against him.

Instead, he fought to control his urges, merely brushing his mouth over hers again, feeling the incredible softness of her lips, catching the faint whiff of mint on her breath. His pulse pounded like a sledgehammer beating away at his ribs. He clutched the countertop with his fists, hanging on as if he were going to fly off into space, trying to keep from placing his arms around her.

A tremor ran through Rebecca. She should stop him. One word and he would move away, but she couldn't say anything. His mouth brushed hers, and heat shot through her. She gasped, her heart pounding. She placed her hands on his hips, lightly; it was the merest touch, yet it set her aflame.

She closed her eyes, relishing his mouth brushing hers, unable to hear anything for the roaring in her ears. She struggled to remember why she didn't want this man to kiss her. And finally she remembered, and she opened her eyes.

Jake felt Rebecca push lightly against his chest. As he leaned away, she looked up at him, her blue eyes seeming to draw him into their crystal depths. "No," she whispered.

Jake stepped back, taking a deep breath while she moved away from him.

At the door to the hall, she turned to face him, her gaze sweeping over him. He knew she could see how aroused he was; it was small wonder she couldn't hear his heart pounding. She raised her chin as if she expected a battle. "I'll get the girls. I better get back to work."

He watched her go down the hall to the living room and then went outside to get his emotions and body under control. When had he ever known a woman he couldn't resist? Not since high school, and that didn't count.

He didn't want to find Rebecca irresistible. How did she constantly slip past all his defenses? She flirted a little, but it was damn little, and it slipped out of her like an unexpected hiccup and was about as wanted on her part.

"Dammit," he muttered, staring at the sunny yard, wondering where Meskell had been when he made the call.

"We're ready," Rebecca said behind him. She stood with the girls at the open door.

"Okay, let's hurry to the barn," he said, holding the door and then placing his arm across her shoulders. They rushed across the yard and into the brightly lighted interior of the barn, which was beginning to feel hot even with the fans stirring the air.

In minutes she was bent over a table, working diligently, and he was relieved that she had shaken her fright over the phone call.

During the afternoon, he gave the girls cold fruit drinks from a cooler filled with ice and canned drinks. He carried a can of cola to Rebecca.

She paused in her work to shake her hair away from her face. As she accepted the drink, her fingers lightly brushed his and he drew in his breath. Every touch was explosive. The slightest meaningless contact could stir desire. He leaned his hip against the table as he studied her.

"Rebecca, would you like to learn to shoot?"

"No," she said, shaking her head. She dug in a pocket, pulled out a rubber band and bent over to shake her hair into a fall in front of her, leaving her derriere within inches of him.

He took another deep breath, trying to tear away his gaze, but he could not stop looking at her round bottom, her smooth legs. She came up, catching her hair up on top of her head to wind the rubber band around it.

He wanted to groan. Now her arms were up, pulling the T-shirt tautly across her breasts. Blissfully unaware of the effect she was having on him, she continued, "I wouldn't be a good enough shot to protect myself from him, and once Lenny Meskell is gone out of our lives, I don't want a gun in the house."

"Would you let me get a dog?"

"I'm so thankful you didn't make that request in front of the girls! Don't even mention dogs around them. I was going to wait until Sissy is just a little older so they can be responsible for feeding a pet, but the thought of a kitten is tempting."

"A kitten doesn't bark at strangers and alert the family if something is wrong. As far as the girls feeding a pet, Tara's old enough to feed one, and Sissy would help."

She laughed, her dimple showing. "Do you own a dog?"

"As a matter of fact, I do. It stays at the ranch—"

"And someone else feeds and waters and cares for it and you play with it when you're there."

"Okay, okay. Point taken. But think about it. You'd at least have a watchdog."

She nodded as she picked up a knife. "I better get back to work. This is due by the end of the month."

When she leaned over the table to cut a piece of glass, he was certain the subject was closed. He gave one lingering glance at her and then walked away to look outside.

That night, after the girls had gone to bed, Rebecca sat working on her books at the kitchen table when Jake entered. "It's about time you took a break. How about a glass of iced tea, or some cola?"

"Tea sounds wonderful," she said, stretching and standing. "My eyes are beginning to blur, but I've paid the bills and balanced my checkbook, and got my billing done."

Ice cubes clinked when he dropped them into glasses. "I'm impressed!" Jake watched her stretch. The window unit still chugged noisily, but he had switched off the one in the living room over an hour earlier and the house was warming. Rebecca wore a bright green tank top and her cutoffs, and when she stretched he felt his own body warmth increase as the clinging shirt outlined her full breasts.

"I wish I could hire you to do my bookkeeping, pay my bills and balance my checkbook. I hate paperwork."

"And I would hate arresting people," she said lightly. He oured the tea and handed her a glass, his fingers brushing ers.

"It's all to keep people like you safe on the streets," he aid, looking at the tidy stacks of papers spread on the table and the neat rows of columns in her ledger. "I ought to ire you. They've probably turned off my electricity by now ecause the bills have been neglected."

"If you could get your bills, I'd do them for you some vening. You have men pick up everything else in town and ring it out here. Have them get your bills."

"You work enough as it is."

She wrinkled her nose at him, and he moved away from er, because he was far too tempted to reach for her. Even ae light bantering was taking a toll.

"I'll be glad to do them," she insisted again, "unless you on't want me in your business."

"I'd be delighted to have you in my business or in anyaing else in my life," he said without thinking, and then nook his head. "Dammit, Rebecca, I'm having as much ifficulty with my conversation as you are. I guess it just omes naturally when two people are attracted to each ther."

The words played over her, making her heartbeat uicken. He rubbed the back of his neck. "Why don't you op working for tonight?"

"And come in and talk to you instead?" she asked dryly, nd he laughed. "We can keep things impersonal if I stay in ere and pay bills and balance my checkbook. But I will be rough in just a few more minutes." She sat down again nd bent over her bookkeeping, her hair shining in the light. he tip of her tongue was in the corner of her mouth, and e stared at her in fascination. The slightest little thing about er could turn him on. And he was going to have a meltown and lose control if they didn't catch Meskell soon.

Frustrated, aroused, he stepped outside and closed the door behind him.

He walked away from the house and the motion-detector lights. If he didn't keep his mind on his job, not only could Rebecca lose her life, but he could, as well. He stopped at the corner of the house and studied the dark expanse of trees. Wishing he could walk for hours or go to a gym and work off some restless energy, he circled the house several times.

When he returned, he entered the house quickly.

"Everything's okay outside."

She nodded and continued working. Jake passed her, curbing the urge to lean down and brush his fingers across her nape, looking at her pale, smooth skin, at the locks of golden hair curling above it.

He gave the house a quick check again and then hovered around the kitchen, watching Rebecca until she finally put down her pen, giving him a radiant smile as she closed her ledger. "All finished for this month!"

"Good. I'll fix more iced tea, and we'll sit in the living room and talk."

In minutes they sat in the darkened living room, their voices low while Jake watched the yard. It was almost three in the morning before Rebecca went to bed. Nothing moved outside, but he felt tense, because it was time for Lenny to make his move.

Or was Meskell taking perverse pleasure in dragging out the wait?

Leaning his shoulder against the wall, Jake watched the moonlit yard and thought about the girls. Someday, when this was over, he could take them out to his ranch on a Saturday and let them ride his horses.

He realized what he was thinking about and groaned. This whole family was getting to him.

He enjoyed Rebecca's company, was dazzled by her beauty, and he was even beginning to enjoy the little girls.

The last thought really jolted him. He ran his fingers through his hair with a sense of frustration.

A whimpering cry made Jake's heart lurch. He raced toward the bedrooms and heard one of the girls cry out. He drew his pistol and halted.

Both girls were in bed with sheets over them. "Mommy! Mommy!" Sissy cried and rolled over.

Jake tucked his pistol into the waistband at the small of his back. He crossed the room to scoop Sissy into his arms. She was hot and damp, tears streaking her cheeks, yet her eyes were closed, and he realized she must be having a bad dream.

"Mommy!"

"Shh, Sissy," he whispered close to her ear. "It's all right. It's all right."

She cried and pushed against him, and her eyes flew open. "Where's Mommy?" she sobbed.

"It's all right," he repeated calmly. "Your mother's asleep," he said, carrying Sissy across the hall and nudging the door completely open. Rebecca lay in bed, her golden hair spread over the pillow, her long legs stretched out, the shirt hiked up across her thighs, and Jake felt his mouth go dry as he looked at her. "See, she's asleep and she's right here."

Sissy snuggled against his chest, and he carried her to the front room and turned on the air conditioner and prayed he could hear if Meskell tried to break into the house. "Now it'll be cooler in a few minutes. Do you want to sit here with me or go back to bed?"

"Sit here," she replied in a tremulous voice.

He sat down and held her close on his lap. Her head was against his bare chest, and she ran her small fingers along his jaw. "My daddy's dead," she said solemnly, and he hurt for her.

"Your mommy's here and she loves you."

"I love you," Sissy said solemnly, and Jake felt another twist to his heart. He bent his head to brush her forehead lightly with a kiss.

"You're sweet, Sissy," he said gruffly, knowing she probably wanted a declaration of love in return.

She twisted around to hug him with her thin arms, her small body pressing against him. "Will you keep that man from hurting Mommy?"

"Yes, I will," Jake answered, looking into her wide blue eyes and praying he could keep his promise to her.

"Will Mommy be safe? She won't leave us?"

"Your mother will be right here with you, and she'll be safe."

With a sigh, Sissy settled on his lap again, seeming satisfied. "Will you tell me a story? I want to hear about the three billy goats."

"Sure," Jake said, relishing the cool air that was puffing over them. He spoke softly, relating the old story until Sissy's head lolled against him and she was asleep. He held her close, smoothing her hair away from her face and finally propping his feet on a chair and falling asleep with her in his arms.

He stirred later and carried her back to bed, lowering her carefully. He smoothed the curls back from her forehead, letting his hand lay against her soft cheek for a moment. He bent swiftly and brushed her cheek with a kiss and then tiptoed from the room.

Feeling uneasy, he circled the house. It was time for Meskell to try to get to Rebecca. As Jake studied the empty stretch of road that passed the house, he tried to think what he would do if he were Meskell. What did Meskell have planned?

Lenny shifted his weight. He hated sitting out in the woods in the dark. Things rustled, and he tried not to think what might be moving around behind him. He was half a mile from where he had left the car, in the thick brush off the road.

If the cops had the place staked, they would change shifts regularly. He figured he had another hour to wait until it was about the same time as it had been last night when he spotted the car turning off the road.

A forlorn cry floated on the air, and Lenny jumped. He leaped to his feet and whirled around, pistol drawn. "Hellfire!" he whispered. The cry came again, and his skin prickled while he tried to peer through the night.

By the third hoot, he decided it was some kind of bird. He swore and sat down again on the fallen log. His skin crawled and he tried to avoid thinking about what might be moving around him, but it was difficult, because every rustle made him think of animals and snakes.

He was scared to smoke, afraid it would draw the attention of night creatures. He moved restlessly, swearing alternately at Delancy and the woman, finally sitting down to wait.

He heard a motor and moved closer to the road, keeping down in the brush. Headlights swept into view, and he could hear the roar of the engine. The vehicle swept past and he had a good look in the moonlight. It was another black car with a spotlight on the right side. He couldn't see the left side of the car. But he would have sworn a man was riding in the passenger seat.

Two guys in a black car going the same place every night. He moved up on the road cautiously and stared at the car as it disappeared over a rise.

Lenny began to jog, still hovering on the edge of the shoulder. He watched as the car slowed and turned, spinning off onto rough ground, sending up a cloud of dust.

Lenny stopped. Cops had the placed staked. "Dammit!" A string of oaths came from him as he stomped the ground and waved his fists. Then he stopped and looked around.

Wait and watch and see if a car returned in a few minutes. He crawled down in a gully beside the road while his mind ran over what he would do if they did have the place staked. They were too far from the house to see it except through binoculars. They wanted to pick him up on the road coming in.

He grinned. They were watching the road. If they were concentrating on the house, they would be closer to it. Either way, they couldn't cordon off every inch around the house.

His grin faded. The thought of going cross-country shook him. He didn't want to walk through the woods to get the woman. But that might be the only way he could get to her.

He mulled the problem over and then forgot it momentarily when he saw a silvery flash far down the road. In seconds a car swung onto the highway. Lenny slid down farther, because he didn't want anyone spotting him.

The car roared past and he saw another dark car with a spotlight on the left. As soon as it was gone, he jogged back to his car and climbed in, locking the door and heaving a sigh of relief to be in a car and out of the open. He started the motor and jammed his foot on the gas, running over bushes as he charged up the slight incline and drove back onto the road, his stormy thoughts forming a plan.

The next few days were stressful. At any moment Jake expected Meskell to come after Rebecca. At the same time, tension was high because of the smoldering attraction he was fighting and knew she felt. They were shut up within the close confines of the house and the barn. He felt his skin crawl several times and he felt Meskell was watching them.

Was there a chance Meskell had learned about the surveillance? Jake raked his fingers through his hair. There was always a chance of anything happening. In his work, things seldom went according to plan.

Late Monday afternoon, thunderclouds piled up on the southern horizon. Jake paced the barn as restlessly as a tiger in a cage, and at half past four received a call from Richard Vance.

Jake stood across the table from Rebecca, and the moment he heard Vance's voice, he turned his back and walked away from her so that she would not hear the conversation.

"The heat's breaking and we're in for a big storm," Vance said.

"So the surveillance might not be as good."

"Right. We think Meskell's on to it, anyway. I'm pulling the teams in closer tonight. They can't watch the roads as well in a big storm. We'll still have McCauley on the place, and the stakeouts on all sides of the house."

"I'll be careful."

"Meskell might have spotted someone, so we'll keep the surveillance team closer from now on, but that means he may stand a better chance of getting past us. We won't be able to see every vehicle that goes down those roads and run a check on them like we used to."

"I agree with you on moving them. Keep Meskell guessing."

"I can't keep this much manpower out there indefinitely. If anything big breaks, you know what I'll have to do."

"I can't imagine Lenny going much longer without doing something."

"Jake, I'm sending Werner out to take your place so you can get some relief."

Jake stiffened, knowing he should accept Vance's offer, but wanting to stay with Rebecca. Jake remembered how much he had protested about taking this assignment, but the thought now of turning over Rebecca's safety to someone else bothered him. He rubbed the back of his neck. "Keep Jay where he is. I want to stay with the Bolens."

"You would rather stay?" Richard Vance's voice was filled with obvious curiosity. "You haven't had a break since this started."

"You heard correctly," Jake answered flatly.

"She's a very beautiful woman," Vance said after a moment. "You're not going to let anything jeopardize your judgment, are you?"

"If I thought so, I'd ask for Werner. I want her and her girls to come through this safely."

There was a long pause, and Jake waited patiently. "If that's what you want, it'll suit Jay and it'll suit me. We'll do our best, but if we cordon this area off completely, or hide her, we never will catch him."

"Meskell's wily, but he can't outsmart the department. We'll get him," Jake said, feeling certain they would. And he wanted to be there when they did.

"Storms are unpredictable. Be careful tonight," Vance said, and broke the connection.

Jake turned around to find Rebecca studying him. She had stopped work and was waiting, so he walked back to stand beside her.

"What's happened?"

"Nothing. That was Richard Vance. They're moving the surveillance teams in closer to the house."

"Is that bad or good?"

"It's not much worse or better than what we had before. We won't know as far in advance if they spot him, but they think he somehow caught on to the stakeouts."

"How could he do that?"

Jake shrugged. "There are dozens of ways he could see someone at the wrong moment."

"Maybe he gave up and went to Mexico and is laughing at the thought of all you guys searching for him."

"Not a chance in hell," Jake said grimly.

"You sound sure."

"I just know him. I was after him a long time. He cased a store—we got the description and staked out the place. He outwaited everyone. Even when he knew he was running big risks, he waited until we pulled the surveillance and then he hit the place. He did that twice, and both times got away with the crime. The third time we nailed him. He's stubborn and damned mean."

"You don't need to remind me."

"I just don't want you to let down your guard," Jake answered solemnly.

Rebecca studied Jake, wondering if he was warning her about the wrong person. She didn't think she would ever let down her guard about Lenny Meskell, but she wasn't doing such a great job of keeping up her guard against Jake Delancy. She thought about the moment in the kitchen at lunch, when he had hemmed her in against the counter and her heart had pounded wildly and she had wanted him to kiss her.

"I'll try to remember," she said solemnly, and something flickered in the depths of his eyes, as if he guessed her thoughts and knew she wasn't thinking about Meskell.

"Meskell will be careful, but we'll get him."

"Is that why Captain Vance called?"

"That, and to warn me about the approaching storm." Jake glanced through the open barn doors, realizing the sky had darkened in the past few minutes. "We're in for a big one."

"What difference will that make?"

"It's more difficult sometimes to see someone moving around at night. It muffles noises and creates noises. If we were to have something really big—wind or flood—it might mean the surveillance teams would have to move. Or if Vance needs manpower for a city emergency, he'd have to pull them."

She frowned and looked toward the north. Her white cotton blouse pulled over her full breasts and was tucked into the narrow waist of her cutoffs. Jake thought about Vance's question and wondered if he could still keep a cool head if Meskell got to them. He felt he could, yet he knew he would never react in the same manner now as he would have the first night or two on the job.

"Things just get worse," she said.

"Let me do the worrying," he replied quietly. "You and your girls are still safe, and you're getting your work done."

She nodded, going back to work.

That night while Rebecca tucked the girls into bed, Jake roamed the house. Feeling uneasier than ever, he switched off the lights, silently cursing Meskell for stretching out the time until his nerves were frayed.

He and Rebecca sat up and talked until three in the morning. Earlier in the evening, thunder had rumbled in the distance, but by three it was closer at hand, thunderclaps rattling the windowpanes.

"I know I should go to bed so I'll be able to work tomorrow, but the storm makes me uneasy. I can tell you that. I can't tell that to the girls."

"Will it wake them or frighten them?"

"I think they could sleep beside the airport runway and never wake up."

Jake hadn't told her yet about Sissy's bad dreams, and he still felt reluctant to give Rebecca one more worry.

"Good night, Jake." Rebecca stood up, and Jake fought the urge to cross the room to her.

"Night." Lightning flashed, and in seconds there was another rolling boom of thunder. Rebecca went to her room, wiping her brow and wishing she could take off the chambray shirt to sleep. The night was steamy, and she longed for a rain to cool the air. She lay down in bed feeling restless, dreading sleep because her dreams were beginning to be filled with Jake Delancy.

A loud clap of thunder rattled the panes, and Rebecca sat up. Rain drummed against the house and she looked at the clock, startled to see that it was almost four. She had dozed and dreamed, and then something had wakened her.

Lightning flashed with a silvery brilliance and then thunder boomed again, and she shivered in spite of the heat. Suddenly she felt an eerie prickling, wondering if everything was all right. The storm would hide the sound of anyone breaking into the house, and the surveillance teams might not be able to see anything in this downpour.

She glanced at her partially closed door and wondered about the girls. Wanting to reassure herself about them, she slipped out of bed.

She tugged open the door, and her heart seemed to stop beating.

Someone was moving in the girls' room.

Chapter 10

All rational thought was gone. Rebecca rushed toward their room as the man stepped into the hall, and she barreled into him.

Jake's hands caught her. "Rebecca? Lord, what's the matter?"

She felt weak with relief when she heard his voice. "I saw a man in the girls' room—"

"I thought you were sleeping. You should have known it was me."

"I should have, but I didn't," she said, shaking now that the crisis had passed. "You've never been in their room late at night."

"Yes, I have. I check on them during the night," he whispered, his first startled moment changing swiftly to an acute awareness of her in his arms. She was wearing only the chambray shirt. The cutoffs she usually wore around the house at night were missing. A faint scent of perfume was on her skin. Jake had one hand on her shoulder, one on her hip. Her could feel her trembling and knew she had been thoroughly shaken.

"The storm must have wakened me, and then I felt uneasy."

"That's not unusual. I've felt apprehensive all evening, and I'm sure it's just due to the storm."

"I had to get up to check on the girls, and when I opened my door wide and looked across the hall, I just could imagine Meskell getting—"

She broke off and looked up at Jake and in the dim light from the small bulb in the bathroom, her eyes looked wide and luminous. Her gaze went down over his chest, which was bare, and then back up to his face.

Rebecca's heart began to thud, and she forgot the storm. The girls were safe, and now she realized she was standing with Jake's hand on her hip, his other hand stroking her shoulder. He stood only inches away, his muscled chest almost touching her. He was strong and appealing and he filled a void in her life. Now, when she was with him, he seemed to fill the emptiness that she had thought she had learned to live with. As she gazed into Jake's eyes, she trembled.

"Jake," she whispered, saying his name tentatively, forgetting her resolve.

Jake's breath went out in a long sigh and his arm slipped around her waist, drawing her to him. The moment her body pressed against his, he groaned, desire exploding into a blaze within him.

Nothing in the world could have stopped him from bending his head and covering her mouth with his. Jake's tongue went into her silken, wet mouth, tasting her fiery sweetness while he shook with need. She felt so right in his arms, as if he had waited all these years for this woman.

Her soft breasts pressed against him, and he let his fingers wind in her hair, tilting her head up so he could kiss her deeply. His arousal was swift, pressing against her while

Rebecca moaned and slipped her fingers across his shoulders.

The moment she wrapped her arms around him and clung to him, he felt on fire. Lightning flashed and he opened his eyes, the silvery illumination catching his attention. He remembered the girls sleeping right behind him and bent his head, kissing Rebecca while he walked them into her room and nudged the door closed behind him.

Rebecca knew he had moved them into her room. She knew they had crossed another threshold, as well. If she kept kissing him, she was going to have to admit that she was willing to explore running risks again. Did she really want to get involved with him? Was she willing to be hurt badly all over again?

As if he knew her thoughts, Jake trailed kisses to her ear. "It's only a few kisses," he whispered, his breath warm against her ear.

"That's what we keep saying," she murmured in return, turning her mouth, seeking his again. Each time they kissed, she opened her heart more to him and became more bound to him. Each day the attraction became stronger. Dimly she remembered that she didn't want this. But right now, in his strong arms, with his hand wound in her hair, she didn't want to stop.

As Rebecca's pulse raced, she wrapped her arms around his neck. His marvelous strength enveloped her, pressing her more tightly against his long, powerful body.

With a racing heart, Jake bent over her and kissed her. She had yielded some of her convictions, or she wouldn't be responding to him. Was he ready to relinquish his freedom? With each kiss he was binding himself to this woman and he had sworn he didn't want to.

He groaned, torn between what his body wanted, what he wanted, and what he had decided he would avoid for years.

Half expecting her to push him away at any moment, he slid his hand along her slender throat. Her pulse beat as wildly as his, and then his hand drifted lower. He caressed her breast, feeling the taut bud pushing against her shirt.

He raised his head to look at her. She was eager, instantly responsive, and he knew she was vulnerable. And he knew they were about to cross a line to a place where their relationship might become so entangled, one of them would have deep regrets. Her arm tightened around his neck, and his thoughts were consumed by desire. In spite of his caution and his careful reasoning, he wanted her.

He turned so that he could get to the buttons on her shirt, twisting them free, still wondering when she would grab his wrist and stop him. He shoved open the blue shirt. He cupped her breast, her softness making him feel as if he were caught in an inferno.

His pulse roared, and he desired her with a desperate need that he had never felt before. He flicked a glance at her face.

Her eyes were closed, her hands on his shoulders, her lips parted. He continued to cup her breasts, his thumbs circling her nipples. Her breasts were full, so incredibly soft, her skin fine-grained and pale. She gasped, clutching his arms, moaning as she held him, and he wondered how long he could maintain his control. He wanted to shove her down now and take her, to feel her softness envelop him, her long legs wrap around him.

He could tell himself she was experienced enough to make her own decisions and take risks. She knew he was not a marrying man. Yet his arguments were useless. Rebecca Bolen was fast becoming a very special woman, and he didn't want to hurt her.

Jake leaned forward to kiss her, taking her right breast in his mouth, his tongue playing over the pink bud. She moaned, clinging to him, her fingers biting into his arm.

Engulfed by desire, he wrapped his arms around her, pulling her against his bare chest, groaning as he kissed her hard and deep.

Rebecca trembled in his arms. He felt so marvelous. She needed his strength, wanted his caresses and kisses. Yet she could remember Dan's death and the pain it had caused and continued to cause. If only Jake weren't a cop. But he was. Completely and thoroughly. Her thoughts spun as he bent his head to kiss her other breast.

"Jake," she whispered, struggling for reason, knowing she must make him stop now. It was impossible to try to remember her resolutions while he kissed her, and in minutes they would be gone like petals in a storm.

She pushed gently against him, and he raised his head to look at her. It was too dark to see the expression on his face, but her hands were on his chest and she felt his pounding pulse and she had felt his arousal. They were both as breathless as if they had run a race.

"Jake, we have to stop. If we make love, it'll go against all good judgment and what we both want."

He trailed his fingers lightly down over her throat, down to the swell of her breast, and she trembled as she caught his wrists and pulled his hands down away from her.

"We have to stop," she said firmly, knowing she was not going to escape getting hurt one way or another by this man. The silence stretched between them, broken by their raspy breath, the tension almost tangible in the air.

"I can't get out of your room until you move out of the way," he said gruffly.

Hurting, wanting him, every inch of her body quivering with a yearning for his hands and lips, Rebecca stepped to one side.

Jake opened the door and disappeared into the hall, closing the door quietly behind him.

She sagged against the wall, wanting to call him back. This was really what she should want—distance between them. She tried to remember the hurt when she had lost Dan, tried to remember her promises to herself to never gain get involved with a man who had a physical job involving risk.

Her skin tingled and her body ached with longing. And he wondered how dreadful it was going to be to go back to her solitary life with the girls, the long hours after they were in bed asleep. When she lost Dan, she had expected that she would never love again. Now Jake had come into her life and had changed so many of her ideas about what she would or would not do.

Another clap of thunder shook the house, and lightning streaked the sky, revealing a bright strip of space around the old window shades. The house was steamy, her body on fire. She wiped her forehead and buttoned her shirt.

If they turned on the attic fan and opened some windows, the house would be cool in minutes. Even a few windows would help. She wondered whether Jake would agree, and she wondered if she could face him again without melting into his arms.

Instead of going to find him, she crossed the room and sank down on the bed, sitting on the side of it, her head in her hands, while she hoped her body would cool. Was Jake in as much turmoil as she was, or was it just his body that suffered? she wondered.

The floor creaked slightly in the hall and she knew he was moving around. She sat quietly, waiting until she was more composed before she went out to see about opening the house and turning on the fan.

Jake stepped out the kitchen door into the rain, feeling the cold drops beat against his shoulders and chest, drenching his jeans. He wanted to cool down. Rebecca set him on fire. Falling into the Arctic Ocean might be the only thing to cool him right now.

He gazed at the woods behind the house. Meskell was probably holed up somewhere avoiding the storm, waiting for a clear night, yet the storm made Jake edgy. And it had frightened Rebecca, or she wouldn't have assumed that a man in the girls' bedroom was Meskell.

Jake walked around the house, his thoughts churning because he had to admit that no woman had been as irresistible to him as Rebecca Bolen. Not one. He had never come close to thinking about marriage. He tried to recall the years when his brothers had been in college, the huge stack of bills he'd thought he would never get through. Freedom. It had always sounded so heady, something he wanted to relish and enjoy for years. Why did it sound empty now?

Jake kicked a pebble, watching it splash into a mud puddle. Lightning flared, momentarily blinding him. His jeans would be soaked, his boots wet and muddy, and he wasn't gaining anything by standing outside in the rain. Except that he needed to cool down.

And he needed to make a decision. It wasn't going to do any good to make a play for Rebecca and figure she could take care of herself. He didn't want to hurt her, and he suspected that before long, he wasn't going to be able to give her up without hurting himself, too.

Rain beat against him, plastering his hair to his head, and he paused, shaking his head. He had left his pistol inside, high on a kitchen shelf. He was standing in the rain, unarmed, getting drenched—all because of gorgeous big blue eyes, blond hair and a luscious body. Only it was more than that. If that had been all, he could have resisted her.

He placed his hands on his hips, stared at her darkened windows and shook his head.

Disgusted, coming to no solution, he stomped back to the kitchen door, his boots splashing in the water.

One thing he knew—he would give up his life to protect Rebecca and her girls, and he would kill Meskell if he came anywhere close to them.

Jake rounded the corner of the house and stopped in his tracks. The kitchen door stood wide open.

Jake charged inside, swearing at his foolishness in going out in the rain to cool down, as well as going out unarmed. Swinging the door shut behind him, he yanked the pistol off the top shelf. "Rebecca!" he called.

As he started across the kitchen, she appeared in the doorway and stopped. "Jake? What's wrong?"

"I was about to ask you the same question. The kitchen door was wide open."

"I couldn't find you."

"I was outside walking around."

"In this storm?" she asked. Lightning flashed, giving a momentary brilliance that bathed them both in light. Rebecca turned on the kitchen light and stared at Jake. His jeans were soaked, his brown hair was plastered to his head, his shoulders and chest glistened with wetness, and the pistol was in his hand.

"What were you doing outside?" she asked, frowning at him.

He gave a jerk of his head, his wet hair swinging away from his face, and then he ran his hand over his face. "I wanted to cool off," he said abruptly.

"Oh!" She felt her cheeks flush. "Won't that rain ruin your gun?"

"It was in here. Why was the back door open?"

She bit her lip, knowing that what she had done had gone against safety. But already the house had cooled. "I turned on the attic fan. I'll switch it off now if you want," she said, her gaze drifting down over his chest again. She could have kept looking at him forever, and she remembered how it had felt to be pressed against his strong body only a short time ago.

"It only takes a little time to cool the house when the windows and doors are open," she added.

"Is the front door standing open now?" He asked the question calmly, but she suspected he was angry. He placed the pistol up high again, the muscles in his back rippling as he stretched out his arm. He turned around and came toward her.

"No. It's slightly ajar and the screen is hooked. I opened the windows and I'll close them right up, but with you here..." Her voice trailed away as Jake approached her. His body was wet, the jeans plastered to his trim hips. There was a look of exasperation in his expression, but his hazel eyes were smoldering, and it wasn't anger she saw in them.

"Jake," she said quietly, in a half protest.

"I'll close the front door." He moved past her and went down the hall, and she let out her breath, feeling as if she had just had a narrow escape. At the same time, she wished he hadn't brushed past her and ignored her. In moments he returned. "I keep another pair of jeans in the pickup. I'll go out and get them, and as soon as the house cools slightly, I want to close it up. It would be safer to run the air conditioners than to have everything open. Meskell would hop in his stolen car right now and beat it out here if he knew the only barrier was a screen door."

"You were just walking around in the rain?"

"Right," he answered gruffly. "Trying to remember that I should keep my hands to myself." He yanked out his radio. "I'll call McCauley and tell him I'm going to my truck. He knows I walk around the house, but anything beyond a few yards from here and I'm supposed to notify him."

"If you want to throw your jeans into the dryer, you can have a sheet to wrap around you and you won't have to go to the truck."

He gave her a level look and put away his radio while she tried to stop imagining his strong body in only a sheet.

"Okay. Get a sheet and I'll start closing up the house again."

In minutes she was in the living room, which was far cooler, listening to Jake moving around in the kitchen, putting his clothes in the dryer. He reappeared with a white sheet wrapped around his hips trailing the floor behind him, and she drew a sharp breath.

"I turned on the window unit in the kitchen because it will get stuffy in here before long."

"Fine," she answered perfunctorily. She couldn't resist looking at him. His legs were bare from the knees down, covered in short brown hair. The white sheet was wrapped low on his hips, revealing more of his flat stomach than she had seen before; his dark skin was a vivid contrast to the expanse of white.

Jake paused and studied her, feeling his body respond to the way she was looking at him. Her gaze lifted, meeting his, and he inhaled, fighting the urge to walk across the room and sweep her into his arms.

"I'll get us some tea," she said suddenly, rushing from the room. He wiped his forehead, thinking the room had grown hotter instead of cooler. He knew she had used the tea as an excuse, and he debated following her and making her forget all about tea.

He groaned and moved restlessly to the window, switching off the lights and opening the drapes so that he could watch the storm. His thoughts jumped right back to Rebecca. He was going to have to come to some kind of decision before he did something that they might both regret.

He thought about marriage. The thought set butterflies dancing in his stomach. But then he thought about going back to his condo without Rebecca. Night after night without her. Never seeing her again. That caused a pang in him that surprised him.

And even if he decided he wanted the lady as his wife—could he ever get past her objections and win her over? He damned sure didn't want to retire now. And he didn't want a desk job. He didn't want a different career.

"You're not ready for commitment," he whispered to himself as he stared outside, watching raindrops streak the window.

"Here's your tea," she said quietly behind him. He turned, and she held the glass out almost as far as her arm would reach. If he hadn't been in such a turmoil over the night, he would have laughed. But there was nothing amusing about the tug and pull on his emotions.

He accepted the tea, aware of his fingers brushing hers. She hurried across the room and sat on the far corner of the sofa, but the room was too small for her to put much space between them.

As he sipped the cold tea, lightning flashed, momentarily bathing the room in bright light. In that moment he saw that Rebecca was curled in the corner of the sofa, her long legs tucked under her, her blue eyes wide while she gazed back at him. The chambray shirt was unbuttoned slightly more than usual—something she might not be aware of.

He sipped the tea in silence, knowing he had to make a decision and stick by it. And if he didn't want marriage, if he didn't want to hurt Rebecca—he might be better off telling Vance to put Jay Werner out here for a few days.

The silence between them was lengthening, and he wondered if her thoughts were just as stormy as his.

"I can get them to put someone else out here," he said quietly.

Rebecca felt a pang of loss, yet she knew in her heart that she should urge Jake to get someone else. It would simplify her life. Why couldn't she answer him and agree?

She sat in the dark, sipping the cold tea, looking at Jake, and lightning flashed again. His long legs were stretched out on a chair, his bare feet sticking up in the air, and something about his bare legs and feet seemed intimate.

Finally she drained the glass and listened to Jake crunching down the last of his ice. She could offer to get more tea, but she didn't want to say anything. She set her empty glass on a coaster on the table and put her head back against the sofa while her stormy thoughts raged again.

How bad was it going to be when he was gone? She had spent the past two years dealing with loss and adjustment, and now it looked as if she were going to have to deal with it again. But *every bit of distance we can keep between us will make it less painful when he goes,* she reminded herself, wondering if her heart was listening.

She should tell him to get another assignment—yet even if she decided that would be best for her, she needed to think beyond matters of the heart and think about safety, because the girls were involved. Jake had been the one person in the courtroom that day who had stopped Meskell from getting to her or hurting anyone. There had been deputies, other detectives, but it was Jake who had leaped over the railing and decked Meskell.

She suspected Captain Vance had tried to place a good man with her. Jake had been one of the men to bring in Meskell before. Suppose his replacement was not quite as competent?

She shook her head as lightning flashed, lighting the room.

"What's the matter, Rebecca?" Jake asked finally.

She realized he had seen her shaking her head. "Just getting my hair out of my face," she answered. "I'm going to bed now."

"Sure. Don't worry. He won't come in this storm."

"How on earth do you know?"

"Just a hunch. I don't think Meskell would want to creep around in the mud. Hard to get away, too. Besides, it's getting far into the night now."

"Do you go without sleep all the time like this?"

"Hell, no," he said, finally standing, the sheet remaining firmly in place. "Under normal circumstances," he said quietly, "I get a regular night's sleep." His voice lowered, and she realized they were skirting a dangerous topic again.

"Good night, Jake." She left the room in a hurry, going to her room to lie in bed, staring at the windows and trying to resolve that she wasn't going to let Jake Delancy break her heart. And she was not going to become more emotionally involved with him than she already was.

After breakfast the next morning, when they stepped outside before hurrying to the barn, Rebecca paused to inhale deeply. The sky was clear and blue, the air fresh, cooled by the rain. "Isn't this a glorious day!" she exclaimed, and then caught Jake watching her intently, his hazel eyes smoldering with the same fires that she had seen in them last night.

"Yeah, it's glorious," he said in a husky voice, his gaze drifting over her in a leisurely manner that made her tingle as if he had touched her. She was aware of her red T-shirt, the cutoffs. Her hair was caught up, twisted and pinned on top of her head.

Tara tugged on her wrist. "Can we go ahead?"

"Yes, go on," she said as Jake gave a nod. He placed his arm across Rebecca's shoulders and hurried her toward the barn.

"It seems too pretty a day for trouble," she remarked, aware of his arm across her shoulders, of their brushing against each other as they walked.

"That's when you really need to keep up your guard," he answered.

"I'll try to remember that," she answered, feeling as if they were talking about two different things at once. "Jake, I want you to stay. I don't want you to get a replacement."

"Is that right?" he asked, his brows arching and his hazel eyes boring into her, and she realized he might have misinterpreted her statement completely.

"I don't want someone else, because I figured Captain Vance sent the best man for the job. I figured the girls and I will be safer with you here."

Jake felt a twist of disappointment. For one heart-stopping second, he had thought she meant she wanted him there for another reason. Inwardly he laughed at himself for jumping to such a conclusion. She had given him damned little reason to think that all of a sudden she would do a complete turnaround.

And he was surprised at the disappointment he had experienced. Was she becoming that important to him? Was he the one who was doing a complete and swift turnaround?

"Okay, Rebecca," he said quietly. Her cheeks flushed, and he wondered why.

Her gaze slid away from him. "Whatever is going on between us personally shouldn't jeopardize the girls' safety."

"Or yours. I'd give this up if I thought I couldn't concentrate."

She glanced up at him, her expression solemn. "Whatever happens, I'm certain you'll keep your concentration on your work."

They had reached the barn and they stepped inside. McCauley had switched on the lights and fans. Jake swung Rebecca around to face him, sliding his arm away so that only his hand rested on her shoulder. His index finger lightly stroked her earlobe while he looked down at her.

"Just what does that remark mean? That I can concentrate on my work no matter what happens?"

"It just means that I think you can put your work first, before everything else in your life. Dan did. If the girls and I had been standing on the curb watching that building burn, he still would have run in there. If the only way you could stop Meskell from shooting me and the girls was to throw yourself between us, I don't think you'd hesitate."

"You're making me into a hero. I might not be able to live up to that image, and that last situation would not be a win-lose one. I would lose either way."

She felt a pang of longing, his words wrapping around her heart. "You know what I meant, and I know I'm right, whether you'll admit it or not. For the girls' sakes, I want you to stay."

"When you twist my arm like that, how can I resist?" he answered, but he wanted to say something else. He wanted to pull her into his arms and tell her he wanted to stay because he wanted to be with her.

"I better get to work." She walked away, and he turned to find Sissy sitting on a bale of hay nearby and studying him. She slid off the bale and walked over to him.

"Are you going to look all over the barn like you usually do?"

"Yes, I am."

"Did you know that Tara and I saw a mouse in the corner?"

"No, I didn't."

"Do you think it'll come back today?"

"Do you want it to?"

"Yes. But Mommy said not to touch it or try to play with it."

"That's right, because it's not like a kitty or a puppy. Sometimes wild things bite. And sometimes they carry germs you can get if you touch them."

"How do they carry germs?"

"In their fur," he answered.

She slipped her hand into his as he walked along. He looked into stalls and knew he was checking for nothing, because McCauley had just done this. But he wasn't going to run the risk that McCauley could have overlooked something or something could have happened between the time McCauley was here and the time they arrived.

As Jake leaned into a stall and looked all around, he glanced at Sissy, who was holding his hand and waiting expectantly, looking all around, the way she had seen him do. A fat lot of good it would do if he found someone hiding. His hand would be in Sissy's and he would have the little girl right at his side. For security's sake, he should tell her to go play with her sister, yet he felt certain the barn was secure and he didn't want to send Sissy away.

His feelings surprised him again, but Sissy was sweet and it was nice to have her tagging along with him.

They looked into the next stall, and as they walked along, she glanced up at him. "You had your arm around Mommy when you came into the barn. Are you going to kiss her someday?"

"I might just do that, Sissy."

"Do you love her?"

He gave that question some thought, debating how to answer her. "I'm getting to be friends with her. Where did you see the mouse?"

"Back there," she said, pointing to the last stall on the west side of the barn.

"Well, mice sometimes follow patterns—"

"What's a pattern?"

"They do the same thing every day at the same time. Did you see the mouse yesterday morning or yesterday afternoon?"

"Yesterday morning."

"All right. Look for him again this morning. But you and Tara will have to be quiet or he won't come out."

"Yes, sir. I'm going to find Tara and tell her," she said, removing her hand from his and running off, calling to her sister.

He looked in each stall and then climbed to the loft to walk over it.

Rebecca bent over her work, but she had watched Jake walking around the barn with Sissy's hand in his. He was in his navy T-shirt and jeans, which made his tanned skin look even darker, and his hair was slightly ruffled. Sissy had looked so tiny next to him, smiling up at him while they talked, and Rebecca tried to stop thinking about their loss. Jake was good for the girls, but she hoped they weren't hurt when he was gone.

As Jake came down from the loft, he paused to gaze outside at the trees behind the house. The day was gorgeous, the weather wonderful, and the threat of Meskell seemed far removed. And that should make him doubly cautious, he thought.

He walked back to watch Rebecca work, looking at her hands moving deftly over the glass, remembering them moving over his chest last night.

At midmorning, the mail truck came as usual. Jake jogged out to get the mail, as always welcoming a chance to work off some energy. He came back to the barn to hand her the mail and stood close by, watching her flip through it and open it. He still expected Meskell to pen a letter or call again, something to keep pressure on her. There were no unusual letters, and he went back to his vigil at the front of the barn while Rebecca returned to her work.

By early afternoon, the barn had become a steam bath. The sun was high and hot, the air muggy and the earth steaming from the rain. As Jake watched her work, Rebecca straightened up and wiped her brow. Even with the big fans, the air was stifling.

She glanced at Jake. He had pulled off his shirt and his chest and shoulders were covered with a damp sheen of sweat. He stood with a cold drink in his hand while he watched her work. Her gaze ran over his chest and she felt her pulse quicken, everything inside her tightening. Her gaze flicked up to meet his, and a mocking gleam was in his eyes.

Picking up her knife, Rebecca bent over her work swiftly, trying to concentrate before she cut a slice out of her finger instead of the glass. Usually, when she worked, she could shut out everything else and focus completely on what she was doing, but with Jake standing close by, she was finding it impossible.

He stood only yards away, leaning his hip against the table, his long legs crossed at the ankles while he watched her.

As she cut carefully, in her peripheral vision she was aware of his hip and legs.

"Dammit," she said finally, straightening up, wiping her wet brow and blowing a wayward tendril of hair out of her eyes. It immediately fell back over her eye, and Jake stepped close and caught the strand, tucking it up under the hair pinned on top of her head.

"You'll have to move away," she said bluntly.

"Sorry," he said with great innocence, his brows arching and curiosity coming into his eyes. "I was just tucking your hair out of your eyes. I can pull it back down—"

"No, I don't mean that!" she snapped in exasperation. "You'll have to move farther away from me," she said, trying to avoid looking into his hazel eyes, which no doubt could see exactly why she was asking him to move, "because I can't concentrate."

"Why can't you concentrate?"

She looked him squarely in the eyes. "You know damned well why I can't!"

"I don't remember ever hearing you swear."

"I didn't have any reason to."

"And now you do?"

"Jake, you're not—"

He grinned and held out his hand. "Whoa. I'll move away. I just couldn't resist for a minute there. Just as I haven't been able to resist time and time again," he added, his smile fading. "Maybe we both should reconsider our views. We might be throwing something away that could really be great."

"I'll keep that in mind," she answered solemnly.

Jake turned to walk to the front of the barn and sit on the bale of hay. He swore at himself silently. He should leave the lady alone. He should stop flirting. And he should make up his damned mind whether he wanted to pursue her or not.

He stared into the hot sunshine and thought about life without her again. And every minute spent with her made thoughts of spending the rest of his life without her an un-bearable proposition. So he ought to consider two things. Firstly, he ought to give some thought to getting married.

For once, no butterflies began a war dance in his stom-ach. That should give him a clue to his true feelings.

And secondly, he should give some thought to whether the lady could ever be won over. She had a true and deep aversion to cops. And that did not indicate great marriage possibilities.

Or he could just cool it, wait until this was over and then try to have a regular, normal relationship with her.

Would he really be able to consider marriage? He turned to look at her. She had moved around the table, standing on this side, bending over it, giving him a good view of her long legs. Marriage to her also meant becoming an instant fa-ther.

He was surprised that he still didn't feel any butterflies at the thought. Actually, the four of them were getting along pretty well, and it was not under the best of circumstances. They were shut up together, day after day—and the days were hot, with little air-conditioning. The girls couldn't play outside or go see their friends or do their activities, yet they were cheerful kids and entertained themselves.

All in all, if he had to become an instant dad, he couldn't think of better children than Sissy and Tara. But even if he wanted marriage and he was ready to become a father—could he ever persuade Rebecca to marry a cop?

It would be a damned sight easier to seduce her. He knew he could have seduced her before now if he had put his heart into melting her mild protests.

But seducing her away from her objections to his job was another matter—and one battle he wasn't certain he could win. All she had to do was look back and remember the pain she had suffered in losing her husband. And he had known she was remembering that several times when he was with her.

He wasn't certain about the answer on that one. She might not ever change her mind. And if he fell in love, asked her to marry him, and she adamantly refused—was he ready for the consequences?

Life was full of risks and he took them often, so he wasn't going to worry about the risk of getting hurt by her refusal. If he decided he wanted to pursue her, he would take that risk. So it boiled down to just one question. Was he in love with the lady enough to want to marry her?

As he continued studying her, she slanted a look at him over her shoulder. She was bent over the table while she looked at him. She straightened up and sauntered toward him, and he wondered if she had the faintest idea how sexy her walk was.

She stopped a yard away. "You're still doing it."

"Doing what, for corn's sake?" he asked, baffled this time.

"Watching me. You know you're watching me."

"I'm clear across the barn!" he said, suddenly pleased that he had that kind of effect on her. "Can't I watch you from here without disturbing you?"

"No, you can't because you're staring. I can't think, Jake."

"You don't say. Do you want me to sit up in the loft?"

"No, I don't," she answered evenly, and he bit back a grin. "Just turn around and look outside for Lenny Meskell."

"I'll try to do that," he answered, and she raised her nose in the air and stomped back to work.

He grinned and turned to watch her. As soon as she picked up a strip of lead, she looked at him. He turned to stare out the front and in seconds glanced over his shoulder to see her bent over her work. She was twisted around so that her fanny was turned toward him, and he chuckled.

He might be disturbing her, but not half as much as she was disturbing him! He glanced outside, still wondering how strong his feelings for her were and suspecting he might have fallen in love.

An hour later, Rebecca straightened up to mop her brow. Her T-shirt clung to her, the waistband of her cutoffs was damp from perspiration. The weather that had been so beautiful in early morning was a tropical heat wave now, and the whirring fans couldn't stir the air enough to make the barn cool.

The girls played only yards away, Tara sitting on a bale of hay and coloring while Sissy was having a tea party with her doll, tiny toy dishes spread on the hay. Out of the corner of her eye, Rebecca saw Jake stand. He opened the cooler and got the girls cold fruit drinks and then picked up two cans of cola and sauntered toward her.

"Time for a break," Jake said, handing her a cold drink.

"Thanks," she said, mopping her brow and accepting the chilled can to take a long drink. "I didn't think it was possible to get this hot."

"I've been listening to the radio. The humidity is ninety-six percent—" He broke off, and she heard the loud rumble of a motor. "What the hell?" Jake said, turning to stride toward the open doors, and Rebecca walked forward, curious who was coming up the drive.

"Stay back, Rebecca," Jake suggested, his hand going to his back, ready to reach for his pistol.

Startled, she moved away, but she had glimpsed the delivery truck lumbering toward the house. Jake placed his hands on his hips and watched as the truck stopped at the house and a deliveryman jumped down with a package in his hand.

"Over here," Jake called, waving at the man.

The man was short, dark-haired and thin, and bore no resemblance to Lenny Meskell. She knew Jake would want her to stay back, so she waited while Jake met the deliveryman.

"Package for R. Bolen."

"That's her," Jake said.

"Can you sign?"

"Sure." Jake scrawled *R. Bolen* and took the box, waiting and watching the man walk back to the truck. He studied the truck, wanting to make certain Meskell hadn't found a way to ride past everyone.

The deliveryman jumped back behind the wheel and swung the truck around, rumbling down the drive and splashing through puddles.

Jake glanced down at the box and saw a neatly typed label addressed to R. Bolen. The return address was the Farthingwood Glass Company in San Antonio, Texas. He carried the box to Rebecca and handed it to her.

"More supplies?"

She accepted it and read the label. She began to peel away the brown paper. "It's not anything I ordered. I don't know a Farthingwood Glass Company." She tore off another long strip of paper, peeling away the wrapping. A plain brown box was taped shut, a string tied around it. She placed it on the table and then picked up a knife to cut the string.

"I don't know why a glass company would send anything to the house, anyway," she said, sliding the blade beneath the white cord.

Jake sucked in his breath, watching her slice through the string. "Run!" he shouted at her.

He whirled around. "Tara, Sissy!" he shouted. "Run!"

"Jake—" Rebecca began, furious with him for yelling at the girls, and then she realized they were in danger. Everything inside her seemed to clench in cold fear as she ran around the table while Jake grabbed up both girls.

"Get out of here!" he shouted at Rebecca. "Run!"

She reached him and he thrust Sissy into her arms, grabbing her arm while he carried Tara and tore out of the barn. Jake was hauling them all toward the house, his long legs pumping the ground while Tara clung to him.

Rebecca's heart felt as if it would pound out of her chest, and Sissy was crying. She ran blindly, terrified for the girls.

The blast behind them was earsplitting, shaking the earth and throwing her off her feet.

Chapter 11

Jake sprawled over the girls, his arm and leg across Rebecca. Her face was pressed into the grass, and she twisted around to see the barn explode. Boards, hay and debris flew into the air, a cloud mushrooming up and an orange tongue of flame shooting skyward.

Horrified, Rebecca scooted closer to cover Tara, protecting her own head with her arm.

Something struck her legs, and she felt a sharp sting in her back. Inches away from her face, a piece of two-by-four hit the ground.

Tara was between Jake and her, and he was shielding Sissy with his body. Both girls were crying.

Jake rolled away, looking at Rebecca. "Are you all right?"

"Yes," she said, getting to her knees as the girls threw themselves into her arms. Sobbing, Sissy clung to her.

Shaking with reaction, Rebecca watched as what remained of the barn burned. Orange flames licked up the walls, the fire crackling while the cloud of smoke thinned and streamed overhead.

"Get the girls into the house!" Jake snapped, whipping out his pistol and his radio, holding the radio to his mouth. "Get Vance. Bomb at the Bolen place."

While the radio crackled and Jake continued to talk to his headquarters, Rebecca picked up Sissy and took Tara's hand, giving Jake another glance. He was covered with grass and mud and had a cut across his arm and another on his cheek.

"Woodson. We're all right," Jake said. "Family's heading for the house."

She hurried toward the house with the girls, and the moment they stepped inside, Jake was behind them, still talking on his radio.

"Get them out here now!" He lowered the radio. "Wait here, Rebecca," he said, pushing past her in the kitchen. He dropped the radio on the table and held his pistol with both hands, sprinting down the hall and disappearing from sight into a bedroom, and she realized he was checking the house for Meskell.

Rebecca hugged Sissy, who clung to her, still crying. Tara stood at the window, staring at the burning barn. Flames engulfed what was left of the structure, and Rebecca thought fleetingly of her work, which had been blown to bits.

Both girls looked terrified, and Rebecca's knees were shaking badly. She held Sissy tightly, placing one hand on Tara's shoulder, squeezing them as if to reassure herself that they were unharmed.

"We're all okay," she said, trying to sound calm and hoping they would calm. All she wanted to do was hold them close and remind herself that they were safe.

"What was that, Mom?" Tara asked.

"It was a bomb," Rebecca replied, feeling a surge of rage, because Lenny Meskell could have killed the girls. The thought made her head swim, and she felt as if she were going to be sick as her stomach rolled. She pulled Tara close, trying to fight back tears, terrified at how close her children had come to being killed.

"I'm sorry that happened," she said. "We're all safe and Jake got us out in time and that's what's important."

She hugged them, fighting to get control of her emotions as she heard the scrape of Jake's boots behind her. He picked up the radio to talk again, and the radio crackled as someone answered him. She wiped her eyes quickly, turning to face him.

The rage in his eyes took her aback momentarily. Her gaze ran over him swiftly, and she said a quick silent prayer of thanks that they were all safe.

Sissy wriggled, and Rebecca set her on her feet.

Glancing beyond them at the burning barn, Jake yanked out his keys. "Give me your car keys, Rebecca. That old garage will catch fire. I have to move the vehicles."

She took the keys off a peg by the back door and Jake grabbed them, sprinting out to move his truck, pulling it up by the house, directly across from the back door. He raced back to get her car, and she prayed it would start. She watched, waiting, wondering if the battery was dead, but in minutes the car began to lurch and roll, and finally he drove up to park it behind his truck.

He came back inside and replaced her keys on the peg, jamming his into his pocket.

He looked at the girls. "Everyone all right?" he asked, hunkering down to get on Sissy's level. He looked at Tara as both girls nodded.

"Was that a bomb in the box Mom got?" Tara asked.

Rebecca drew a deep breath, unable to stop shaking with rage. She clenched her fists while Jake nodded.

"It was, but it didn't hurt anyone," he said. "You can replace the barn, and even your mom's work can be done again. The important thing is that everyone is all right. Now the fire trucks are on their way. And a lot of policemen will come look at what's left of the barn, so everyone will have to stay in the house for a time, and out of the way."

Both girls nodded solemnly.

"You're covered in dirt," Sissy said, studying him.

"Your face is cut. Doesn't it hurt?" Tara asked, and Rebecca hugged her arms to her sides, knowing they should get to satisfy their curiosity, yet finding it unbearable that they had been put in so much jeopardy.

"No, it's just a scratch." Jake was good at answering children's questions. He sounded unruffled as if this weren't an unusual occurrence.

"Did the bad man send the bomb?" Sissy asked.

"Yes, he did."

"Was that what the man delivered from the truck?" Tara asked, and Rebecca realized they had paid attention to the arrival of the delivery truck.

"Yes, it was," Jake answered calmly. "So from now on, when packages and mail are delivered, I'll check them over first."

"How will you know if it's a bomb?" Sissy persisted.

"Your mom can tell me if a package is from someone she knows or something she expected to get. If it's not, we'll send it down to the police station and they can put it through an X-ray machine that will show what's inside, like they do at the airport."

Both girls nodded at that answer. Rebecca still couldn't control her shaking. Every time she thought how close she had come to opening the box and remembering that the girls had been only several yards away, tears welled up. She walked over to switch on the air conditioner, knowing that before long there would be so many police in the yard that she wouldn't have to worry for several hours about Lenny Meskell.

Sissy reached out to touch Jake, and he pulled her close and hugged her, stretching out his long arm to enclose Tara in the same embrace. He looked past them at Rebecca, and she drew a deep breath, wanting to hold her girls, too, and feel his strong arms around her at the same time.

He released them and studied them. "Okay now?"

"Yes, sir," Tara answered politely.

"We're going to catch him soon," Jake said firmly. "And if you get scared, come tell me or tell your mom. And just remember, he hasn't gotten close to you and he didn't hurt you today. He caused some excitement, but all of us are all right. Barns are replaceable. Okay?"

Both girls nodded.

Eventually the girls moved into the other room, after a few more minutes of being reassured that everything was okay. When they were alone, Jake's gaze met Rebecca's and he stood, walking over to her. He took her arm. "Come in here," he said quietly.

He led her to her room, stepping inside and closing the door, pulling her into his arms to hold her tightly.

She wrapped her arms around him, for a moment yielding to the reassurance of his strong arms around her. And she let go of the tears she had been fighting to hold back, suddenly sobbing against his chest. "Jake, when I think what could have happened—"

"Nothing happened. And we won't give him that chance again."

"He came so close. All this time, I thought I was the only one really in danger, but today, that bomb would have gotten the girls."

"It didn't, Rebecca. That's what you have to remember," he said quietly, and she could hear the rage in his voice. She cried softly and Jake stroked her head, holding her tightly against him with his other arm.

"Sorry about your work, honey, but I couldn't take the risk of tossing the bomb outside."

"My customers will understand. Jake, how could anyone do something like that? He didn't know who or how many people he would kill."

"Meskell doesn't have one shred of remorse. He's a monster. Just concentrate on the fact that no one was hurt." Jake held her tightly, trying to control his rage. He hoped that when he finally cornered Meskell, he resisted arrest. Jake longed for a chance at him.

Right now, he wanted to get back out to the barn, to be there when the detectives arrived, but he needed to reassure Rebecca.

She had looked as pale as snow and as if she might fly apart at any minute. He knew it wasn't fear for herself that was undoing her. It was the thought of the girls playing so close at hand and being in danger.

He swore silently at himself again for not realizing what was in the package when she said the box wasn't something she had ordered. He should have quizzed her about the package when he saw it was from a glass company. He should have picked up on the fact that it had been delivered to her house and not to her shop in town.

Just as she slid the knife beneath the string, he had realized what could be inside. As long as he lived, he would remember that moment of cold panic when he'd tried to get them all out of the barn and as far from it as possible.

"Jake, if I had a gun and Meskell broke in, I think I would gladly shoot him."

"I think you would, too," Jake said dryly. She was more of a fighter than she realized.

"Why didn't the bomb go off in the delivery truck?"

"It was set to go when you tore it open. I'd guess when you cut the cord, it started the countdown."

She shuddered, and he squeezed her close, wiping a tear off her cheek with his thumb. "We're both covered in grass and mud," he said.

Her blue eyes were wide as she gazed up at him, and suddenly she threw her arms around his neck and hugged him tightly. Startled, he wrapped his arms around her, relishing her soft body pressed against him, wondering what was running through her mind.

"Thank you for saving us," she said, the words muffled because her head was buried against his chest.

"Anytime," he said dryly.

Someone knocked on the door. Jake arched his brows questioningly as he released Rebecca and turned around to open the door. Tara gazed solemnly up, looking from one of them to the other.

"Your radio is making noises," she said.

"Thanks," he answered, and turned to wink at Rebecca. "Are you all right now?"

When she nodded, he strode past them down the hall.

Tara gazed solemnly at her mother. "Did Jake hug you, too?"

"Yes, he did," she said, wondering why Tara had gone from "Mr. Delancy" to "Jake," and wondering if he had told her to at some point.

"Did he hug you like he hugged us?"

"Yes, he did."

"Or was it like Daddy hugged you?"

"Maybe a little of both," Rebecca answered, knowing Tara understood a lot of things and wanting to be honest with her.

"Do you love Jake?"

"Not yet, honey," Rebecca said quietly. "We don't know each other that well, and everything is so crazy right now. We'll see what our feelings are someday when things are normal."

Tara nodded. There was still something on her mind, so Rebecca remained silent and waited for the next question.

"I like him, Mom."

"I'm glad you do," Rebecca replied, and meant it. Whatever happened in the future, she was glad the girls liked Jake. And she was glad he was good with them, even if it was in a professional way.

"Maybe you better wash up," Tara said, and Rebecca smiled.

"I'll do that."

Tara went back to the kitchen, and Rebecca went across the hall to the bathroom to study herself in the mirror. She was smudged with dirt, and Tara was bound to have guessed that she had been crying, because tears had made streaks in the dirt on her cheeks. She studied herself, thinking she didn't look any different, yet she wondered if she would ever be the same or forget how close they had come to tragedy this afternoon.

She washed her face and then stripped down to shower, wishing she could scrub away what had happened and knowing she might have nightmares about it for a long time to come.

And the thought of nightmares made her think of Sissy. Rebecca drew a deep breath and said a small prayer. "Please don't let the girls have nightmares. Please let them forget this. Thank you that we all survived."

She stood under the shower, taking down her hair and washing it, hurrying because Jake might want to clean up, too. She dried, wrapped herself in a large towel and scooped up her clothes, opening the door to look up and down the hall. She heard the girls' voices from the kitchen as she rushed into her room.

Dressing in jeans and a blue cotton blouse, she hurried so that she could get back to the girls. In minutes she had returned to the bathroom and dried her hair, pulling it up into a ponytail, then gone to the kitchen. Tara was standing at the window, looking at the barn.

"The garage is burning, Mom."

"The garage is good riddance," she remarked, moving to the window to see the small structure blazing away, firemen pumping water on it.

Fire trucks were in the yard, and Rebecca was thankful again that she had remained inside the city limits, where they could get the fire trucks out quickly. Firemen moved around, and she wondered if any of Dan's friends were out there, but doubted it.

Police cars were parked all over the drive and yard, and an official-looking white truck was parked near the barn. She wished she could join them and hear what was being said, but knew Jake would want her and the girls to stay in the house. One media truck was in the yard.

Tara must have spotted it at the same time she did.

"Will we be on the news, Mom?"

"We might," Rebecca answered.

"Can I go out there and maybe get in the picture?"

"Not yet, Tara. Jake said we should stay in the house. It's safer here."

Rebecca's gaze swept up the road away from the barn, and she noticed a police car parked on the drive with a man seated inside, and she guessed he was there to watch the house while Jake was with the others.

She realized she was stroking Tara's head all the time she was looking out the window.

She thought about Jake yelling at the girls, taking time to grab them both up and holding her arm before he started out of the barn. He had taken the time to get them out with him, risking his life for them without hesitation.

She closed her eyes, knowing that she would always be grateful. And yet this reinforced her opinion about not getting involved with a man with a dangerous occupation. She shuddered, wrapping her arms around herself and closing her eyes. She did not want to fall in love with a man who had to deal over and over with men like Lenny Meskell. Never!

Deep inside, she hurt, because she knew Jake already had won a bit of her heart and she was going to miss him. When he took her to her room a short time ago and pulled her into his arms, it had been like coming home to security and love. But he thrived on danger, and it was too much for her. She knew the only reaction he was having to the bomb was rage. He wasn't frightened or shaken or repulsed.

She turned away to start something for dinner, wishing she could busy herself enough to get her mind off what had happened. In minutes she had cut strips of chicken breast and sliced vegetables, preparing everything for a stir-fry that wouldn't heat the house or take long when the time came.

After getting the food cut and washed and back in the refrigerator, she asked Tara to set the table.

After an hour, Rebecca went to the front room to watch the news, and Tara came in and plopped down on the floor. "Will we be in the news?"

"I don't know. We haven't been so far."

They watched until the end of the program, and nothing was on about the explosion.

"We weren't in the news," Tara said, disappointment filling her voice. "Isn't a bomb important?"

"It's very important, but they might think in the interest of our security it would be better not to have what happened on the news."

"I don't see that it would make any difference. It's over now."

"It might cause a lot of curious people to drive by to look. The police would have more to deal with about our security. Maybe they don't want Lenny Meskell to know what happened today."

"Why not?"

"They might prefer for him to wonder about it. He might do something to try to find out, like come by the house."

Tara turned to look at her. "In the house?"

"No, just drive by on the road, but if he does, they'll arrest him."

"How would they know?"

"They're watching the road for him. And I think he always steals the cars he drives."

"Do the police know when a stolen car goes past?"

"Yes. Since they're watching, they can find out quickly by checking the license number."

Rebecca heard a deep male voice and stood, heading down the hall as Jake came in. His gaze raked over her, and he smiled. The rage had gone out of his eyes.

"Better?" he asked quietly.

"Yes, I am," she answered, her pulse jumping as if all her decisions about wanting to avoid getting involved with him meant nothing.

"The girls seem to be taking it in stride."

"Better than I will."

"Some of the people are still out there. They'll check things over for a while. We'll have more cops around the place tonight. You're top-priority right now," he said softly.

"I don't know if that's a plus."

"Well, you can relax. There are cops behind every tree at the moment."

"But I'm still a prisoner in my own house, while Lenny Meskell can build bombs—"

"Hey," Jake said, placing his hands on her shoulders.

"I'm all right, Jake. Just angry. And I can't stop thinking about the danger the girls were in. When I do, I get frightened again."

"Chin up. When he finds out this didn't work, he may come out in the open."

"That's not necessarily good news."

"It is to me," Jake said grimly. "I'm going to bathe and get rid of the dirt. Tara asked me if I had a souvenir of the bomb."

"Oh, for heaven's sake—"

"I don't," he said, grinning with a flash of white teeth, "because the department hauled away every last scrap they could find, but she's enjoying herself at the moment."

"I know, and I'm glad. I'll get dinner."

"If you'll wait until I shower, I'll get dinner."

She studied him, determined to keep the barriers up around her heart. "All right. I'll take you up on the offer."

His eyes narrowed slightly as he looked at her, and she turned away.

Jake had clean jeans, T-shirt, socks and briefs in his hand. He went to bathe, knowing Rebecca was shaken. And he knew the barricades around her heart were up again.

And maybe it was better for both of them, because if he fell in love with her and asked her to marry him, she would have to accept him as he was. He couldn't give up his job, yet he was beginning to be unable to imagine life without Rebecca.

He stripped and stepped into the shower, feeling water sting his back. Pulling aside the shower curtain to look in the small mirror over the sink, he saw the cut across his shoulder. There was another one low on his back and one on his cheek, but they were all just scratches.

He shaved and finally dressed in his jeans and a T-shirt.

He put his other clothes in the washer and turned it on, crossing the kitchen. The girls had gone to watch television, finally settling back into their routine. Rebecca was stirring something that smelled delicious as he walked up behind her.

He placed his arms around her waist. "I don't know which smells better, you or dinner. On second thought, I think you definitely do," he said, brushing his lips across her nape.

Rebecca closed her eyes. Her body tingled and warmed, and his arms around her felt so right, but she couldn't erase the moments in the barn.

"Jake, don't, please," she whispered, afraid to turn around, because if she did her resolve might vanish.

He moved her away gently, reaching around to take the big wooden spoon from her hand. "Whatever the lady wants," he said solemnly. "But I did promise to cook dinner, so you should have waited and let me do it all."

He stirred and glanced at her to find her studying him as if some inner battle were being waged inside her. "I'm off-limits again," he said finally.

"Yes. I can't live with risking my heart to a man who lives like you do. I told you I couldn't. And you don't really want me to, anyway. You're not a marrying man, as I recall." She moved away from him and he let her go.

He stirred the pan and studied her as she stood with her back to him and filled glasses with water. He knew he was falling in love with the woman, whether it was wise or not.

Chapter 12

As they ate, she seemed to relax, and after dinner he shooed them from the kitchen and cleaned up. While he worked, his cellular phone rang. He answered to hear Richard Vance's voice.

"Wanted to check on things."

"The place is swarming with FBI, as well as your people."

"Just want to make it tight tonight. Tomorrow we'll go back to the regular surveillance."

"Yeah. That package shouldn't have ever gotten into her hands. After this, I screen the mail. Lenny's changed his M.O."

"He must have discovered the stakeouts. I'm moving them again, but there will still be a man to the north of the house in the woods, one to the south, one to the west and one a little farther away to the east, because there's no close cover there."

"Thank heaven for small favors."

"How are the widow and kids?"

"The kids are fine. Disappointed it wasn't all on the tube. The widow is fine, but having something come that close to her kids really shook her."

"Still want to stay out there?"

There was a momentary pause, but not because Jake wanted to be relieved. "You can't imagine how much I'd like to get Meskell. Yes, I want to stay."

"Well, today you showed you still have a cool head."

"I should have intercepted the package before it ever got to her."

"You didn't know, and Meskell's never been that subtle before. If you can call a bomb being subtle. I think he was ready to move, somehow made the stakeout and pulled back. He sent the bomb. Now, you tell me, what's his next move? You think like he does."

"Thanks a hell of a lot," Jake said, but his mind was already running over what Meskell might do, and he had thought about it while he was in the shower.

"Are you keeping it out of the media?"

"Yes, and they've agreed to cooperate."

"If I were the one who had sent that bomb, I'd want to know if it did the job."

"So how would you find out?"

"Meskell can watch the obituaries, but I don't think he's into that." Vance waited in silence while Jake thought. "I think he'll make a pass of the house. He'll want to see what's out here."

"We agree with you. We think he'll go past on that road in front of her house so he can see which cars are at her place."

"And when he can't tell from that, I think he'll come after her if he has to come cross-country."

"You didn't think he'd do that before."

"I would bet next month's pay that Meskell's patience is gone."

"Yeah, so keep up your guard. We're giving him about forty-eight hours. Hopefully, we can pick him up when he drives past to check out the place."

"Sometime tomorrow."

"Jake, there's something else."

"What?" Jake asked, suddenly wary.

"A convenience store was hit on the south side of town today, and then a bank. Sixteen thousand dollars was taken from the bank. The jobs fit Meskell's M.O."

"Dammit. He'll have enough money to do whatever he wants now."

"With sixteen thousand, he could stop stealing cars."

"He can, but he won't," Jake replied tersely. "He's pushing his luck, and we'll get him."

"One more thing—we have an informant, and he's trying to keep in touch with Meskell."

"That's great."

"If our guy can, he'll let us know when Meskell makes his move."

"I hope it's soon."

"I'll keep in touch." The connection was broken, and Jake put the phone on the counter. He looked out the window across a yard bathed in the glow of a setting sun. It looked peaceful until he saw the blackened boards and smoldering rubble of the barn and garage. A fire truck was still parked in front of the barn, and he knew one would return again later for a final check to make certain the last embers had burned out.

He glanced toward the door to the living room and felt a tightness in his chest. He was in love with the woman. When he thought of marriage now, he didn't have any qualms. But he knew that if he married, he wanted a wife who loved him and accepted him as he was. And that might not be possible with Rebecca.

He thought about changing jobs or retiring and he knew he couldn't do it. He liked his work. He was meant for this sort of job.

Forget the lady, he told himself. She was as off-limits now as she had been the first hour of his arrival. Common sense said to forget her before she became impossible to forget, but he suspected it was far too late for that.

If he tried, how long would it take to get over her? It shouldn't be long or too devastating when they had known each other a short time and there had been no real intimacy between them. He had a feeling that he was wrong—in spades.

He wiped the counter swiftly and headed for the front of the house.

He found her sitting in the living room, working a puzzle with the girls, when he stepped to the door. "I'm going out to talk with McCauley. There are plenty of men around here, so everyone will be all right."

Rebecca nodded and Jake left, moving across the yard in the dusk, pulling out his radio to talk to McCauley and learning he was with the firemen.

Jake circled the house once, trying to think what he would do if he were Meskell. It was hell to get past surveillance, but not impossible on a dark night. He would come at night. But how could he get inside her house without everyone hearing him?

Jake's thoughts shifted to Rebecca again. He loved the woman. It was as simple as that. And it seemed so damned right. Right for him. He would have to become a super salesman to convince her it was right for her. So much for his plans to wait until he retired for marriage. He was in love, madly and hopelessly, and the more he thought about it, the more certain he became about his feelings.

He circled the house, knowing he'd better get his mind back on Meskell and off Rebecca until this was over. He had probably been thinking more about her long legs this afternoon than he had her mail. He turned to walk down to the barn.

That night, after Rebecca put the girls to bed, she returned to the living room. Both air conditioners were going and the house was reasonably cool.

She moved across the room and sat in the chair, looking at the television as if it were of great interest—something she had never done before. Jake was sprawled on the sofa, and he was watching her. She was hunched forward, her fingers locked together in her lap, and she was ignoring him completely.

Standing, Jake crossed the room to the television, leaned down and switched it off. He received a startled glance and then a frown as he walked over to her.

While Rebecca watched him stride toward her with a purposeful gleam in his eye, her heart began to thud. Without a word, he leaned down to pick her up in his arms.

Her pulse jumped, and she folded her hands primly on her knees, as if she wanted to avoid touching him. "Jake, put me down. What are you doing?"

He crossed the room and sat down on the sofa, settling her in his lap. "I'm holding you. That's all, Rebecca. It's nothing earthshaking. It doesn't mean commitment. It's just something I want to do, and you look like you need someone to hold you for a little while. You're still in shock, whether you realize it or not."

Rebecca knew she should get up and move away from him. She didn't want to like being in his arms, but she couldn't move. He tightened his arm around her waist and stroked her hair, and she felt the tingles on her scalp that radiated through her.

"Just relax, honey," he said quietly. "I won't do any more than this, but you've been a bulwark all afternoon and night for the girls. Now you need a little care yourself, so let me do it."

She sat stiffly on his lap, her hands still on her knees. Words failed her, because everything was bottled up inside. She felt tense, wanting to keep a wall between them. She wasn't going to let Jake charm his way into her heart again.

"You're a great mom, Rebecca, and the girls got through the whole ordeal in pretty damn good shape."

"You'd make a good father, Jake," she said stiffly without looking at him.

"Thanks," he commented dryly. "I've been a dad since I was nine years old."

"Zach lives in Round Rock, and you said another brother works at a bank in Austin. What about the third brother?"

"Bill lives in Cedar Springs and sells farm machinery," he said, answering her questions. She was as tense as a coiled spring and she avoided his eyes when she spoke. Her voice had the polite tone of someone conversing with a complete stranger, and he knew he had a long way to go to coax her back to the place they'd been before the bomb.

They were silent a moment while he stroked her hair.

"Someday when this is over," Jake said, "you can take the girls out to my ranch and take them horseback riding. I'll be at work, but I can give you the name of my foreman, and he'll get gentle horses. There's a small mare Sissy can ride. Puff is the laziest horse on this earth, and great with children. And if Sissy doesn't want to ride alone, she can double up with Tara."

His voice was soothing, and his hand moved through Rebecca's hair and then down to massage her back. His arm was still around her waist.

"Come on, honey, ease up a little," he said quietly, pulling her over against his chest and continuing to stroke her back.

She leaned against him, and in the cool living room the warmth of his body felt good. And his strong arm holding her felt good.

"Put your head on my shoulder. Relax. I won't do anything."

She did what he told her, and she listened to him talk in his deep, steady voice while the tenseness gradually left her and she relaxed, but she kept her hands folded in her lap, trying to avoid touching him, trying to keep from responding, wishing her pulse hadn't quickened when he picked her up.

He finally became silent and sat quietly stroking her back, still keeping one arm firmly around her waist.

"I'm afraid that when I close my eyes, Jake, and go to sleep, I'll have nightmares about today. What's worse is, I'm afraid Sissy and Tara will have nightmares. Sissy was just beginning to get over the ones about losing her father."

Jake heard the quaver in Rebecca's voice and knew some of the horror of the afternoon was returning. He tightened his arm, holding her close. "Don't worry about it until it happens."

She twisted to look up at him. "Why don't you have nightmares?"

"People are affected in different ways."

"You don't have nightmares because it isn't horrible to you. You thrive on it," she said bitterly, and he remained quiet, knowing he couldn't argue with her.

"If the girls have nightmares, I'll hear them," he said finally.

"If there are so many police around here, you have a chance to get a regular night's sleep."

"I'll do that when this is over. I don't care if an army is surrounding this house, I'm staying awake most of the night."

He shifted her slightly, holding her close, his hand massaging her back and his other arm still around her. She knew she should move away from him, because her body was responding to his touch.

"Rebecca," he said softly, drawing out her name, his head bent close to hers. "Let's see how the girls get along tonight. Then, what do you think about sending them to stay with Zach and Sally tomorrow for just a couple of days? It would put them out of harm's way."

She drew a deep breath. She didn't like the thought of being separated from the girls, but even as she opened her mouth to say no, she thought about their safety. "Jake, that would be like ripping out part of me and sending it off. On the other hand, I know I need to think about what's best for them."

"Meskell really has no interest in the girls. And Sally and Zach would bring them right back here if they seemed unhappy. You saw how good Sally is with kids."

"I know they had a good time that night they stayed with your family. They've asked about going back," she said, thinking aloud and barely aware of Jake, her thoughts on the girls. She rubbed her forehead.

"I've never really been away from them for a long period of time. Dan and I didn't take vacations away from them. We were a together family. Part of it was finances. We couldn't afford to go off, but I'm so accustomed to having the girls with me that it's difficult to think about sending them away in a crisis."

He sat quietly rubbing her back, his hand drifting to her nape. Rebecca inhaled, aware of his fingers trailing back and forth so lightly across her skin. If she wanted to keep barriers between them, she needed to stop his caresses, but his touches were reassuring, and she was torn between what she had decided earlier and what she wanted now.

"I don't ever want them in jeopardy like they were today," she said, knowing she should send them to his brother's. "Do you think Sally and Zach would want to keep them?"

"You know the answer to that one. Talk it over with the girls. Tara is old enough to tell you what she wants, and Sissy will do what Tara wants."

"And if Tara says no?"

"If they're going to be miserable, then keep them here," Jake answered, but he hoped the girls had enjoyed themselves enough with Sally and Zach to want to go back.

"You're right. They should be where it's safe! I'll talk to Tara in the morning, but you talk to Zach and Sally first. I don't want to interfere in their lives or put them at risk."

"They won't be at risk. It's you Meskell is after, Rebecca."

Jake tilted her chin up. "You were great today. I was afraid you wouldn't run when I yelled at you. Quick reflexes and all that. After this, I'll get the mail, and anything unusual we'll send to the station first and let them check it out."

"As far as I'm concerned, you can send all my mail there," she said, looking into his hazel eyes. He was only inches away, holding her in his arms, his fingers playing across her nape, and she felt her body yearning for him.

They kept staring at each other, tension growing with a silent clash of wills. "Come back to the world, Rebecca," Jake said softly, his deep voice coaxing.

"I don't want to live in your world."

"It's not always as bad as today. That's the only bomb I've had to deal with, except one tiny little thing that blew a hole in a safe. You took risks before and had a happy marriage. You've focused on the bad part of it and blanked out the rest."

"No, not completely."

"I can understand why you did, but now it's time to let go." His voice was gentle and her heart drummed and she was torn between what she wanted and what better judgment screamed at her to do.

"I don't know why men like you come in such attractive packages."

Amusement curved one corner of his mouth slightly. "Thank you. I didn't know I was an attractive package."

She wiggled and slipped off his lap and moved away from him, walking to the kitchen to get a drink of water. Jake followed her and crossed the room to stand behind her.

"You're like Dan. You're understanding and good-looking and sexy—"

"My, oh, my!" he exclaimed, bending his head to brush his lips across the nape of her neck.

She whirled around to face him, and even in the dim light of the kitchen he could see the sparkle of tears in her eyes. "But you love risk. That bomb didn't scare you today."

"The hell it didn't."

"All right. To put it another way, your only reaction afterward was anger. You weren't terrified or appalled. You won't have nightmares."

"No, I won't." He moved closer and slid his arms around her, reaching up to wipe a tear off her cheek.

Rebecca ached, because Jake was so many wonderful things. He was good with the girls and he was understanding and sexy and appealing. But he wasn't into commitment or marriage and she couldn't have an affair. "You don't want a long-term relationship," she stated.

"I'll take sexy and good-looking and understanding, Rebecca, but don't say I'm not into anything long-term," he answered quietly. Gazing at her solemnly, he pulled her closer. "I love you."

Stunned, she looked up at him in surprise. The words poured over her, shaking her. There was no mistaking the look in his eyes. He bent his head, cupping her head with his hand as he placed his mouth over hers. His lips parted hers, his tongue sliding into her mouth, thrusting over hers.

Heat shot through her, and she moaned, her body clenching with need. Her hands raised and rested on his arms, feeling the bulge of his strong biceps. She trembled, relishing his words, but shocked by them, as well, because he didn't seem like the kind of man to say them easily.

His arm tightened around her, pulling her up against him as he bent over her and his kiss deepened. And she fought responding to him, torn more than ever because of his declaration. She pushed his chest lightly, and he raised his head as she gasped for breath.

"You can't mean that! We don't know each other that well."

"Oh, yes, we do. It doesn't always take a lot of time, Rebecca. And we've been living together under the most trying circumstances possible."

"Jake, I don't even know if that's something you tell all the women you date. I don't know if you've dated around a lot, or even if you've ever been engaged."

"I've never been engaged," he said, his hand sliding to her hip while his other hand stroked her throat, caressing her, sliding across her nape and over her shoulder. His fingers drifted across her lips, making them tingle. "I haven't told all the women I date that I love them. I've had a couple of relationships that have been somewhat long-lasting, but I wasn't wildly in love and neither were they. Sort of friend-lover relationships. I've been burdened with bills and brothers and our ailing mother and responsibility—"

"And you said you wanted your freedom from all that for years," she said, still astounded and trying to sort out his feelings.

"That was before I met you. Somehow you don't seem the same as sending my brothers through college and dealing with all that. And that came in my early years, when I was a kid and I wanted to go to college and couldn't because I had to support them. Now I have a decent job and some savings and have the ranch on a paying level. I'm in a different situation."

"That isn't what you said to me when you came here. And that was only a short time ago."

"I have a whole different perspective now. Do you think I haven't thought about this? Do I look like the type of man who doesn't know what he wants?"

"No, you don't," she said warily, her heart pounding. Part of her wanted to melt into his arms. The other part was frightened because she did not want to fall in love with Jake.

"I love you," he said quietly. His hands slid over her shoulders and then down to her hips, and he pulled her closer. "And I think you're a warm, wonderful woman who needs to let go of the past." Jake bent his head, his arm sliding around her while he kissed her.

Rebecca's heart thudded, and she stood stiffly in his arms, yet her body was melting, her heart pounding. His tongue invaded her mouth, sliding over hers, thrusting deeply, while she quivered and heat pooled low within her, turning into flames that licked through her veins.

"I can't," she whispered, knowing she didn't want to yield to him. It wasn't just letting go of the past. It was facing a future like today over and over again.

His hands drifted down, unfastening her blouse and pushing it off her shoulders.

"Jake, I can't change. And all I have to do—" she said, closing her eyes, holding his arms as he unfastened her lacy pink bra. Jake pushed it away, cupping her breasts in his big hands, and her words ended on a gasp of pleasure.

His thumbs flicked over her nipples as Jake bent to kiss her. His declaration of love felt so right. He wanted her and he was willing to risk his heart to try to win her over.

"I want you, Rebecca," he whispered, trailing kisses along her throat to her breasts, cupping her right breast and taking the nipple in his mouth to tease and suck gently, hearing her moan of pleasure, which set him on fire.

He was hard and he wanted her, but he would give her the time she needed. And he prayed he could overcome the objections she was going to raise.

Rebecca shook as he kissed her. She didn't want to be in love with him. He was a wonderful man, but he also was what she disliked most.

She pushed on his shoulders and he moved away a fraction. He was breathing hard, a lock of brown hair falling over his forehead. His hazel eyes smoldered with desire.

"Jake, stop," she said, but the word held no force, and she was breathless. She pulled her clothes into place again. "You know you can destroy all my thoughts when you love me, but I don't want this."

He stroked a lock of hair from her cheek and tucked it behind her ear, his warm fingers brushing her face. "You took risks before and you were happy," he said in a husky voice. "What have the past years been like without Dan?"

"That isn't a fair question, because I was deeply in love."

"They were empty, weren't they? I know you have the girls, but there were empty nights, lonely moments. You live out here in isolation and you work alone. You're warm and giving, and you weren't meant to go through life hiding from love."

"Don't tell me how to live my life!" she snapped, taking his wrists and moving his hands away. His words had hit a nerve. And after having him under her roof constantly, it would be worse than ever when he was gone.

He caught her face, winding his hands in her hair and holding her tightly, moving close to look down into her eyes. "You need love in your life, Rebecca. And I need you."

She trembled, the words pouring into her heart, making joy leap within her. Yet, in spite of her longing, she wasn't going to yield to him. He would be gone soon, and she would adjust.

"Jake, you don't really want—"

He placed his finger over her lips. "Yes, I damned well do. I love you, lady. And I'm going to fight for you." He bent his head, his tongue parting her lips and sliding deep into her mouth in a demanding kiss that carried the same promise as his words.

Her heart pounded, because he was the most temptation she had ever had in her life. She wanted him in so many ways, wanted to throw good sense aside, toss all her fears away.

His arms wrapped around her, and he pressed her softness against him. She felt his long, lean strength, his hard arousal, and she knew he wanted her, and she was dismayed that he said he loved her.

Unable yet to push him away, Rebecca relished his kiss, returning it as his tongue slipped into her mouth, playing over her tongue. She moaned, her hips thrusting against him, desire a burning ache deep within her.

Finally she placed her hands on his arms and pushed him away. She stepped back. "I mean it, Jake. I won't get involved. I think I better go," she said.

Her breathing was as ragged as his. His eyes seemed to bore into her. He stepped aside and let her go, and she trembled as she rushed from the room.

Jake watched her disappear into her bedroom and wondered if he could get her to turn her fears loose. And how badly was he going to be hurt if she didn't?

He ached for her, his body on fire with need, but that was nothing compared to the longing in his heart. Now that he had made his decision, it felt so right.

He moved through the house, knowing with all the cops outside this would be a night he could get some sleep, yet he was too wound up. And he wanted to see how the girls and Rebecca got through the night.

Would she even agree to see him when this was over? He suspected that if he didn't win her over while he was under her roof, he might not ever get another chance. He raked his fingers through his hair, combing it back from his face. The last thing he had expected when he took this assignment was to fall in love with the woman, but fall in love he had. He wanted her, and he knew he couldn't sleep now even if they told him Meskell was behind bars.

Jake sat down to pull off his boots so that he could move around without making noise. Finally, at about five in the morning, he stretched out on the sofa and fell asleep, suspecting he was going to need his rest in the nights to come.

When Rebecca entered the kitchen for breakfast the next morning, Jake was pouring milk over Sissy's bowl of cereal. Coffee was brewing, orange juice was poured for all four of them, and glasses of milk were at each of the girls' places. Jake's hair was damp from a shower, and he wore a T-shirt and jeans and looked as appealing as ever. She felt a pang, wishing he was an accountant or salesman or teacher, because he was perfect in every other way.

"Good morning," he said cheerfully, holding out a glass of orange juice to her.

"Thanks for getting breakfast," she said. His gaze flicked over her, taking in her red T-shirt and cutoffs, and she saw the approval in his eyes as he looked at her and winked.

She turned away, going to the kitchen cabinet to get bread to make toast, wondering if the girls had noticed his wink and would make anything of it.

"Are we going to build another barn?" Tara asked.

"It wasn't covered in the insurance," she answered lightly, "so no, we're not. We didn't need it, anyway, and soon I'll go back to working at my office in town."

She sat down at the table and picked up her writing tablet to go over the daily tasks. "I'll have to call my customers and tell them there will be a delay getting their orders." She ran her hand across her forehead. In all the upheaval over Jake's declaration of love and the bomb, she hadn't realized that she was temporarily out of business.

"It won't be a long delay," Jake said, and she glanced up to meet his gaze, realizing he expected Lenny Meskell to do something again soon.

She listed the customers to be notified and jotted notes about work she could do at home. As soon as they'd finished eating, the girls carried their dishes to the sink and left to get dressed.

"I'll go help Sissy and talk to the girls about going to your brother's."

Jake caught her arm and pulled her close, sliding his arm around her and kissing her lightly. "That's the way I wanted to greet you."

"I'm glad you didn't. I'd be answering questions for the rest of the day!"

"I'd be glad to answer them. I'd be glad to shout my feelings from the rooftop." He grinned and looked into her eyes, and her pulse drummed. Trying to resist his charm, she wiggled free reluctantly.

"I better go."

He reached out again to catch her arm. "I called Zach and Sally and talked with both of them, and they would love to have the girls. I've talked to Vance. If you agree, Vance himself will come out with Sally and get them. And Vance won't let anyone follow him to Zach's house."

She nodded. "I'll talk to them about it. I know that would be the safest thing for them."

She hurried down the hall, her thoughts as stormy as they'd been the night before. If she could just hold out and resist Jake until this was over, then she could think rationally. It would be easier to tell him no then. Now her emotions were raw and everything was so confusing and Jake was pouring out charm.

She entered the girls' room and picked up a hairbrush. "Come here, Sissy, and let me put up your hair. Bring your shirt and I'll help you put it on."

She helped Sissy into a pink T-shirt that matched her pink shorts and then began to brush her hair. "Tara, how would it be if you and Sissy went to stay with the Delancys again?"

"Hey, neat!" Tara said, smiling broadly. "They have all kinds of books."

"Sissy, would you like that?"

Sissy laughed and clapped her hands. "Let's go to the Delancys!"

"Tara, what about if you and Sissy stay there overnight? Jake thinks it would be safer. Probably for two or three days. You could come home anytime you wanted, but it might be better if you're there."

Tara studied her solemnly and nodded. "We could come home anytime?"

"Of course you can."

Tara smiled and crossed the room to Rebecca to hug her. "We'll go. It'll be fun, and we'll call you when we want to come home."

Rebecca laughed. "Well, I might call you first and tell you that it's time you come home. I'm going to miss my girls, but I bet you'll have fun with Mrs. Delancy."

"She has a dolly that I can play with, and she reads to me," Sissy said.

"All right, pick out what you want to take with you and I'll go call them as soon as I finish doing your hair," Rebecca said, tying a pink bow around Sissy's ponytail. Now, come here, Tara, and I'll braid your hair."

When Rebecca returned to the kitchen, Jake was stacking the last dish in the dishwasher. "I could have done that, Jake, but thanks."

"Told you, it keeps me in practice."

"They want to go. The Delancys captivate again."

Something flickered in his eyes and he studied her as he reached for his cellular phone. "I'll phone Vance and let him know. How about midafternoon?"

"Sure," she answered, realizing it might be more diffi-
ult to deal with Jake when the girls were no longer under-
oot and she didn't have her work to do. "I want to call your
ister-in-law first and make absolutely certain this is all
ight."

He handed her the phone and waited to call Vance.

The rest of the day until the afternoon, Rebecca couldn't
top hovering over the girls. At two o'clock, Richard Vance
nd Sally arrived in an official car to pick them up.

While Vance and Jake talked, Rebecca gave the girls'
ings to Sally. "They stay up later in the summer, but they
sually go to bed around half past eight or nine o'clock. I'll
all them tonight. And thanks again for taking them."

"It'll be a treat for us," Sally said, her eyes sparkling, as
he let Captain Vance take the girls' belongings from her.
ebecca hugged Tara and kissed her and then turned to hug
nd kiss Sissy. "I'll call you tonight," she said. She fol-
wed them to the door, wanting to go outside, but halting
hen Jake took her arm.

"Let's go, girls," Captain Vance said. "I'll help you get
uckled up, and you can ride in a police car."

"Awesome!" Tara said as he took Sissy's hand and they
ent to the car. Sally remained at the step, the sun making
er red curls a bright halo around her head.

"Don't worry about them. If they get homesick, I'll call
ou at once."

"I have a feeling they're going to forget all about me,"
ebecca said with a smile.

"Impossible," Jake said, dropping his arm casually
cross her shoulders. "What's going on, Sally? You look
ke the cat that ate the cream."

"I told Zach I was going to tell you. I'm pregnant!"

"That's great," Jake said warmly, and stepped forward
hug her.

"Well, we know what you think about starting a family, but you know we've been wanting children for a long time now."

"I think that's great," Jake repeated, and Rebecca smiled at her, giving her a quick hug.

"It's wonderful!" she said. "Congratulations."

"We're so excited. We'll talk later. I'll take good care of your girls," she said, bounding across the yard to the car.

"I really am glad for them, but I have a feeling it will take the next nine months to convince them," Jake said. "Hey, Sally!" he called. "Just a minute, Rebecca," he added as he left her and stepped outside. The sunlight was bright on his thick brown hair when he crossed the yard in long strides to catch up with Sally.

Sally turned around and came back, and Jake stood talking to her. Rebecca wondered if he was trying to convince Sally that he was happy about her news. In minutes he turned around, grinning at Rebecca, and returned to the kitchen.

Rebecca waved when they drove down the driveway and Jake closed and locked the door. He turned to look at her. "Now I've got you all to myself," he said quietly, reaching for her. His fingers closed lightly around her wrist, and he pulled her around as he leaned against the counter and placed his hands on her waist.

"Let's talk about this phobia you have about my job, because I don't think it should rule your life."

Chapter 13

Rebecca's heartbeat quickened as he pulled her close. He leaned back against the kitchen counter and placed his hands lightly on her hips.

She shook her head at him. "Why don't we postpone this conversation until Meskell is caught?"

"Why don't we talk about it right now? I know what I want, Rebecca," he said softly. His voice became husky, and her body tightened in response. "You're the woman I want in my life. I want you now and always—"

She placed her fingers on his face, feeling the faint stubble on his jaw, looking at his thick lashes. "I don't see how you can be certain of love! We haven't known each other a long time."

"Time isn't always necessary. Not in my life. I'm not a kid caught up in first love. I may act like it because of what you do to me, but I'm not."

Rebecca's heart pounded with his words. Jake's eyes were solemn, his voice was husky and earnest, and something inside her ached to open to him even as another part of her battled to resist.

"I know what I want," he declared again, and the look in his eyes left no mistake that he wanted her. She found it hard to get her breath, and his hands resting so lightly on her waist were a fiery contact.

"Jake, just a short time ago you were saying you weren't a marrying man."

"I hadn't fallen in love then," he answered solemnly, and she closed her eyes for a moment, wishing with all her heart that things were different. His words sounded marvelous, and in so many ways he was a very special man. But in one important way, he was what she had promised herself to avoid forever.

"You weren't a marrying man," she repeated firmly. "You've had nothing but responsibility since you were a child, and you want your freedom." She recited the litany, knowing he had already gone over it last night. She couldn't believe he had really fallen that deeply in love with her. In so many ways, the idea of his being in love with her was like a heady wine, intoxicating, tempting.

"That was different, Rebecca. I've fallen in love, and that's changed my whole perspective. My walls are gone. Now let's work on yours."

She was astonished he had overcome all his objections to love and marriage. She gazed into his clear hazel eyes and felt shaken all over again. "I can't let go," she whispered.

"You said last night that everything else was all right except my work."

"So?" she asked, suddenly holding her breath, wondering if he was going to offer to quit his job.

"So try to get past that a little. Think about all the other pros of being together—because there are plenty of pros."

"But you won't think about changing careers?"

"I've given it some thought, and I don't want to," he answered bluntly.

Disappointment rocked her. She had hoped he was going to capitulate and say he would leave the force. She tried to focus on what he was telling her.

"But you said you have a ranch and that someday you want to be a rancher."

"Someday, when I retire from the force, but not yet. I'm not ready for retirement, and this is what I know how to do. I don't want to retire to the ranch now."

Jake gazed into her wide blue eyes, and he could see the pulse beating fast in a fine blue vein in her throat and he knew the only barricade between them was his work. All his objections were gone. Marriage began to seem something desirable, a heady prospect, when he thought about spending his life with Rebecca.

"There are so many other considerations you should think about that would counterbalance your worries over my work," he said, tilting her face up to his and feeling as if he could never tire of looking at her. He leaned back against the kitchen counter and spread his legs apart, watching her, seeing her lips part, and knowing she was torn between wanting his love and fearing his work. "You're strong enough to cope with being married to a cop, Rebecca," he said softly, and bent his head to place his mouth over hers.

As his mouth brushed hers and then covered hers, his tongue touching her lips, desire burst within her. Rebecca yielded to him, her thoughts swirling over what he had said to her. *Marriage.* He had gone from saying he wouldn't marry for years to asking her to marry him! She might be strong enough to cope with his dangerous work, but was that what she wanted to do?

His tongue slid over hers, and her heart raced as she wrapped her arms around his neck and let him pull her close against his hard body.

Each time he kissed and caressed her, he bound her more completely to him and shattered a layer of her defense. She

should have resisted him from the start, but she couldn't.
His strong arms were marvelous. Jake was good to her, good
to the girls. She liked his companionship, wanted his kisses.
The arguments raged in her as his hands slipped down to tug
her shirt out of her cutoffs and then went beneath her T-shirt
to caress her breasts.

Thoughts and reluctance melted away, and she trembled,
letting him touch her, wanting to touch his body, to love him
and be loved.

Jake felt her tremble, felt her resistance go as her body
softened and her lips parted and her tongue met his. Her
mouth was wet and hot, and he wanted to stroke every inch
of it with his tongue, to taste and touch and love her.

He felt as if there were an emptiness in his life that went
soul-deep and Rebecca was the only person who could ever
fill it. And he was going to help her fight her fears, because
he knew she was strong.

He leaned over her, determined to demolish her objections. He had always been so careful with her before, stopping the instant she made the slightest protest. But now he
wanted to kiss her until she forgot all her fears, to caress her
until she wanted him, because he felt she was filled with a
love that he was so close to winning.

He turned his head, trailing kisses to her ear, running his
tongue over the curve of her ear. "I'm going to love you,
Rebecca. I want your love, and I'm willing to risk my heart
to win yours. I'm giving you all of it." He caught her hand,
watching her.

Rebecca opened her eyes, taken aback at the hunger she
saw in the depths of his eyes, which had darkened to a deep-
sea green now, with only tiny flecks of gold. He placed her
hand against his chest and through his T-shirt, beneath his
warm flesh, she felt his racing heart.

"There. You feel that? That's what you do to me. And
my heart is yours. I've already taken that risk, Rebecca."

A tremor rippled in her, and she met his gaze, her heart pounding from the words that tore at her. How badly she wanted to say yes to him, to yield, to let him love her! Her body shook with need for him, and she ached, her hips thrusting against him. For days now the slight physical contact, his kisses and caresses, had built fires of passion within her that were finally blazing out of control.

His mouth covered hers again, his kiss hot and demanding, while his hands slipped down to take hold of the hem of her T-shirt. He pulled it over her head, leaning back to look at her as he unfastened the clasp to her bra. His eyes had darkened, turning a stormy green while he cupped her breasts and bent his head to kiss her, his tongue flicking over her nipple.

Rebecca moaned softly, swept away by the passion fluttering in the pit of her stomach, burning lower between her thighs. She wanted him, wanted his fierce loving, yet at the same time she battled against yielding, because she knew she would give him more than her body.

Jake trembled, wanting to go slow, to have it last forever, because this might be the only chance she would give him. He wanted to set her on fire. She was beautiful, perfect, loving and giving and sensual. And he suspected there was far more warmth and passion in her than he had seen so far.

Kissing her, he unfastened her jeans, pushing them over her hips, letting them fall around her ankles. As he bent to kiss her breast, to suck gently and feel her soft flesh beneath his tongue and lips, he caught his T-shirt. He straightened to yank it over his head and drop it on the floor and heard her quick intake of breath.

Any moment he expected her to stop him, but then her gaze met his and the burning blue fires in her eyes made his heart thud against his rib cage. He saw in the depths of her eyes that wanted to be loved, and it turned him rock hard, making him tremble and fight for control. He felt as if this were a one-time chance, knowing he might not ever get past the barriers in her heart again, wanting to destroy them, to bind her to him body and soul.

Her gaze drifted down over his chest, and her fingers fluttered there.

"Damn," he whispered, his fingers kneading her soft buttocks. "I could eat you alive, Rebecca."

He leaned forward to kiss her, his tongue going deep while his hands stroked her hips, sliding down to caress her inner thighs, pushing aside the narrow strip of lace to stroke her moist, soft flesh. He found the feminine bud, his fingers stroking as she grasped his forearms and cried out.

Her cry of passion tore through him like a flame. He shook with wanting her as he stroked her, driving her to the brink, watching her bite her lower lip with her white teeth, her eyes closed in passion as her fingers dug into him and her hips moved frantically.

"Jake!"

"That's it," he whispered hoarsely, leaning close to her ear. "That's it. I want to hear you call my name. I want you to cry out for me. I want to set you on fire, Rebecca."

He knelt, pulling down the flimsy panties, his tongue following the path his fingers had taken while he felt her fingers wind in his hair and she gasped with pleasure.

He stood and looked at her, seeing that her eyes were closed. Perspiration beaded her upper lip, and a fall of golden hair covered her cheek. Her face was flushed and her nipples were hard buds, and he relished every sensual peak he had brought her to. He picked her up in his arms, aware of her bare body against his, of her soft cries of need and her hands fluttering over his chest.

He set her on her feet beside her bed and knelt to slide his hands down her legs, caressing their silken smoothness, wanting her as he had never wanted anyone. "I want you," he said gruffly, looking up at her as his hand closed around her ankle and he lifted her foot to push off her shoe and slide off the jeans and lacy panties. Then he did the same with her other foot, handling her as if she were precious crystal.

Rebecca's heart pounded, and every caress made her ache for him. As he straightened up, her gaze ran over his broad chest, the powerful muscles, and she reached out, her fingertips feeling his smooth skin, his flat, hard stomach. She touched the top of his jeans and heard his deep intake of breath.

Looking up at him, feeling the heat in his gaze, she began to unbutton his jeans, twisting the flat copper buttons loose, freeing him, while his gaze ran over her like a warm caress.

"You're a beautiful woman, Rebecca," he whispered hoarsely.

She glanced up and met Jake's burning half-lidded gaze as she pushed open his jeans, sliding them off his narrow hips. She caught her fingers in his briefs to slide them away, freeing him.

He was virile, throbbing, ready.

She drew a deep breath, shaking, wanting him to love her, to feel like a complete, desirable woman again, if only for this one moment in time. She closed her slender fingers around him, her flesh pale against his darkened skin. She drew her hand up slowly, stroking him.

Jake groaned, winding his fingers in her hair, and then he picked her up and placed her on the bed, bending over her to hold her slender foot, his fingers stroking her ankle as he trailed kisses along her leg.

Knowing that if she did this she could never go back, that her heart would be bound to him whether she accepted his love or not, Rebecca's heart thudded. She wanted his loving, even if she couldn't accept his proposal.

She pushed the pillow behind her head to watch him as he flicked his tongue along the inside of her thigh, tingles radiating from each stroke. Jake watched her, his gaze steady while he kissed her, making her heart drum.

"I want to marry you," he whispered. "And I'm not going to give up easily."

Her heart pounded at his words. The sensual touch of his hands and his lips drove any answer from her as she closed her eyes and gasped with pleasure, spreading her legs and opening herself to him.

She felt his weight leave the bed and watched as he removed a packet from his jeans. He came back, kneeling between her thighs. He was poised over her, watching her. She knew that she was making an ultimate commitment, that her battle with him would be a thousand times more difficult now. And then he trailed his fingers along her inner thigh and between her legs, and she moaned with pleasure and closed her eyes and stopped battling with herself. Thought vanished, yielding to pleasure as she felt his warm body above hers, and she wrapped her legs around him, pressing them against his firm buttocks.

Jake's heart thudded so violently, he felt as if it would burst out of his chest. He looked at Rebecca, her lower lip caught again in her even white teeth, her eyes closed with passion. "I'm going to make you mine, Rebecca, for this moment and forever," he whispered, wanting to bind her to him heart and soul.

He lowered himself and felt her fingers close around him, guiding him into her as her hips arched and her hand slid away. She pressed against him, and he fought for control, trying to go slowly, feeling her tightness.

Rebecca wound her hands around his neck, feeling his shoulder muscles tense as he slid into her, hot and big, filling her, moving slowly.

She cried out with pleasure, her body arching against him, and then they were moving, climbing to a peak, their bodies bound together as need buffeted her.

"Rebecca! Love," Jake said, his voice hoarse as he ground out the words, and they moved with a frantic rhythm.

Waves of pleasure washed over her, rocking her body as she clenched and spasmed around him. Jake shuddered, climaxing and finally slowing, his weight lowering. He turned his head to kiss her throat, his arms wrapping around her.

Rebecca stroked his smooth, damp back as their breathing returned to normal, and she wondered how much change the past few moments would wreak on her life.

Jake held her, feeling her heart pounding as violently as his. Satisfaction and love burned in him as hot as passion had only moments earlier. And a fierce determination to win her love.

He stroked her hair from her face and kissed her cheek, trailing light kisses to her mouth. Rebecca turned her head to look at him, and his breath caught at the heat in her gaze. He leaned down to kiss her deep and hard, as if he could convey all he felt by his kiss. He raised his head and touched her cheek lightly with his index finger, looking at her smooth, fine-grained skin, her wide blue eyes. "I love you," he whispered.

She closed her eyes, and he felt a sudden stab of pain. It was as if in that moment she had slammed a door in his face and shut him out of her life.

Rebecca wanted Jake's love. He was a wonderful man and his lovemaking had taken her to dizzying heights. She wanted to be able to return his love, knew that she was already far more in love with him than she wanted to admit, but she was never going through anything like what she had with Dan. Never. She was not going to sit back and watch Richard Vance drive up someday to tell her that her husband had been blown up by a bomb while he was trying to save someone.

Tears stung her eyes, and she didn't want to cry, because she knew Jake was watching her. She felt his thumb trace across her eyelid and wipe away a tear, and she turned, twisting beneath him, unable to keep her emotions under control as her throat burned and more tears came. "I can't let go of it, Jake. No matter how lonely I am or how much I need you or even if I love you, I'm not putting my heart at risk again."

"Shh, Rebecca," he said softly. "Don't cry, honey. You don't have to do one thing today. Just take it a little bit at a time."

His words calmed her. She twisted around to look at him. "Bully," she said gently, amazed by his patience, because he could be such a hard, arrogant, commanding man at other times.

He grinned, white teeth showing, creases appearing in his cheeks, that coaxing twinkle coming into his eyes. "That's my girl," he said with hearty approval. "I'm counting on the passionate woman in you to win the battle going on inside that pretty head of yours."

"I ought to kick you out of bed," she snapped, but there was no bite in her words. It was delicious fun to be in bed with him, to have this intimacy.

"Give it a try," he urged, the twinkle changing to a wicked gleam as his legs pressed hers down. "I don't think you can get a kick anywhere that will have any effect."

She smiled at him and realized what possibilities lay before them if things would only change. "Oh, Jake!" She sighed, suddenly relishing his strong body covering hers, the feel of his weight on her. She slid her hand over his smooth back and then couldn't resist letting her fingers drift over his buttocks.

The moment she did, she felt him stir inside her, and her amusement vanished as she gave him a startled look and saw passion flare in his eyes again.

"See what you do to me?" he asked in a husky voice.

"Me?" she asked, astonished that she had that kind of effect on him. She felt her cheeks flush, and he leaned closer, his gaze going to her mouth.

Suddenly she wanted him again, wanted to feel his hard body, wanted him to take her through the same dizzying spiral to release.

Jake's body became hard, and he moved slowly, intending to draw out their loving this time and make it last longer. Rebecca arched beneath him, her long legs holding him tightly while she clung to him, and then her fingers slid down over him, tugging at his buttocks as he moved with her.

She cried out, arching when he thrust deeply into her, and they climaxed again, Jake shuddering with release and sagging on top of her, wanting her in his arms every night for the rest of his life.

This time they were quiet for a long time, and then Jake turned to kiss her again. "And you were saying, love?"

She stuck her tongue out at him. "I have no idea what I was saying when you so sexually interrupted."

He chuckled and hugged her, rolling over so that they lay on their sides and he could look at her. "This is one of the best days of my life."

Instantly her blue eyes clouded, and Jake kissed the tip of her nose. "Stop worrying. There's no ring on your finger, no contract in front of you. You're no more bound than you were yesterday...." The words floated into the air, his voice changing and becoming serious as they gazed solemnly at each other.

Rebecca knew that she was more bound to him than ever, and that he was to her. Their lovemaking had created invisible bonds that would take time and effort to sever. Even if she took things one step at a time for the next year, she didn't think she would get any closer to the decision Jake wanted her to make.

She rolled over, running her fingers through her hair while worry plagued her. He propped his head on his hand to look at her, running her golden hair through his fingers and kissing her shoulder and throat lightly.

"Just give it some thought. Think about the future. What we had together just now was very special."

She had to agree with that, but she couldn't talk about it. She didn't want to say anything, to get into an argument. She dreaded facing the issue and coming to a permanent decision, because when she did, it might shut Jake out forever.

She wound her fingers in his hair, feeling its softness, the slight wave in the locks. "I'll go—"

He placed his finger over her mouth. "Don't go anywhere yet. I just want to lie here and hold you against me, to feel your warmth and softness." He wrapped his arms around her and pulled her close and stroked her back while he held her.

Jake knew he was going to have a tough battle with her. He had told her she was a strong woman and he knew she would be adamant about standing by her decision to avoid marrying a cop. But he was strong, too, and he wasn't going to give up easily. He had already won part of her. Maybe more than either of them realized.

He felt stunned, shaken by their lovemaking. He had never wanted a woman the way he had wanted Rebecca. Now, as he lay with his arms wrapped around her, his amazement deepened, because he wanted her even more than before.

He studied her. She was what he had always tried to avoid—someone who hated his work. Someone who was earnest and into lasting relationships. Someone who already had children and obligations. Rebecca's life-style and his were poles apart, yet here she was in his arms, seeming to fill the needs and voids and emptiness in his life. And until he met Rebecca, he hadn't even realized these were voids in his life.

Rebecca nestled against him, feeling relaxed, satiated, and mildly worried, because she suspected they might both be in for heartbreak. She stroked his back, enjoying being able to touch him and being held in his arms.

Finally she knew she should move away. "Jake, are you awake?" she whispered, not expecting any answer. He had been so still, she was certain he was asleep.

"I'm awake."

"I'm going to shower."

"Good idea," he said, stirring, and she pushed him down.

"You stay right here. I need to shower alone and make some phone calls and see about what we'll eat tonight." She slid off the bed and yanked up her T-shirt to wrap it around her, hurrying to go shower.

She returned a few minutes later, wrapped in a towel, her thoughts still churning. "Jake, did you know we spent hours in bed? It's six o'clock!"

"We weren't in bed all that time," he drawled. "We spent a lot of the time standing around and kissing before we ever got in bed. We can try that again."

"We certainly cannot!"

He chuckled and came out of bed, crossing the room. Rebecca glanced at him, her pulse jumping at the sight of his lean, muscular, naked body. He left to shower, and she stared at the empty doorway.

She dressed in a blue cotton shirt and jeans and sneakers. Studying her reflection in the mirror, aware of the rumpled bed behind her, Rebecca brushed her hair, putting it up in a ponytail.

As she turned to leave the room, she looked one more time at the bed, rumpled from their lovemaking. In her mind she was remembering Jake, his dark hands on her body, his powerful body.

She turned and went to the kitchen to start dinner. At the sink, she looked across the yard at the blackened ruins of the barn. Just outside the kitchen, sunlight was bright on Jake's big pickup, her small, oddly colored green car looking pitiful next to his truck. She shook her head, her thoughts on Jake. Nothing had changed except she was going to be hurt even more now.

She moved around the room automatically, getting out the chicken breasts she had marinated this morning, putting rice on to cook, making a quick corn casserole. Pipes rattled, and she guessed Jake had turned off the shower.

She knew every minute with him now would be more difficult. She had merely compounded her troubles this afternoon by making love with him. He seemed to think she could cope with being a cop's wife because she had been married to Dan. But she had been younger then and hadn't stopped to think about the consequences.

She heard the scrape of boots in the hall, and Jake came striding into the room, and her heart thudded.

His hair was damp and clinging to his head. He had on a navy T-shirt and fresh jeans, and he smiled at her, giving her a wink that sizzled through her like an electrical current.

He crossed the room to her, wrapping his arms around her as he leaned down to kiss her. "Hi, good-looking," he said lightly.

His mouth silenced her answer as he brushed her lips with his, and then he shifted, tightening his arms around her and really kissing her. "Maybe we should go back to the bedroom," he said in a husky voice.

She pushed against his chest and turned around, unable to give him a light answer. "Jake, I can't change. I just cannot do it!"

His hands closed on her shoulders, and he kneaded them gently. "Will you stop worrying about the rest of your life? Just think about the next few hours, honey," he coaxed.

"That's what I did when I married Dan!" she snapped, and then was sorry she'd been so abrupt with Jake. She wiped her eyes. "Sorry to sound sharp," she said, turning around.

Jake's eyes had darkened, and he frowned slightly as he studied her.

"That's about the only view I had of life when Dan and I married. We were so young and had so few responsibilities."

"Maybe it's time you get back to some of that," he said gently. "Honey, you were hurt badly. I know it was terrible, but it's time to turn loose and take some risks again. Life is always a risk. You know that." He smiled at her and kissed her temple. "And you're not going to throw a damper on my spectacular day. I'm a fatuous male and I'm in love."

"A fat male?" she teased, suddenly unable to resist him, and he grinned.

"That's more like it. Let's call the girls."

Rebecca smiled and turned to the phone, feeling better and wondering if she was worrying too much. And was she cheating the girls of a man who would be a wonderful father? The thought startled her, and she realized there was a lot more to consider about his offer.

After dinner they cleaned the kitchen together and Rebecca felt the electric tension sparking between them constantly. Every touch now was magnified more than before. Jake was relaxed, flirting easily, trying to charm her.

They sat in the kitchen at dusk, sipping iced tea, when his cellular phone rang. He picked it up, and she moved away to refill their glasses with tea.

"Jake, it's Werner. If Meskell passed the house today, he wasn't in a stolen car and we didn't spot him. The snitch is still in touch with him, and we hope we can give you warning and cordon off the area."

"Thanks. Nothing happening here."

Jake replaced the phone as the connection ended and watched Rebecca move around the kitchen and sit down facing him again. He stretched out his leg to rub slowly against hers, and her eyes flickered.

Rebecca sat quietly, but her pulse raced as Jake's leg rubbed hers sensually. Now just a touch could make her heart pound. She tried to ignore the jump in her pulse, yet she couldn't move away from him.

"No news on Meskell?"

"None. Enjoy the cool air, because when dark comes, we have to turn the air conditioners off."

"It seems strange to not have the girls here. But I know they're enjoying themselves. They barely had time to talk on the phone because of something they wanted to do with Sally."

"Zach and Sally are floating above the earth anyway, over the expected baby."

"And you really do approve?"

His gaze met hers, and he gave her a level stare. "I do, because they've wanted a child for a long time. Zach has a good job, and they've saved their money. They're adults and should make their own decisions. And it's nice."

"I think you've mellowed since I met you."

He raised the glass of tea in a mock toast. "See what you've done for me."

"I can't take credit for your change of heart about Zach and Sally."

"You can a little. I feel different about the whole world now. Well, almost the whole world."

She was astounded at the effect she must have on him. How could he change so completely? He would have to be wildly in love, and that thought started fires dancing in her. He looked desirable and handsome, sitting back, his hazel eyes studying her as she looked at him.

His eyes darkened, and he leaned forward and reached for her wrist. "Come here, Rebecca."

He tugged lightly, and she moved to his lap. He wrapped his arms around her and held her. "When night falls, I need to give security my undivided attention," he said in a husky voice. "Until then, I want to give *you* my undivided attention."

He shifted, turning her so that she was cradled against his shoulder as he leaned forward to kiss her. His mouth opened hers, his tongue meeting hers as she slid her arms around his neck and returned his kiss.

Her heart raced, and heat gathered low in her body, her stomach fluttering as their tongues touched.

She wound her fingers in Jake's soft hair, thinking that was the only soft thing about him. His body was hard, he was hard. His hands trailed over her breasts, and she moaned, moving against him, everything inside her tightening because she wanted him.

Struggling as if she were coming up from the depths of the sea against a strong current, Rebecca pushed against him and sat up, facing him. "Wait. You have to give me room. We've loved, Jake, and now every touch is explosive. I want you and there's no denying it, but I don't want to marry you. I haven't changed my mind, so just give me some time to think things through."

She slid off his lap and picked up her glass of tea, walking to the window to look outside, afraid that if she didn't get away from him he would charm or kiss away her protests within seconds.

He stared at her back solemnly and nodded. "Okay, honey. I'll give you some time to think, but keep in mind what I said. And stop conjuring up the worst scenario. I do a lot of mundane, routine things in my work."

She turned to give him a look, and he shrugged. "Okay, but I'm careful and I'm not in constant danger." He stood, and Rebecca's pulse skittered, because he was so damned appealing. His body was lean and hard and fit. He stretched and drank down the last of the tea, his Adam's apple bob-bing as he finished the drink.

He set the glass on the counter. "I'll go circle the house, check with McCauley, who should be on duty in a few min-utes. When I come back in, I'll have to shut off one of the air conditioners."

She nodded and watched him go out the back door. She saw him pass the window and wondered what he satisfied himself about when he circled the house, because there wasn't any good place to hide around it. Someone could hide underneath it, but that would do him little good. The house was silent, and she felt alone. She tried to think what it would be like when this was over and the girls were at their lessons and she was home alone.

And she knew it would be dreadful. Which did she want—hours of loneliness or the risk of another incredible heartbreak? As cheerful and optimistic as Jake was about his work, she couldn't view it that way. She watched his dark head disappear around the corner of the house.

Jake walked around, seeing the bright horizon in the west, the gray-blue sky to the east. To the south a bolt of light-ning streaked in a mass of clouds, and he wondered if an-other storm was blowing in or if it was merely heat lightning. His skin prickled, and an uneasy feeling settled on him.

He frowned, pausing to look over the expanse of yard, the burned rubble of the barn, his pickup and the green car. He retrieved his radio and called McCauley.

"Everything all right so far?"

"Yes, sir," McCauley answered. "Lowman is on surveil-lance to the south, and he'll be relieved about midnight."

"Have you heard any weather report?"

"Yep. Thirty percent chance of rain around here."

"That means we probably won't get any. Keep your eyes open."

"Yes, sir."

Jake replaced his radio on his belt and stared at the sky to the south, over the tops of the trees. In a few minutes he saw another streak of lightning and the massive thunderheads. He glanced at the house, wondering about Rebecca and if he was going to lose her. Just thinking about it hurt. He wanted to go inside and pull her into his arms and kiss away her protests.

He looked over the road and trees, knowing Meskell's next move was overdue. His skin prickled again and he wondered whether it was some atavistic gut instinct or just the weather that was giving him the jitters.

He opened the door. He wouldn't take her to bed against her wishes, but he was going to kiss her again a few times tonight, and he suspected her objections would be short-lived.

Jake closed and locked the kitchen door. "Time to close the house!" he called. Silence came and he turned around, his skin prickling as he yanked out his gun. "Rebecca!"

"Yes?" she answered, coming out of her bedroom and smiling at him, and he relaxed, but the moment she saw the pistol, her smile faded.

"What is it, Jake?"

"You didn't answer me."

"Sorry. I didn't hear you," she said as he put the gun in his jeans. He wanted to swear at himself, because she had been smiling and cheerful and now a frown was back.

"I just said let's close up for the night. You didn't answer, and I couldn't imagine why you didn't hear me."

"Just didn't. I'll pull the shades."

In minutes they were seated in the living room. Jake had switched off the air conditioner in the front, leaving the one on in the kitchen for a time because the air was muggy and hot. They moved later to the kitchen to talk, and then back to the living room. Finally Rebecca told him good-night, and when he reached for her, she stepped back.

"Jake, you have to give me time. I have to be able to think, and I can't when you kiss me."

"That should tell you something."

She ran her fingers across her brow. "You're rushing me and trying to change my life completely."

"I hope so," he said quietly, and she saw the determination and desire in his eyes. "You've changed my life, honey," he said, in a tender tone of voice that almost made her walk right into his arms.

"Oh, Jake, I just have to think about it."

"You know what you feel."

"And you know exactly, too, because you can see it in my eyes and feel my heartbeat. You know I can't resist you."

"You're resisting right now, Rebecca. Just keep thinking about it," he said, knowing she wasn't one to toss aside her convictions lightly.

"You're willing to become a father? Just like that?"

"Just like that," he said in a husky voice that made her insides flutter. And she could see what he felt, the blaze of desire in his eyes, the reaction of his body to nothing more than what they were doing right now.

"I'll think about us," she said, knowing she would for the rest of the night.

He reached for her. "Just one kiss. Just a good-night kiss."

"Oh, Jake," she said, knowing he was going to barrel right ahead and do what he damned well pleased.

"Come here, honey," he whispered, and wrapped his arms around her, and she yielded for another ten minutes before she pushed against him.

She stepped back and hurried to her room, putting space between them before she turned at her open door. "That was a lot more than one good-night kiss, Jake! You're going to do everything you can to get your way."

"Not quite *everything*," he drawled, and she felt as if he had reached out to stroke his hands over her body again with his sexy tone and insinuation.

"Night," she said, and entered her room and closed the door and wondered if she would get one moment's sleep during the night.

"Night, honey," Jake said softly as the door closed. He ached to take her to bed and love her and hold her in his arms all night, but he knew he had to do what she wanted. She was determined enough to stick by a decision once she'd firmly made it. And that was the bad side to falling in love with her, he reminded himself. He wasn't going to give up without the fight of his life.

Switching off the last lamp, he walked to the window to gaze outside. Nothing but heat lightning. No rain. Jake sat down, placing the pistol on his lap, listening to the house creak occasionally and thinking about Rebecca stretched out in bed only a short distance away.

The next morning he was pouring a cup of coffee and talking on the phone to Zach when he heard a noise in the hall and turned around. Dressed in a blue T-shirt and cut-offs, she appeared in the doorway, and his pulse jumped.

"Gotta go. Thanks, Zach. Rebecca will call in a little while to talk to the girls."

Jake replaced the receiver and set down the cup, looking into her wide blue eyes as he went across the kitchen to her. "Morning, love," he said, taking her in his arms and kissing her soundly.

His body responded the moment he pressed her against him, and he wanted to pick her up and carry her back to the bedroom, but Rebecca pushed against his chest after a few moments and looked up at him.

Jake felt like groaning, because he could see the worry in her eyes.

"I told you last night," she said, in a breathless voice that made him feel better, "I have to be able to think."

"Think away, sweetie. Just a little kiss now and then to remind you."

She gave him an exasperated look, and he turned around. "Breakfast awaits. I'll put on your usual toast."

"You don't need to wait on me," she said, her tone was lighter. He brushed his hand across her nape and touched her ear.

"I'm doing what I want to do," he said.

"I'm well aware of that, Jake."

She moved around the kitchen, and in minutes she was poring over her To Do list and then making calls to her customers while Jake fought the urge to continually touch her.

He glanced over her shoulder between calls and saw the list of names of customers. All around the names were doodling and scratches. His pulse quickened, because his name was written over and over. And he spotted something scratched out and leaned closer to study it.

"What are you doing?" she asked, twisting around to look at him.

"Trying to decide whether I dare kiss that tempting spot on your neck or not, and I'll have to admit, I'm giving in to temptation." He bent and brushed a kiss across her nape and looked again at the tablet, turning it so that he could read it.

She tried to take it from his hand, but he held on. "Does that say Mrs. Jake Delancy?"

"It doesn't mean anything!" she snapped, yanking the tablet from him and looking at him with sparks in her blue eyes and pink in her cheeks.

He leaned down, catching her chin and holding her. "I hope to hell it means a lot. You must be thinking about something." He leaned down quickly as she opened her mouth to protest. He kissed her, and in seconds she was on his lap and he had his hands beneath her T-shirt.

"Jake—"

"I know. Let you think," he said. "And how's the thinking going?"

"It goes one way until something happens to remind me of your work, and then it goes the other way." She stood and tucked her shirt into her cutoffs again. "Jake, can you ask for a desk job?"

He studied her and knew he'd better wait a few seconds before answering. "Rebecca, there's a lot of things I've changed my mind about since I met you, but that isn't one of them."

She inhaled as if he had hurt her, and turned away abruptly, and he wondered if he was going to lose after all.

Rebecca kept busy all day, while Jake constantly paced the house. It was cool and comfortable and he had no qualms about running the air-conditioning during the daylight hours.

She wondered if she would ever get out of debt. She would have a huge electrical bill. The barn was burned. Her business was closed temporarily. She ran her hand across her forehead and heard Jake whistling in the front room and suddenly everything else barely mattered. It was Jake and the golden promises he held out to her that were important, yet his offer was all tied up in risk.

All day long Jake had continually stolen kisses, teased, flirted, touched her, and she knew her resistance was crumbling, yet it was for the wrong reasons. Once this was over, she would be able to think clearly and make a rational decision. But it hadn't done much good to tell him that repeatedly.

Jake had someone deliver hamburgers, and they had dinner at sundown. She talked several times a day with the girls and finally made one last call at bedtime.

When she replaced the phone, Jake was seated at the kitchen table. He wore a white T-shirt and jeans and had an iced tea in his hand and his feet propped on a chair. He had switched off the air conditioner in the kitchen and turned on the one in the front room for a while to try to cool it down.

"The girls are having a wonderful time. Not a word about coming home."

"The charming Delancys, I believe you said."

She smiled and wrinkled her nose at him as she sat down facing him.

Jake raked his fingers through his hair. "The humidity must be high tonight." The floor creaked above him, and he looked up, knowing that the house continually made noises as it settled.

Rebecca heard it, too, and she looked worried, and he wondered what was going through her mind. She had grown increasingly quiet. Did she miss the girls? Or was she thinking about his declaration of love?

He heard the rumble of thunder in the distance and got up, moving across the room. "Mind if I switch off the lights?"

She smiled at him. "That's the first time you've asked. And no, I don't," she said, and Jake flipped the switch. He raised a shade and watched as lightning flashed in the distance.

"More heat lightning. McCauley said it isn't supposed to rain," he said, dropping the shade into place and switching on the lights again, wondering about Meskell and where he was.

A mile away, Lenny Meskell moved through the brush and mesquite and halted. He was becoming adept at creeping around in the dark, now that he had tried it for several nights. And he had spotted the stakeout. He suspected there were other stakeouts, probably across the road, but all he cared about was one. It was to the north of the house—the best place, anyway. The way he had planned to go in the first place.

He took another step and was still. Something rustled nearby and he frowned, drawing his breath, yet telling himself it could only be a rodent.

It was the cop yards ahead he'd better worry about, not wild creatures. Meskell took another step. He was hot in the black clothing, but it would hide him. He heard a distant rumble of thunder and wanted to swear. He wanted a clear night. He had mailed money to a friend in Laredo, and a car with good plates would be waiting. He'd make the change of cars there. Now all he needed was to kill the cop and take the woman and life would be good again.

He moved forward and paused, easing his foot down carefully. The trick to getting through the woods in the dark was to not think about what was out there.

Lenny moved slowly, easing through the trees, taking out the binoculars. Finally he spotted the stakeout. He crept forward until only yards ahead, at the edge of the trees, he could see a cop dressed in black, seated on a camp stool.

Clutching a rock in his fist, Meskell moved closer, taking his time. When he got within yards, he pulled out his pistol, turning it to hold it as a club.

He eased forward. The guy had been watching for several nights now, and his attention was focused on the house. Meskell crept up behind him and tossed the rock. It arced and fell, rolling across the open ground, which had only a few small mesquite.

The cop leaned forward and then stood, and when he turned around, Lenny was already behind him, swinging the gun, bringing the butt down across the man's skull with a dull thump.

The cop fell and Lenny yanked out a roll of duct tape, working swiftly. Taking the cop's pistol, he straightened. He looked at the house, and his pulse leaped, because he could see the lighted kitchen windows. He prayed it was the cop. Might be too early, though. He wanted a good start tonight, before the next shift for the stakeout came.

Meskell calculated how to cross the open space, knowing how he would get into the house if he made it that far without being noticed. He dropped to his hands and knees and began to crawl forward, eagerness filling him.

Jake stood at the kitchen window, staring into the night.

Silence stretched between them while he studied the road and watched a car drive past, only the beam of the headlights showing, and then the red of the taillights.

Rebecca sat at the kitchen table. She rubbed her bare feet over a rung of the chair absentmindedly. It was quiet, and again, Rebecca tried to imagine how it would be when Jake had gone.

She shivered, wondering again if she ought to do what Jake suggested and stop looking at the past, stop worrying about the future. Lightning flashed, and she saw the bulk of his shoulders in a dark silhouette against the night sky.

She felt alone and uncertain for the first time. The house was too quiet without the girls, every creak making her uneasy. Jake would be gone, and she suspected he would persist in trying to win her over for a while and then vanish out of her life. The thought of life without him hurt, and she wondered if she was making a huge mistake. A board creaked overhead.

Disturbed, feeling a need to be near Jake, to feel his solid strength and vital energy, she crossed the room to stand beside him.

Jake looked down, surprised to see Rebecca, suddenly curious why she was close to him. She had kept him at a distance all evening.

Dropping the window shade back into place, he set down his tea and turned around, sliding his arms around her waist.

The moment Jake touched her, Rebecca felt swamped with need for him. She moaned, turning into his arms, clinging to him tightly while she turned her face up for his kiss.

His heart thudded as Jake leaned down to kiss her. He wasn't going to ask questions, but joy spilled through him. He tightened his arm around her, winding his fingers in her hair, sliding his hand over her as if she had come back to him after weeks of separation.

Her tongue played against his, and her hips thrust against him with an urgency that matched his own. He bent over her, molding her soft body to his, sliding his hand over her derriere and pulling her up against him.

Rebecca clung to him, still uncertain about what she should do, because whatever decision she made, it would affect the girls. She twisted her head to look up at him. "Jake, I just don't know anymore. If I can't cope with your life-style, we'll all be miserable. I've been sitting here in the dark and quiet and thinking how empty it will be when you're gone. Whatever I do, I'm not just doing it for me—it'll change the girls' lives. If I tell you to leave, they'll lose someone wonderful. If I let go and love you, they could get hurt so badly all over again. It isn't just me."

"I know it isn't, Rebecca," he said gently. "I want to marry you, and I want the girls."

"Oh, Jake! I just have to think about it, and these aren't the best circumstances for making a lifetime decision."

"You'll see, honey. It's hard to let go of the past, but once you do, you won't regret it," Jake whispered, kissing her throat, wanting her, and feeling jubilant because she was considering the possibility of marrying him.

His cellular phone was a jarring note, and Jake wanted to swear at the interruption. He kept his arm tightly around her waist while he reached out and picked up the phone. "Jake."

"This is Werner. The snitch said this is the night."

Chapter 14

"He'll make the hit and then head south."

"We'll be waiting," Jake said, feeling a rush of eagerness. Tonight and it would be over, and they would have Meskell.

"The SWAT team is moving out now, the chopper is waiting. Just hole up until the troops arrive, and we ought to get him...except..."

Jake groaned. "What's gone wrong?"

"Nothing yet, but the snitch is dead drunk. We don't know how long ago our man headed your way."

"Everything is quiet here," Jake said, suddenly feeling his skin prickle, knowing the quiet could be deceptive.

"No more details other than that," Jay added.

"That's good enough," Jake said, and heard the click as Werner broke the connection. He lowered the phone to the table and saw Rebecca watching him and wondered if this would destroy the tiny bit of progress he had made with her. Every time danger loomed, she pulled up the walls.

"What is it?" she asked, and he suspected she had already guessed.

"The police have an informant. He said Meskell is coming here tonight."

She inhaled deeply and gripped his hand. "When?"

"We don't know specifically," he answered, thinking how nice that would have been. And also how nice it would be to know how Meskell planned to get to her, and which direction he would take to get to the house.

"I'll never sleep now."

Jake could think of a way to put her to sleep, but he needed to give all his attention to guarding her, not seducing her. He turned to her, running his hands over her arms. "Don't worry. They'll have an army out here in minutes. And before they arrive, we've got a lot of men watching for him. We'll get him. Just stay close."

She turned away, and he wondered if her barriers were up again. But regardless, he knew she had had some kind of change of heart tonight—even if only a fleeting one.

"Should you look around the house?"

"We'd hear him if he tried to get in. I checked all the windows and doors tonight."

"I can't relax now."

"You will in a few minutes, when the novelty of the idea wears thin."

She frowned, and he suspected he had said the wrong thing in reminding her how accustomed he was to this. She moved away from him and went to the window, and he went to stand behind her, his hands on her shoulders while he nuzzled her neck.

"Stop worrying."

"He's out there somewhere, Jake. And he wants me."

"It'll be over soon, honey. I want to turn off the air in front. Let's move in there."

They went down the hall, and he glanced in the bathroom. He would have preferred that the night-light not be on in the bathroom, but it was her usual routine and he knew it made her feel better, so he hadn't said anything about it when she switched it on.

"You sleep in here tonight, where I can be with you," he said.

"All right," she answered, and he guessed she had intended to stay right there anyway.

Rebecca's nerves were stretched thin. Her hands were cold and clammy, and Jake's continual looking out the window didn't assuage her fears. The night seemed long, and she wondered what would happen if daylight came and Meskell hadn't been spotted.

She leaned back against the sofa. "Jake, I'm going to get my shoes," she said, suddenly feeling vulnerable, worrying if she might have to run like they did the day of the bomb. "I'll be right back." She left the room and went to the darkened bedroom, moving across the room to the closet to slip on her sneakers.

She turned to go back to the front room, hurrying toward the door that was slightly ajar. A shadow separated from the darkness, and Rebecca gasped.

From behind the door, a man stepped toward her, grabbing her, his arm going around her neck. He jammed a pistol against her head as she screamed and tried to break free.

Chapter 15

Jake heard the rustling and yanked up his gun. Rebecca screamed, and he saw a dark shadow move in the doorway. "Freeze!" he yelled, sprinting forward, holding out his pistol and steadying his wrist.

Meskell stepped into the hall. He had his arm around Rebecca's throat and a pistol at her temple. "You freeze, and drop the damned gun."

Jake looked at the pistol at her head.

Her blue eyes were wide as she stared at him, and he hated what he had to do, but he had dealt with Meskell before. "If you shoot her, I take you out right now."

Meskell jammed the gun against her harder, and Rebecca gasped. Jake's head swam with rage as adrenaline rushed through him.

"Toss her your car keys. I'm taking her with me. Go ahead, do it!" Meskell yelled.

Jake fished out the keys, keeping his gun trained between Meskell's eyes. He gave them an easy toss, and Rebecca caught them. Meskell grabbed them from her.

"Get back or she's dead!" he yelled, walking backward. "You call the rest of the bastards. You tell them my gun is at her head. Anyone tries to stop me and she's dead. Now get back!"

Without hesitation, Meskell walked backward through the house, and Jake remembered the dead bird and knew that Meskell had been all over the house and was familiar with it. He wanted to know how the hell he had gotten into it tonight, but the thought was gone once he looked at Rebecca's ashen face. He wanted to lunge at Meskell, to shoot him and grab her. But he knew that Meskell would shoot her at the slightest provocation.

The instant they went out the kitchen door, Jake yanked out his radio. "McCauley! Meskell's got Rebecca and he's taking my truck!"

Jake sprinted after them, knowing that McCauley would notify the others. The truck motor roared to life, and Jake leaped out the kitchen door and ran toward it. Meskell pulled away as Jake caught the back of the truck. The truck sped down the drive, and his feet bounced.

For a terrifying second, he was afraid he would fall off, but then he got a toehold and rolled into the truck bed. He slid forward, knowing that Meskell had to know he was in the back. He had seen only one head in the brief glimpse he'd had of the cab.

He didn't dare shoot, because he was certain Rebecca was down on the floor of the passenger side, with the barrel of the pistol against her head.

And he wouldn't risk a shot at Meskell as long as she was in that position.

Jake pulled up the radio, and in seconds Vance's voice came on.

"I'm in the truck. He's got her and he has a gun pointed at her head. I'll give you directions."

"We're already moving in."

Jake swore, wondering what had gone wrong, how Meskell had slipped past the surveillance, yet he knew from experience how many things could go wrong, and how quickly. And the longer Meskell could hold her, the more dangerous the situation would become.

"Hang on, honey," Jake whispered, aching to fire at Meskell and get her, praying she wasn't terrified senseless. And he knew that she was probably terrified for the girls, afraid they were going to lose their only parent.

Jake swore, remembering his promise to Sissy to protect Rebecca and keep her safe.

The truck swung around, skidding out of control and then righting on the pavement. Jake picked up the radio to give directions. "He's heading toward town."

Wind rushed over him, and the roar of the motor drowned out all other noise. He cursed the day he had had a powerful engine put in the customized pickup. Meskell could outrun anyone in a chase, but there wouldn't be a chase with Rebecca inside.

And what would happen when Meskell stopped? Jake knew that they might end up in a final standoff in the same position they had been in the house, with Meskell pointing a gun at Rebecca and Jake pointing one at Meskell.

Jake closed his mind to that scenario, hoping that Meskell had some money stashed that he wanted to live for.

"Hang on, Rebecca," he whispered again, in agony for her, clenching his fist and wanting to get his hands on Meskell.

He raised himself up enough to survey his surroundings, knowing Meskell didn't dare take the gun from Rebecca to shoot him, because she would do something. If she was conscious.

He swore and raised the radio to his mouth. "He's turning. We're entering I-35, headed south. He's going for San Antonio or Laredo or the border."

"We've got you in sight."

Jake turned and spotted the lights of a chopper off in the distance to the east. It was too noisy in the back of the truck to hear the chopper's motor, and he didn't know when they had picked up Lenny's trail.

"Hang on, honey," he whispered.

Rebecca was squeezed on the floor, the barrel of his pistol jammed against her throat. Lenny had ordered her to put her hands behind her head, and her arms were getting tired and her legs were aching from being folded beneath her.

Would the police just let him take her away, since he had a gun on her? She shivered violently, knowing it was up to her to get away, because the police could do little as long as Meskell was holding her hostage.

"How'd you get in the house?" she asked.

"Shut up!" he said, jamming the pistol against her, making her choke and cough.

"Get your hands up! Put them behind your neck."

She locked her fingers together and propped her head against her knee, trying not to think at all.

"I came in through your attic fan."

Startled, she turned a fraction. The glow of the dash lighted his face. He had black smudged on it, and his hair seemed to have been dyed black, because she didn't remember it being black in the courtroom. He wore black gloves, jeans, and a long-sleeved black T-shirt. The smell of sweat was overpowering.

"The attic fan?" she repeated, not understanding. The attic fan was above the hallway.

"Came up through the attic fan opening over your porch. Had to wait until the cop wasn't looking out the window. Then I came down in your closet. I been all over your house that day I was in it. Saw your clothes, your things."

She shivered and remembered the house creaking, boards creaking in the attic. But the house always groaned and creaked in the dead of night.

"I been in your house for hours, just waiting for you to come back to your room, hearing you and that cop talk. He's in the truck right now," he said, his voice sounding sly.

Startled again, she looked up at him. His hair was standing up wildly. He must have worn a cap over it part of the night. He grinned, looking wolfish in the light from the dash, and she shivered.

Jake was in the back of the truck? She couldn't twist around, but her pulse jumped and hope climbed within her. But common sense made her realize there was little Jake could do.

"Where are we?"

"Heading for Mexico. And when we cross that border, no one can touch us. You and me'll have fun."

They must be on the freeway. And no one could stop him now. Because he had her as a hostage. She prayed that the fact she had been taken hostage didn't go out over the news and frighten the girls.

"My arms hurt."

"Tough. That'll be nothing. Go ahead and cry."

She clamped her mouth closed and heard him laugh.

The truck sped through the night, and the ache in her arms and legs became unbearable. Her legs became numb, and she wondered what was going to happen. Would they stop him at the border? She looked at the gas gauge. He was going to have to stop and get gas before he reached Mexico. She didn't want to point that out to him, but when he did, what would he do about Jake in the back?

Jake heard the crackle of the radio and held it to his ear.

Vance's voice came on. "Just north of San Marcos, we're setting up roadblocks. We expect him to drive right through them, but he won't be able to drive through a row of patrol cars. We've shut off the freeway for a stretch there. No one is getting on or off—all the exits are blocked, and we'll have the roadblock in the middle of nowhere. We're going to try to slow him and force him off the road. If he's on foot, even with a hostage, we can get him."

Jake felt cold. If Meskell had to go on foot, he would shoot Rebecca. "He might squeeze the trigger if the truck goes off the road."

"He's got money waiting. He may want a hostage. He knows he's dead if he kills her. He can't get away on foot. He has to keep her. Jake, if he goes off the road, he might put both hands on the wheel."

Jake drew a deep breath. He knew that was what Vance and the others were hoping for. "All I need is for him to get that pistol away from her for a second."

"We know that. How much gas has he got?"

Jake tried to remember. "I think half a tank. The motor is powerful."

"Dammit. At the rate he's going, we expect him to reach the roadblocks in another twenty minutes."

Jake glanced at his watch.

"Good luck. The chopper should be in sight, and men are waiting, but it's going to be up to you when he goes through the roadblocks. We'll stop him there."

"Right."

Jake hunched back against the truck. "Hang on, Rebecca. Twenty more minutes, and we'll get the bastard."

He glanced at his watch, looking at the sweep of the second hand, counting down the minutes, his muscles tensing as he got ready. Everything would happen in seconds. It took only seven or eight seconds to wreck a car, from the first slide until the smashup. Jake closed his eyes and prayed for her safety.

Twenty minutes ticked past, and still Meskell was barreling along. The wind roaring over him, Jake raised up and leaned over the side and saw nothing but darkness and a stretch of empty highway ahead. And then he saw the headlights shining on the orange-and-white boards that stretched across the highway.

The truck didn't slow, but kept racing toward the roadblock. Jake twisted around, kneeling, bracing his body against the truck, trying to get to where he could raise up and get a shot at Meskell, yet knowing that any second now the truck might go spinning off the road.

"Be ready, baby. Be ready," he whispered, wishing Rebecca could feel what he was saying.

They smashed through the boards, sending them flying. Jake had no idea how many Meskell was smashing through. Jake ducked as boards fell into the bed of the pickup and came flying over the roof.

Then they went into a sliding skid and Meskell turned. Jake felt the truck lurch, then spin as they wheeled around. He lost his balance, hitting his arm against the truck.

Desperate, he scrambled to gain his balance, kneeling and leaning against the truck as they bounced, trying to steady himself and look through the back window. He saw Meskell turning the steering wheel. He couldn't see Rebecca, but both of Meskell's hands were on the wheel.

Jake steadied his wrist and raised his hands.

Suddenly Meskell whipped around, holding his pistol, and fired at Jake. The glass shattered, and Jake felt his shoulder burn.

He squeezed the trigger. His shot hit Meskell squarely in the head. The body slumped down, sliding down in the seat, and Jake felt the lurch of the truck. The weight of Meskell's body must have pushed down the accelerator. They were off the road, bouncing over rough ground; the truck could roll or smash at any minute.

Jake threw himself across the pickup, trying to reach around to grab the door handle and yank it open, but the truck was bouncing too much.

Headlights waved up and down eerily with each bounce, and directly ahead was a stand of tall, aged oaks, their trunks large and looking as solid as concrete posts. The pickup rushed straight at them.

"Jump, Rebecca! Jump!" Jake bellowed, fighting to grab the door handle.

Chapter 16

Rebecca screamed when the blast of Jake's gun shattered the back window and killed Lenny Meskell. He slumped down, his body pressing the accelerator.

The truck was bouncing over rough ground. Frantically she tried to wiggle up on the seat. Her legs were numb, and pain shot through her arms. She tugged on Meskell's body, struggling to shove it away so that she could get to the brakes.

And then she looked up and saw the oaks looming in front of them. There was no way to avoid hitting the trees unless she turned. With the speed they were traveling and the rough ground, if she tried to turn the truck, it would likely roll, and Jake was in the back. Sobbing, she pulled at Meskell's inert deadweight, trying to shift him away so she could get to the brake. She reached across him and opened the door. Yanking herself across Meskell's body as the door swung wide, Rebecca scooted back onto the passenger side. She held the seat and the dash and put her feet against him and pushed.

She felt as if she were pushing against a wall.

"Jump! Rebecca, jump!" Jake bellowed.

Sobbing, she shoved. She felt the body shift, and then the deadweight gave and the body slid out of the truck.

"Jump!"

She jammed her foot on the brake and scooted across the seat, throwing on the emergency brake, as well. The truck plowed into the ground. A mesquite hit the windshield and was gone.

Headlights were bright, clearly showing the solid oak that loomed up only yards away now. She kept her foot jammed against the brakes, getting ready to throw herself out the door as the truck slowed.

Suddenly Jake swung into the seat beside her, squeezing in, almost on her lap.

The pickup plowed up the ground while the brakes locked. Dirt flew up around them as they finally stopped. The nose of the pickup was within an inch of an oak.

Rebecca turned, throwing herself into his arms. Jake wrapped his arms around her, crushing her to him, showering her with kisses, and his strong arms were the most wonderful feeling on earth to her.

"Thank God you're safe," Jake said, squeezing her tightly, wanting to hold her forever. "It's over, honey. It's all over forever. He won't bother you again."

Rebecca tilted her face up to his and Jake kissed her hard, and she returned his kisses.

"I'd like to take advantage of the shock you're in and ask you once again to marry me. I love you, baby."

"Well, are you?" she asked, running her fingers over his face.

"Am I what?"

"Going to take advantage of me?"

His arms tightened around her, and he knew he would have to ask her again when she had calmed and thought it over, but he wasn't going to hold out for fair play now. "Will you marry me?"

"Yes! Yes, oh, yes! I'll have to ask the girls, but I'm sure their answer will be yes."

Jake kissed her, hearing voices, knowing the police were about to surround them, but he didn't give a damn. He didn't want to stop holding her or kissing her yet. He didn't know when she had decided she wanted to accept his proposal and all that went with it. If it had been in the past terrifying hour, he would have to let her reconsider.

He tightened his arms around her, feeling certain she wouldn't change her mind now that she'd decided to marry him. She belonged to him, heart and soul, and nothing in his life had ever seemed so right. And then he stopped thinking and kissed her.

Finally Rebecca realized there were men talking around them. She pushed against Jake and looked around. Uniformed patrolmen, men in black clothing with rifles, cars with flashing lights behind them, were all around the pickup.

"Jake, there are men all over the place!"

A highway patrolman stepped up to the open door, and Jake climbed out. "I think I ruined a damned good pickup tonight," Jake said as he thrust out his hand. "Jake Delancy. We've been in a bit of a dilemma."

They were taken to an emergency room, where Jake's shoulder was treated. Meskell's bullet had merely grazed him. Then they were taken to Jake's condo.

"We'll go out to your place tomorrow," he said, entering his condo, which had been cleaned and straightened. Things were not the way he kept them, but in order. As soon as he closed the door, he turned to Rebecca to take her in his arms.

"I remember something back there about an acceptance of my proposal."

She nodded, raising her lips as he bent his head to kiss her. After long moments, she twisted her head. "I'll still have to talk to the girls about it."

"Sounds great, honey," he whispered, his hands moving over her hips lightly.

He bent his head forward to cover her mouth with his, his kiss hard and demanding as he held her tightly.

They looked at each other again, and she knew there were no words necessary for what they were feeling. And her decision seemed all the more right.

Jake drew her to him again to kiss her slowly and thoroughly, and Rebecca wound her arms around his neck. Then remembered his wound. She pulled away. "I'm sorry. Did I hurt you?"

He drew her back to him. "Never," he whispered as he picked her up and carried her to his bedroom.

The next morning, while she showered, she heard Jake talking to someone. When she stepped out of the shower, she wrapped a towel around herself. She wanted to burn the clothes she had worn the night before. While she stood staring at the heap of clothing, Jake knocked on the bathroom door.

She swung it open, and his gaze went over her, desire flaring in the depths of his eyes. "Oh, honey, how I wish!"

"Wish what?"

"That we had all day alone. Unfortunately, we don't. I have to go to the station to give my reports, but first I'll take you to Sally's to get the girls, and then I'll take you home."

"Did I hear you talking to someone?"

"Yes, you did," he said. He was dressed in a white shirt and dark slacks and he looked handsome and sexy and as unruffled as if nothing had happened the night before. He held folded clothing in his hand. "That was Zach. Sally sent some clothes for you to wear today."

"Thank heavens! I can't bear to touch the clothes I wore last night."

"Don't touch them. I'll get rid of them." He drew his hand across the top of her towel, over the curves of her breasts. "As much as I hate to," he said in a low voice, "we have to get dressed and go."

"Right," she said, pushing him away and closing the door.

She emerged in a blue cotton skirt, sandals and a blue blouse. Jake whistled as she stepped into the living room. "Wow! Do you look good!"

"I feel much better now. Even the sandals fit all right. I'm ready. Should we call Sally and tell her we're coming?"

"Nope. She knows."

He walked over to her and put his arm around her. "Remember when Sally picked the girls up and I went out to talk to her?"

"Yes," she asked, wondering what was on his mind, because he looked solemn.

"I told her I wanted something, and to have Zach call me. And then I made a few other calls. When Zach came by just now, he brought those clothes for you, and something that I had him buy awhile ago and haven't had a chance to pick up." He reached into his pocket and produced a small black box that he placed in her hand.

"I told Zach what kind of ring I wanted, and he suggested a jeweler, and we had a few conversations that I didn't want you to overhear. Zach picked it up for me."

Rebecca stared at the box, knowing her life was going to change. No matter what hurt was involved, she knew she couldn't give up Jake. Opening the black velvet box, she looked at a sparkling emerald-cut diamond set in a gold mounting. Jake removed it from the box. "Hold out your hand," he said in a husky voice. "Please."

She extended her hand, holding out her slender fingers. "Jake," she whispered, watching his strong, tanned fingers take the bright ring and hold her hand. He paused and studied her. "Rebecca, you consented last night in wild circumstances, and you were in shock."

Feeling as solemn as he looked, she shook her head. "I know what I want, too. I love you, Jake."

"Will you marry me, Rebecca?"

Looking into the depths of his hazel eyes, seeing the love that was shining in them, she was ready to take chances. And her chances seemed pretty good at the moment. "You know my answer is yes," she said softly.

His brows arched and he studied her. "Without reservations or ultimatums or conditions?"

"I can't put conditions on my love," she whispered. "You won that battle so long before I wanted to acknowledge it."

"And how will you handle the police work?"

"The same way I handled the fire fighting. The best I can. But it will worry me sometimes."

"I love you, Rebecca," he said quietly, leaning forward to kiss her hungrily.

Her pulse was drumming and she wanted him, seeing the desire she felt reflected in his smoldering eyes.

"Rebecca," he said, her name coming out in a rush, his voice sounding torn with emotion. With shaking hands, he slipped the engagement ring on her finger. She closed her hands over his, looking at the sparkling ring and then up at him. "I love you," she whispered again, feeling so certain.

He kissed her, and then leaned back. "Let's go tell the girls."

As he sped across town in his car, Jake glanced at her, watching her wiggle her fingers as she looked at the ring.

She smiled at him, her dimple showing. "Oh, Jake, I can't believe—"

"Yes, you can. Love won. You're getting what you want and I'm getting what I want. Rebecca, I have a question."

Giving the sparkling diamond one more glance, she looked up at Jake. "What is it?"

"You have your family. You've already had two girls," he said solemnly. "Do you think you might ever want one more?"

She slid her arms around his neck carefully. "I would love one more with you," she said. "I started young, so there's still time."

"It'll be good, love, so good," he whispered.

The moment Rebecca saw Sissy and Tara run across the living room to her, she felt light-headed with joy. Unable to keep from crying, she gathered the girls into her arms and hugged them. Tara wiggled to get away, and Rebecca released her, trying to curb her emotions, hastily wiping tears away because for just a few minutes last night she had thought she might not ever see them again.

"There are my girls," Jake said, walking to them to hug them both. Sissy threw her arms around him and squeezed him. As he moved away from them, he pulled Rebecca to his side, placing his other hand on Tara's shoulder.

"Your mother and I have a surprise," he said, glancing at Rebecca, waiting so that she could tell them.

Rebecca watched Tara. "Jake and I are going to get married. Jake will be your stepfather."

Tara's grin widened while Sissy shrieked with glee, and Jake hugged them both. Rebecca let out her breath, because it was obvious her announcement made both girls happy.

"Welcome to the family!" Sally said, hugging Rebecca. "I can't believe it!"

"See the ring Jake gave me," Rebecca said, showing the girls and Sally her engagement ring, suspecting the ride home would be spent answering questions.

"I can call you Daddy, too, just like I did my daddy?" Sissy asked.

"You can call me Daddy, Dad, or Jake. Whatever you want."

"I think I want to call you Dad. I always called our real father Daddy," Tara said solemnly, and Jake gave her shoulder a squeeze.

"I think that would be nice."

"I think I'll call you Daddy," Sissy announced. "I have two daddies now. One is in heaven and one is here." She squinted her eyes at him. "Suppose someone shoots you again?"

"I intend to see that that doesn't happen, so we won't even consider it. Okay?"

"Okay."

He stroked Tara's hair. "I want to adopt both of you legally so you'll officially be my little girls. All right?"

"Yes," Sissy answered happily, but Tara gave it some thought.

"I don't want to forget Daddy."

Jake sobered, his arm sliding around her shoulders. "Tara, you won't ever lose or forget your daddy. Not ever. Your mom and I will talk it over, but it'll never change the relationship you had with your daddy."

She nodded and ran her hand along his arm. "I'm glad you're getting married," she said shyly.

Jake hugged her lightly, hugging Sissy with his other arm. "I'm glad, too."

"When's the wedding?" Tara asked, and Jake looked at Rebecca.

"Soon, I hope. Very soon."

"We have a lot to consider... your brothers and their families, and I'll be months behind in my business... When?"

"Saturday," he said, his eyes dancing.

She laughed. "I have plans to make, and the girls will need dresses."

Jake grinned. "Your list will be ten feet long!"

Sally disappeared and returned with a calendar to hand it to Rebecca.

Rebecca studied it, her insides fluttery with excitement. "It's June now. How about the third week in August?"

Jake stepped to her side and ran his finger along the calendar. "I'll help you get dresses."

Sally laughed. "Don't fall for that one, Rebecca!"

"How about the third week in July?" he suggested.

Rebecca looked up at him, knowing there were so many plans to be made, but it all seemed insignificant at the moment, because the four of them were safe and were going to be a family.

Jake's hazel eyes were filled with love. He put his arm around her and pulled both girls to them to hug.

"All right, we'll marry in the third week in July. You always win."

"No, I don't. You just notice it more when I do." He winked at her.

"Let's go home so you can start planning this wedding," he said, looking into her eyes, his gaze filled with love.

At the house, he was afraid that Rebecca's memories of the night before would resurface, but to his relief, she didn't seem to have any problem.

"You can put this house and the neon car on the market," he said, standing in the kitchen doorway.

"You might come to like my car."

"Not in the next—" He grinned. "Who knows—I seem to remember telling you I wasn't going to marry for years. I'll be back when I'm finished at the station."

They kissed again and she watched him drive away and couldn't wait for him to return. She could hear the television and Sissy's laughter and the house seemed right again. And she wasn't going to think about last night.

Three hours later, she heard a car roar up the drive. She hurried to the window and then dashed out the back door to watch Jake drive up and stop. He stepped out, bounding around the car to wrap his arms around her and swing her off her feet. "Good news, beautiful fiancée!"

"Oh? You must have gotten a pay raise."

"Yes, I am getting one, but it's better than that. And I have the rest of the week off. After I tell you my news, I'm packing all of you up and we'll go look at my ranch. We'll stay out there tonight."

"The girls will love it," she said, wondering whether Jake didn't want her staying in the house tonight because of her ordeal yesterday. "I have a million things to do, but—" she shrugged "—this comes first," she said, placing her hand against his jaw and kissing him.

He set her on her feet, keeping his arms around her. "Look, honey, we can stand out here in plain sight in the sunshine."

"I know, Jake, I've been thinking about that all day. And it's nice of you not to say, 'I told you so about our being safe again.' Now, what's the big news?"

"Richard Vance has a promotion in mind. He's offered me a captain's job. It won't be as hazardous as what I've been doing."

"How marvelous!" she cried, but then she sobered when she thought about Jake and all he had told her about loving his job. "You're not going to like it. I don't want you to change if it's something you won't like."

He ran his fingers along her cheek, and suddenly hope blossomed in her, because he looked satisfied and not at all as if he were making a sacrifice. "I'm suddenly tired of getting shot at, and my priorities have changed, and I think I'll have enough excitement at home that I won't need an adrenaline rush at work."

"Oh, Jake," she said, tears of joy filling her eyes. His arms tightened around her, and he leaned over her to kiss her passionately.

Rebecca stood on her toes to kiss him back, knowing their house would be filled with love because of this very special man.

* * * * *

INTIMATE MOMENTS®
Silhouette®

COMING NEXT MONTH

Trained to protect, ready to lay their lives on the line, but unprepared for the power of love.

Award-winning author Beverly Barton brings you
Ashe McLaughlin, Sam Dundee and J. T. Blackwood...
three rugged, sexy ex-government agents—each with a
special woman to protect.

Embittered former DEA Agent Sam Dundee has a chance at
romance in GUARDING JEANNIE, IM #688, coming in January
1996. Hired to protect Jeannie Alverson, the woman who saved
his life years ago, Sam is faced with his greatest challenge
ever...guarding his heart and soul from her loving, healing
hands.

And coming in April 1996, the trilogy's exciting conclusion.
Look for J. T. Blackwood's story, BLACKWOOD'S WOMAN,
IM #707.

Silhouette

SPECIAL EDITION™

CELEBRATION
1000

Nora Roberts

THE PRIDE OF JARED MACKADE

(December 1995)

The MacKade Brothers are back! This month,
Jared MacKade's pride is on the line when he
sets his heart on a woman with a past.

If you liked THE RETURN OF RAFE MACKADE (Silhouette
Intimate Moments #631), you'll love Jared's story. Be on
the lookout for the next book in the series, THE HEART OF
DEVIN MACKADE (Silhouette Intimate Moments #697)
in March 1996—with the last MacKade brother's story,
THE FALL OF SHANE MACKADE, coming in April 1996
from Silhouette Special Edition.

These sexy, trouble-loving men
will be heading out to you in
alternating books from Silhouette
Intimate Moments and Silhouette Special Edition.

NR-MACK2

HEARTBREAKERS

We've got more of the men you love to love in the Heartbreakers lineup this winter. Among them are Linda Howard's Zane Mackenzie, a member of her immensely popular Mackenzie family, and Jack Ramsey, an *Extra*-special hero.

In December—HIDE IN PLAIN SIGHT, by Sara Orwig: Detective Jake Delancy was used to dissecting the criminal mind, not analyzing his own troubled heart. But Rebecca Bolen and her two cuddly kids had become so much more than a routine assignment....

In January—TIME AND AGAIN, by Kathryn Jensen, *Intimate Moments Extra:* Jack Ramsey had broken the boundaries of time to seek Kate Fenwick's help. Only this woman could change the course of their destinies—and enable them both to love.

In February—MACKENZIE'S PLEASURE, by Linda Howard: Barrie Lovejoy needed a savior, and out of the darkness Zane Mackenzie emerged. He'd brought her to safety, loved her desperately, yet danger was never more than a heartbeat away— even as Barrie felt the stirrings of new life growing within her....

INTIMATE MOMENTS®
Silhouette®

HRTBRK4